On the Sunset Rim

Harlan Hague

CHAPTER ONE

They stood in a meadow of brilliant bluebonnets. A scattering of Indian paintbrush pushed up through the blue carpet. One of the two men held the reins of his horse, the thumb of the other hand hooked in his belt.

The day was still, sunny but cool for April. Quiet but for the chittering of an unseen swallow. A faint wild scent wafted from the live oak wood behind them.

The men looked across the flat at a column of cattle moving northward at a slow, steady pace, close herded by riders on each side. A thin film of dust lifted from the trail by their hooves, appearing as a gray tunnel, then drifting back to the ground as the end of the herd moved ahead.

Most of the cowboys rode quietly beside the column, heads hanging, daydreaming. Some whistled or hummed, occasionally calling out or cussing an animal that stopped too long to graze or decided to head out on its own away from the herd. The rider had to pull away from the column to convince the errant bovine to obey the rules, and order was soon restored, meaning that the wanderer was back in line, and the cowboy once again was lost in his private reverie.

1

These were longhorn cattle. Horns of the young cows in the column looked like the shorter horns of the Hereford cattle, just being introduced in Texas, but the mature animals, the bulk of the herd, had long, almost-horizontal horns that turned upward at the tips. The length varied but often reached six feet or more.

They were the colors of the rainbow. Some were almost completely white with touches of black in their ears and around their noses and eyes. Others were mostly brown, shades of yellow or tiger-striped, streaked with color. Some were almost solid red, flecked with white and brown. Not a few were a pale, smoky silver, almost a mouse color.

The two men watched the end of the herd pass. One of the three cowboys riding drag at the end waved, and the two men standing in the meadow returned the wave. The man holding his reins turned to the other, extended his hand, and they shook. He clapped the other on the shoulder, mounted and rode away at a lope toward the herd. He turned in the saddle, looked back and waved.

Will returned the wave, watched until the herd disappeared around a distant stand of cedar. He looked across the flat, dust above the trail swirling slowly in the light breeze that had come up with evening, to the orange sun ball that had just descended below the tops of the mesquite thicket beyond the meadow. The gray-green mesquite foliage trembled in the light breeze, glowing, like tiny dancing flames. He stared at the horizon, watched the sun disappear, shadows vanishing.

An observer might call Will a good-looking fellow. He had a pleasant face, brown eyes that squinted when he smiled and longish sandy hair that was rarely neat. He had a ruddy complexion that he had acquired from seasons of hard work in the sun. He was muscular and trim, almost slender, that spoke of an active life. This evening, watching the setting sun color the cloud layers at the horizon a dozen pastel shades, he looked older than his twenty-three years.

He took a deep breath and exhaled. "What do you think, sweetheart? We gonna do this?"

Up to you, cowboy.

He lowered his head a long moment, stared at the bluebonnets at his feet, raised his head and looked up at the cloudless blue sky, darkening at the end of day. He walked back to the oak, head hanging, where his horse's reins were tied to a low limb. Loosening the reins, he mounted and set out at a lope through the bluebonnets to the cattle trail where he turned southward.

Will sat on the ground at a small fire, staring into the flames, chewing on a chunk of dried beef. His bedroll and saddle lay behind him, the bay hobbled nearby in a patch of good grass at the edge of a dark oak copse. Light from the fire shone dimly on the low heavy oak foliage, creating the soft appearance of a room.

What's the plan?

"The plan. Well, we catch up with the outfit tomorrow, we pick up the herd at the Rio Grande a few days later, we trail the herd north, deliver it to the buyer and get paid off."

Then what?

"Don't know. Do we come back to Texas? Or do we settle in Montana? I've heard some people going up the trail decide to set up their own ranch thereabouts. What do you think? You ready to settle down in Montana?"

Don't have much choice, do I?

He stirred the fire with a stick, dropped it, stared at the dancing flames. "Honey, you'd break my heart, but you can leave any time you like, any time you decide that's what you want to do."

Silly, I'll never leave you . . . at least, not till you decide it's time for me to go.

He watched the flames until they became embers, rocking back and forth, tears rolling down his cheeks.

Next day, Will rode into the cow camp at sundown. A passel of cowboys sat around a campfire, partially filled supper plates in laps, silently watching him ride in, pull up and dismount. Holding his reins, he looked at the upturned faces. They were a taciturn lot, or at least they appeared so as they watched this stranger who appeared unannounced.

"I'm looking for Charlie McBride," Will said to nobody in particular.

"That would be me," said McBride. He set his plate on the ground, stood with a grunt, walked to Will and extended a hand. McBride was stout without any fat showing, with slanting shoulders. Wisps of brown and gray hair splayed out below the sweat-stained hat that sat back on his head. A week-old scraggly brown beard was flecked with gray. Will noted that, in contrast to the other hands, McBride's shirt and pants appeared to be clean. He would learn later that the boss's obsession with clean clothes caused no snickers from the hands.

"And you would be Will Bishop," McBride said. Will smiled, took the hand, and they shook. That mystery solved, the cowboys sitting at the fire returned to their supper without a word. McBride and Will, holding his horse's reins, strolled away from the fire.

They stopped at the edge of firelight. "Passed your brother two days ago," said McBride. "He said to expect you. He got the jump on us this year, but I betcha we catch him up. He only had a couple thousand head and a small outfit. Anyway, he said you wanted to join us, and anybody Scott Bishop recommends must be a good man. Both of us are lucky, by the way. One of my best men broke some ribs just a couple weeks ago, so I'm a man short. And you're lucky I'm a man short.

"I'm curious why you didn't go with your brother. You two don't get on?"

"We get on fine, and we talked about it. We agreed that it would be a bad idea. He was afraid the other men would think he played favorites for his little brother. I knew he would work me twice as hard as anybody else so they wouldn't be able to think he was playing favorites with his little brother. I didn't think much of that idea, so here I am.

"Saw Scott up the trail, probably right after you talked with him. He said that Charlie McBride is so slow, he would be in Dodge before McBride crosses the Red River. He smiled when he said it."

McBride smiled. "That's Scott. He's a good man. But you know that. Okay, here's what's comin' down. Since I don't know your work habits, I'll take a chance on you as far as two weeks. If you don't make the grade, I'll pay you what's coming to you and tell you goodbye. If you make it, you're in. How's that?"

"Sounds good to me. I won't disappoint you."

"You got a six-shooter?"

"Sure do."

"Know how to use it?"

"I do. I've used it on everything from coyotes to bad bulls. Sorry to say I've used it to satisfaction on a couple of Comanches and one thief."

"That's all good. I hope you'll have no use for it on this drive, but you never know. I've not made a drive yet that we've not had some little excitement.

"Now, lemme introduce you and get you some supper." Will tied his reins to an oak sapling and followed McBride to the fire circle. The men seated on the ground around the circle looked up from their plates. He introduced the group by first name, pointing to each in turn: Rod, Brad, Win, Kirk, Jimmy, Cowboy Mack, Bobby, Lester and Fred.

Some of the men silently acknowledged the introduction with a wave of a fork or a nod. Others simply stared at Will or concentrated on their plates. Cowboy Mack touched his hat, his eyes fixed on Will. He did not smile. The broad-brimmed brown hat that sat low on his forehead made his black face even darker.

Bobby, who sat back from the fire, was the only one to smile. He was slight, smaller than the others, with a softer and lighter face. Will figured he had not been cowboying long. Bobby had watched Will from the time he rode into camp. The young cowboy turned away quickly, embarrassed, it seemed, when Will made eye contact.

"You won't remember a damn name," said McBride, "but you'll be able to attach names to faces before long. Three names you should remember from right now. Win is *segundo*. He'll be in charge if I get shot by a Indian or drown in a crossing. Just hope that don't happen." Win, who had watched McBride and Will and listened closely, grinned.

"A more important name you should remember from right now is Cookie, also known formally as Teddy." The cook looked up from the pantry at the back of the nearby chuck wagon and waved, unsmiling. "I don't mind saying to his face that he's the best cook west of the Mississippi. And he better be. I pay him more'n any cowhand here."

"Go t' hell, Charlie," Cookie mumbled. He turned away, dropped his chin, hiding an embarrassed smile. McBride looked aside at Will and smiled.

McBride took Will by the sleeve and pulled him away from the fire, out of earshot of the others. He released the sleeve and looked toward the men at the fire circle. "And there's Cowboy Mack." He looked soberly at Will. "You got any problem with Mack? If there is, we don't need to talk anymore, and you can be on your way."

"No problem at all. I've worked with nig—"

"Hold on. I need to tell you what Cowboy Mack is and what he is not. He's not a helper, he's not a boy, he's not a flunkey. He's a cowboy, the best in the outfit. I call him Cowboy Mack so nobody will be confused on that point. He's been punchin' cows for ten years, and he's been up the trail with me twice and saved my life last year. I'll tell you about that sometime. If you're still with us, that is. What do you say?"

"I'm fine. I've worked with . . . colored men before. I found them good workers."

"I'll say okay to that. I usually have two or three black men in my outfit, and they pull their weight. Just by chance that Mack is the only one this year. Now get your plate, and come back over here. Got more to talk about."

Will walked toward the chuck wagon. Cookie saw him coming and beckoned. "Come on over, and we'll see if that bunch has left anything in the pot." Cookie wore a stained clean apron over an ample belly that spilled over the apron tie. His ruddy, deeply creased face and short, thinning gray hair told of a hard life outdoors.

He dished up a plate of roast beef, boiled potatoes, beans and stewed dried apples and gave it to Will. He poured coffee into a cup and handed it to him. "That lot didn't leave no biscuits or gravy," Cookie said.

Will smiled, took the plate and cup. "Best meal I've had in a long time. Appreciate it." He walked to McBride who had waited where he left him. McBride was looking westward where wispy cloud layers were tinted a dozen shades of pink and red, painted by the sun's memory.

McBride stared silently at the horizon. He turned, nodded to Will. "If I live to be a thousand years old, I'll never get tired of west Texas sunsets." He sipped his coffee, turned serious.

"Okay, to business. We're picking up 3,000 head at the Rio Grande. I have a contract to deliver the lot to the Crow Reservation in Montana. That's where you'll be paid off. You got spending money till then? I can give you some little advance, if you don't."

"I have all I'll need. I don't expect to need much."

"That's what they all say, son, till they get to the railroad towns. We'll be going through Dodge. We'll see. Spend wisely, and let me know if you change your mind." Will nodded.

"Mounts. We'll choose horses at the Rio Grande.

9

Ten for each man. Take good care of 'em. They're mine. I'm lending 'em to you." He smiled.

"Since you never been on a long drive before, you got a lot to learn. You'll watch night herding two nights to learn the ropes. After that, you'll *do* night herding. Daytime, you'll have an assigned place at the herd, and ask questions of anybody while you're learning what we do. Shouldn't take long."

McBride pointed at a second wagon near the chuck wagon. "We're a pretty big outfit, so we got two wagons. The hoodlum wagon over there carries bedrolls and personal gear. Also some tents that we'll need to put up in bad weather. We'll have some of that for sure.

"Cookie drives his own wagon. Bobby usually drives the hoodlum, but he also alternates with the other hands because I want Bobby to know everything he needs to know about tending cows. Bobby pretty much takes care of the mules and does the hitching. He does lots of other stuff around camp, pitches in wherever he can help. Can't say that about most of the boys. They do what they're told to do, what they're paid to do, and they do a good job of it, but they don't generally go out of their way to do somethin' extra.

"Not so, Bobby. Seems he wants to be busy. He also helps Rod with the horses. Rod's the wrangler. Bobby's little, and he don't say much, but he's a good hand. This is his first long drive, but he's been around cows and knows the ropes."

Bobby hadn't been around horses much, but had a good teacher in Rod. The wrangler rode his first horse before he could walk. He was shy and said little, but when he offered anything about horses, everybody listened. He was usually reluctant to contradict anyone who said something he knew was wrong; he just smiled. Everbody knew what the smile meant.

There was one notable occasion to the contrary when Fred commented on the qualities of a particular horse, and Rod frowned. "That's the dumbest thang I ever heard," Rod said, and that was the end of that conversation.

McBride sipped his coffee and poured the last bit on the ground. "Now we both need to get some shuteye. Lots to do tomorrow." While they were talking, the men around the fire had finished supper and wandered off to the bushes and back to their bedrolls.

Will touched his hat to McBride and walked to his horse. He untied the bedroll from behind the saddle, carried it toward the fire that had died to glowing embers. Stopping at the sound of light snoring, he walked away from the fire and dropped the bedroll on the ground between the wagons. He went back to his horse, removed the saddle and saddlebags, blanket and bridle and patted the hose's rump, sending him toward the remuda. He carried the horse gear and dropped it near his bedroll.

Only then did he see the bedroll laid out behind the hoodlum wagon. Bobby lay there, eyes open, watching him. When they made eye contact, Bobby immediately shifted his covers and turned over.

Will unrolled his bed and made a pillow of his saddle blanket and saddlebags. He sat on the bed, removed his boots, unbuckled his belt and lay down on his back. He stared at the sky, sparkling stars seeming to pop from the dark ceiling as his eyes became accustomed to night. He tried to look past the stars, wondering what was out there.

Pretty, she said.

Yes, it is.

Everything seemed to go okay today. Are you pleased?

I am. Seems like a good bunch. I believe I can work with them. What do you think?

Yeah, guess so. A couple of them don't seem to have much behind the eyeballs, but a good lot on the whole. I like Bobby the best. He seems a sensitive kid, bit insecure. I wonder what persuaded him to sign on to a job that calls for big, tough fellows.

You think I'm a big, tough fellow?

Oh, my, honey, you can be a real test when you want to! Remember that day when I was trying to get away from you in the hayloft, and you caught me, and we rassled, and—

Don't, Ellie . . . don't . . . don't.

He turned over to lie on his stomach, his face buried in the blanket.

*****

The hands sat their horses quietly, bunched up on the north bank of the Rio Grande below old Fort Brown. The river at the ford called Paso Ganado was two hundred yards wide, the current slow, hardly noticeable. The bank at water's edge was thick with reeds and low bushes. The riders stared at the stream, some glancing nervously at each other.

"Looks like it's swimming all the way," said McBride. "Hard to tell, water's so dark, but I'd bet on it." He turned in the saddle. "We'll camp over there at the edge of those trees." He pointed at an oak grove back from the bank.

"Win, you go across this afternoon and see if you can find our supplier. Take a couple of boys with you. I sent word down two weeks ago, so he should have the herd just about ready to move. Agree on the moving day, and tell him we want to begin crossing 'em at first light on that day. Send one of the boys back with the word. I'll dispatch two or three more men over to help with the crossing, but the vaqueros should do most of that work."

McBride turned to the others. "You boys that I pick to go over, take your best swimmers. Now, on that point. We need to select our mounts. Come on." McBride walked his horse, followed by the others, to the remuda near the wagons where Rod and Bobby held the horses. The riders pulled up, dismounted and tied reins to anything stationary, walked to the horses.

"You've ridden them on the trail," McBride said,

"so you know 'em. Ten to each man. I've already picked mine. The rest of you, you'll roll the dice to set the order for choosing. Use three dice. If there's a tie, roll again. Then you'll choose your mounts in turn, one horse at a time, till you've got your ten. If you're riding one of my horses now, and you like him, keep him and choose nine more. If you're riding your own horse, choose ten.

"Bobby, you're in the dice-rolling, and you take five mounts. You'll be on your wagon most of the time, but you'll ride herd nights and help Rod when he needs help in camp with the remuda. You'll ride enough day herding so you'll know the ropes. We'll be needing you from time to time." Bobby nodded, retreated a step when the others looked at him.

The dice tossing ended with more grumbles than grins, but the results were accepted and mounts chosen in good order. When all was finished, no one appeared overly disappointed with his string. Will walked away from the remuda, smiling at his good fortune. He had been second in line of choosing and was pleased with his selection.

Will, Fred and Jimmy, holding the reins of their mounts, walked toward the campsite pointed out by McBride. Both wagons were already moving in that direction. Bobby, driving the hoodlum, glanced sideways at Will when he passed. Will raised a hand in greeting, and Bobby looked abruptly back to the front, shaking the lines. Will frowned, shrugged. He fell back a few steps behind Fred and Jimmy.

Pretty pleased with yourself, aren't you?

"Yes, I am." Will smiled.

Fred turned around and frowned at Will. At that moment, Jimmy, walking beside him, said something to him, and he turned back.

Crossing the cattle over the river sounds like fun. Fun to watch, I mean.

"Don't you want to go swimming?"

Fred stopped, jerked around. "What hell you talking about, swimming'?"

"Oh, sorry," said Will, "sorry. Talking to myself."

Fred glared a silent moment. He stepped toward Will.

"Goin' swimmin' sounds pretty good to me." Mack stood behind Will who had not heard him come up. Fred looked from Mack to Will and back to Mack.

Jimmy looked at Mack, shook his head. He took Fred by an arm, and they walked away. Fred looked back over his shoulder, frowning.

"Fred's harmless," said Mack. "He's a good man, but his tongue gets ahead of his brain sometimes."

They walked toward the campsite where Bobby was already unhitching the mules while Cookie worked on a fire pit.

Two days later, first light. All hands in the outfit were mounted and lined up along the bank near the Paso Ganado ford, looking across the Rio Grande.

"Gawdamighty, I never saw so many cows in one

place," said Lester, a bewhiskered wiry character, the oldest man in the outfit. "And I seen some pretty good size herds."

"That's two herds, actually, maybe more," said McBride. "Most of them are ours, but another outfit is also picking up a herd tomorrow, and there's some mixing, no doubt. Just be sure we get all the cows with our trail brand. Remember, that's a dot inside a square on the left hip, the square dot I call it. Anything else, cut 'em out."

It hadn't taken McBride long to decide that Will was a quick learner and eager to take the initiative. He paired Will and Cowboy Mack who spoke some Spanish to swim over and help Win with the crossing. When McBride gave the word, the two shed their boots and britches, tossed them under a bush, mounted and entered the water.

Will and the bay had some experience in swimming the creeks around his home place west of Fort Worth and entered the water with no problem. Mack's horse was hesitant in testing the cold stream, but with a little urging and a touch of the quirt, the gelding was soon swimming alongside Will's horse.

On the south side, they found the Mexican in charge of the herd, *Jefe*, the vaqueros called him, and talked about the process for moving the cattle to the river. The vaqueros had built a brush fence that ran hundreds of yards along the flat straight into the river. Jefe explained how they use the fence as half of a funnel with the riders forming the other side of the funnel, pushing the cattle toward the water.

Jefe said he would demonstrate the process by first crossing a group of only about three hundred head. All seemed to be going as described until the thirsty cattle in the lead stopped at the bank to drink, and the herd bunched up behind them.

Will had a quick parley with Cowboy Mack who called Jefe over and talked with him. Will and Mack, accompanied by five vaqueros, moved the cattle back from the bank, then turned them and shouted and quirted them into a headlong rush for the river. The lead cattle balked only a moment, then plunged in and swam toward the far bank. The remainder of the group followed.

On the north side, cowboys close herded the three hundred near the bank to serve as magnets for the cattle on the south side. Will and Mack plunged back in the river, swam their horses for the south bank, each in the water behind his horse, gripping the horse's tail and enjoying the tow.

Successive crossings were made with bunches of four or five hundred head. The vaqueros swam their horses with the cattle to midstream, then turned back.

The final bunch totaled six hundred. Just before reaching midstream, Will heard a muffled cry and turned in the saddle to see the vaquero next to him swept from his plunging horse. Will saw the water moccasin swimming away from the horse. The vaquero, arms flailing and shouting, and the terrified horse, head high and eyes bulging, disappeared beneath the churning surface.

Will slid off his horse, grabbed his horse's tail and reached toward the swirling water where the man had disappeared. The vaquero's horse surfaced and swam frantically toward the north shore. Will swirled his hand below the surface, back and forth, but the vaquero was gone. He never came up.

Cowboys stood at water's edge on the north shore. They pulled Will from the water and helped him stand, assuring him against his protests that he could have done no more than he did. He shook his head, led his horse from the bank and tied him to the bush where he had stashed his clothes.

He pulled on his pants, sat on the ground and dried his feet with a bandanna, then pulled on his boots. He looked back at the river, now free-flowing, unencumbered with cows or people.

Pretty scary.

Will looked up, looked around at the other cowboys, talking, smoking, pulling on clothes. He stood, put on his shirt and buttoned it.

Yes, it was. It happened so fast.
I didn't know you could swim.
I can't.
Pretty dumb.
Yeah.

He smoothed his wet hair back with both hands,

rubbed his hands on his pants, staring at the empty river.

Cowboy Mack is quiet, she said.

Will looked at the group of cowboys standing back from the bank. Mack stood apart, staring at the river.

He probably spent a good part of his life being told to be quiet, before he came west. I suppose he was a slave. He looks to be about forty or so.

I haven't seen him smile.

I imagine he's having trouble forgetting. I think I'm going to like him.

Are you trying to forget, honey?

Will looked down, shook his head slowly. He saddled the bay and untied the reins. Mounting, he rode toward the huge milling herd not far from the bank. Mack saw him coming, mounted and walked his horse to him. They rode together toward the herd that was being held in a mass back from the bank.

"Too bad about the vaquero," said Mack. "Didn't look like the snake even bit nobody, but that horse sure didn't like what he saw." He straightened, pointed toward a small cluster of men near the herd. "Look yonder. They're gettin' ready to count. Took two hours to cross the herd. I 'magine it'll take longer than that to count."

McBride beckoned to Mack while Will rode to the herd.

Under Win's tutelage, Will and the other cowboys

worked the herd slowly, moving the cows in a single line through four counters. Representing the sellers, Jefe counted, moving a pebble from one hand to the other after each hundred count. McBride, the buyer, held a string lined with knots. He slipped past a knot after each hundred.

Standing beside McBride, Bobby also counted with no aids but his head. McBride had assigned Bobby to count as a backup to his own tally. He had already told Will that Bobby was the brightest cowboy in the bunch, after myself, he said, grinning. He added that Bobby was probably going be the best hand after Cowboy Mack, after he's learned all the ropes. The fourth counter was a representative of the United States Custom House. At McBride's instruction, Mack stood nearby in case there was any difficulty communicating with Jefe. No one had ever asked Cowboy Mack where he learned his Spanish.

The cattle, tired from the swim and heavy from drinking, were more docile than usual and gave the cowboys no problem as they lined the cows past the counters. All were tallied in less than an hour. Bobby and Jefe counted 3,078. The Customs man was one head more, and McBride one less. All agreed that it was a good count and accepted the 3,078 figure.

"Win," said McBride, "there's a good patch of grass up near where we're setting up camp. Move the herd up there. It's getting on dark, and they should bed down pretty quick. I'm going with Jefe to town where we'll meet the sellers to close the deal. I'll be back late tonight. Don't wait up."

"Should I come lookin' for you if you don't show up by breakfast?" Win said, grinning.

"None of that, amigo. Another time, another place maybe, but not at the settin' out. We need to get the herd moving at first light tomorrow. You'll take care of that. You know the delivery date, September 1. We got a long way to go."

He walked to Jefe who had waited, shifting his feet, looking often in the direction of the town downriver, where lights had begun to flicker on in the gloaming. McBride clapped Jefe on the back, and they strode along the bank toward the town.

CHAPTER TWO

For the first few days, the herd was driven slowly in a northwestern direction on the trail alongside the Rio Grande, breaking the cattle into a routine that would become commonplace on the long drive. Each morning, they moved the longhorns from the bed ground slowly, then threw them onto the trail. They generally kept the herd moving at a steady pace, but occasionally slowed and let them graze on a particularly good patch of grass.

The drovers watered the herd at odd times. After leaving the Rio Grande, watering times depended on when they found a stream or pond. The best time to water was in the evening, just before a stop for the night. If they were lucky, they would find good grass near the stream. Then the cattle, full of water and grass, tended to bed down without any fuss.

Cowboys were paired for night herd. They rode in opposite directions to try to intercept any restless maverick that decided to head out into the darkness. Sometimes, when the herd was restless, McBride doubled the night riders. Night herders usually sang or whistled a soft tune to calm the cattle. Each pair of night herders slept beside each other so they would not bother any-one else when being called for their round and when they returned to their beds.

McBride paired Will with Bobby. He repeated to Will, though half a dozen other cowboys were within hearing distance, that Bobby, being the smartest cow-boy in the outfit and the fastest learner, would teach him the ropes quickly. The cowboys standing nearby looked at each other, frowned, shook their heads. Bobby ducked his head, looked aside. McBride grinned at everybody's discomfort.

On the first night herd, Bobby and Will rode side by side. "We normally ride in opposite directions," Bobby said, "but I thought we should ride together for the first hour so I can explain what night herd is all about. I'll bet you already know, but Mr. McBride said we should do this."

"I understand, and I'm glad for the help. I've been on some drives of a few miles with small herds in north Texas, but never on long drives with big herds."

"Okay. Mister McBride says we are here to keep the cows quiet and bedded down so they don't get up and scatter. Hell, we couldn't do anything if they wanted to get up and scatter, so we try to convince them that everything is in order, and just go to sleep and dream about green grass and shallow streams with gravel bottoms."

Will smiled. "By damn, Bobby, you're a poet!"

"No, I'm not, just a cowboy who enjoys the work.

You got any questions? I don't think I can teach you anything you don't already know."

"I'm ready. I'll ask if something comes up."

They rode together, silent, then chatting about nothing in particular, passing the time. After completing a couple of rounds, Bobby pulled up and turned to him.

"Can you sing? Or whistle?" Bobby said.

Will grimaced. "Do I have to?" Bobby cocked his head. "Okay, I'll give it a try. "Good thing the cows can't see me. Hope my singing doesn't cause a stampede."

"You sing soft and slow on night herd. The only time you sing loud is during a stampede. The old hands who told me this said singing loud during a run sure won't do much to calm the cattle, but it helps everybody know where the other cowboys are. I've no experience with this. Anyway, your singing at night herd is not going to cause a stampede. Just sing or whistle sort of low. The cows just need to hear a soft voice."

Bobby turned his horse and rode off at a walk in the opposite direction, skirting the edge of the bed ground. He began singing, a slow, plaintive melody that Will did not recognize. *Nice voice, sings on key, sure better'n me.* He watched as Bobby became a shadow, then was swallowed by darkness. He was whistling now, the same melody.

Will pushed his horse to a slow walk at the fringe of the bedded cattle. He rode silently for a long stretch, then remembered that he was supposed to sing or whistle. He started to hum, then found the lines and sang softly, tentatively:

My foot's in the stirrup, my pony won't stand.
Goodbye, old paint, I'm a-leave'n Cheyenne.
Goodbye, old paint. I'm a-leave'n Cheyenne.
I'm a-leave'n Cheyenne, I'm off for Montan.
Goodbye, old paint, I'm a-leave'n Cheyenne.
Goodbye, old paint, I'm a-leave'n Cheyenne.

He looked around, as if to see whether anyone had heard this first attempt at night herd singing.

Oh, my, you never sang to me, sweetheart. I didn't even know you could sing.

That's because I never sang where anybody could hear me.

Where'd you learn it? I never heard anybody singing it around our place.

From an old boy at the saloon in Fort Worth that I went to a lot. He was there every time I went in. He was always there, sitting in the corner with his old guitar. He'd been up the trail a few times. He said that all the trail taught him was this song and to stay at home.

You sing good, honey. Not as sweet as Bobby, but you've got a nice voice.

"I think I better whistle from now on."

"You don't have to." Bobby suddenly emerged

from the darkness, riding toward him. "You have a nice voice." He pulled up beside Will. "I don't know that song. I hope you'll to teach it to me someday."

They sat silently a moment, watching the cattle, looking off into the dark night, glancing back at each other.

"We need to keep moving," Bobby said. He pushed his horse into a walk past Will. The dark overcast parted, and soft moonlight illuminated the moving horseman for a moment. Then he was gone. Will turned in the saddle and rode off in the other direction.

Will removed his hat and mopped his face and the top of his head with a bandanna. He replaced the hat and stuffed the bandanna into a pocket. He looked up, squinted at the sun ball overhead. The heat was searing, the hottest spring day he could remember.

McBride had told Will that he would ride at each of the trail positions until he had learned them all. He was a flank rider today, about two thirds of the distance from the front. He backed up the swing rider, who rode about a third of the distance from the front. Swing rider today was Mack, who looked back occasionally and traded waves with Will. The flank rider's job was to keep the cattle bunched, preventing them from wandering away from the column. He also ate the dust raised by the bulk of the column.

It could be worse. His first assignment was to ride drag at the back of the herd. During the drive, slow cows lagged at the end of the column, and it was these that the drag riders had to push to keep them moving.

Drag riders ate everybody's dust. Because this was the most unpleasant position, it was always assigned to the newest hands and, sometimes, a cowboy who had gotten on the wrong side of McBride or Win. Will had been relieved when he was moved after a few days to flank. He knew that after getting a taste of each position in the drive, he would return to drag for an extended time.

As the day wore on, it became increasingly difficult to keep the cattle moving and bunched. They had not watered since the previous afternoon, they had bedded in sparse dry grass last night, and they had found no grazing today. Stands of oak and cedar on each side of the trail suggested water, but riders who were sent ahead came back shaking heads.

By afternoon, the cattle were dragging, heads hanging, lowing and beginning to drift away from the column. Only with difficulty were the cowboys able to keep them bunched and moving.

At dusk, supper was hurried as the outfit prepared for what could be a busy night. Most of the cattle had not bedded down. They paced in circles, lowing softly. McBride doubled the night riders and extended their hours. Cowboys expected they would be up most of the night.

McBride stood beside the campfire, staring at the darkening horizon. A dry breeze had quickened and now flapped wagon canvas and blew sparks from the fire.

"Boys, I don't like the looks of this," said McBride, "not a little bit. I've seen this before. We could have some dry lightnin' tonight. Keep your horse saddled, and be ready to ride. You won't need your slicker. It's not gonna rain."

A sudden brilliant flash of lightning was followed by a burst of thunder. The lightning struck a mesquite thicket half a mile away, igniting small fires in the sparse dry grass at the base of the trees.

The cattle were immediately in motion. They shook their heads, milled, bellowing as cowboys ran for their horses. Two lightning forks shot earthward simultaneously from the churning black cloud, one striking the ground at the far end of the herd. Thunder exploded overhead.

The cattle burst from the bed ground, almost overtaking the cowboys who had mounted and now were galloping furiously ahead of the stampede, riding for their lives. Lightning sparked and sizzled about the horns of the cattle and the horses' ears. Only after they could get control of their horses and their heads could the cowboys begin to try to control the herd, now scattering in three or four ragged columns, all the while riders wondering whether their horses would step into a gopher hole or crevice that could spell the end of the road for horse and cowboy.

Galloping headlong in the darkness, two or three

riders here, two or three there, attached themselves to a stampeding bunch and began to turn leaders, trying to slow the run and turn the dash into a milling herd. And this in a landscape that was almost totally dark, illuminated only by a weak moon that appeared after the angry black clouds had thinned.

Will rode near the leaders of a bunch of running cows. He saw Mack just ahead pull his six-shooter and fire into the ground beside the leaders, trying to turn them to the right. Will drew his pistol and imitated Mac, firing into the ground at the feet of the racing cattle.

He looked up. Mack and the leaders in the plunging column had disappeared in the gloom. Then he remembered that McBride said everybody should sing loudly during a stampede so cowboys could locate each other. Will thought it a little silly to be singing and shooting at the same time, but he began to sing at the top of his lungs:

Goodbye, old paint. I'm a-leave'n Cheyenne!
I'm a-leave'n Cheyenne, I'm off for Montan!

More shout than song, he felt foolish.

"Who's that? That you, Will?"

Will looked across the herd and saw the shadowy mounted figure on the other side of the surging column. "Yeah! That you, Bobby?"

"Yeah! Back off! I'm turning 'em your way!"

Will reined leftward, away from the column, and the leaders followed him. He pulled back, saw Bobby on the other side of the bunch. They soon had the cattle circling wildly, lunging, charging. The herd slowed and settled into a steady, tight milling.

Will and Bobby rode through the herd, trying to break the mill so the cattle would settle. They pushed through the tight mass, back and forth. The cattle were parted, but they closed in again into a tight churning mass.

Finally, the compact bunch of circling animals slowed and widened. Cows milled slowly, finally stopping to stand spraddle-legged and heads hanging. A few began to graze on the sparse dry grass.

"Whoo," said Will, exhaling. "How many head do you think we have?"

"Can't say in the dark. I 'spect about two or three hundred."

"You done this before?"

"Couple of times, but only in the daytime."

"Saw Mack ahead," said Will, "but lost him. Just you and me now." He looked around and saw nothing but the dark shapes of cattle and the night. "I have no idea which way camp is or the rest of the herd. What do you say we stay here and try to keep this bunch quiet till morning?"

"Sounds good," Bobby said. "They should settle down. They're still thirsty, but they're real tired from that run. And there's a little grass here. Let's just ride around the bunch, just like night herding till they settle. That sound okay?"

"Yeah."

They set off in opposite directions around the herd. In the soft moonlight, they could see the cattle milling slowly, heads hanging, some grazing, some still heaving from the run, some bedding down.

That was exciting.

Yeah, little too exciting. I kept expecting my horse to step in a hole, and we'd both go down. I was lucky.

Glad that didn't happen.

He pulled up, listened. He heard nothing but the soft lowing of a few cows. Then in the distance a coyote howled, followed by a sharp yip yip, and it was quiet again. He looked up at the cold moon, felt the cool breeze on his cheek.

Aren't you supposed to be singing?

You're right. Forgot. He cleared his throat.

My foot's in the stirrup, my pony won't stand.
Goodbye, old paint, I'm a-leave'n Cheyenne.
Goodbye, old paint. I'm a-leave'n Cheyenne.
I'm a-leave'n Cheyenne, I'm off for Montan.
Goodbye, old paint, I'm a-leave'n Cheyenne.
Goodbye, old paint, I'm a-leave'n Cheyenne.

"Hope the cows don't mind," he said. "It's the only song I know."

"All they want is the voice," said Bobby. "They

don't have to know the words." He had just emerged from the darkness and pulled up beside Will. "How did you know I was there? I couldn't even see you when you spoke."

"I . . . I was . . . talking to myself, I guess. I do that. I've . . . been alone so long, I sometimes talk to myself."

They sat their horses, quiet, nervous. Bobby stared into the darkness. "I know what you mean." He started to move away, stopped, looked back at Will. "Why don't you try to sleep a while? I'll keep riding. I'll wake you later."

"Good idea. I'm bone-tired. You sure you're okay?"

"I'm okay. I'll wake you." Bobby rode off at a walk, whistling softly.

Will watched him go, then walked his horse to a flat beside a clump of sage. He dismounted, removed the saddle and saddlebags, then the blanket and dropped everything beside a large sage. He pulled hobbles from the bags and led the horse to a patch of grass a few yards away. After hobbling the bay, he went to where he had dropped his gear, spread the blanket and sat down. He pulled his boots off and lay down with a tired groan, resting his head on the saddlebags.

He closed his eyes and exhaled deeply. His eyes opened, and he saw only darkness.

Ellie?

I'm here, honey.

What the hell am I doing here?

Oh, sweetheart, you talked about going on a long drive for months. You were still talking about it when I . . . when I . . . went away. Then you said you had to go.

Ellie, don't . . . I thought I could forget. I didn't know you would come with me. I'm glad you did. Probably would have shot myself by now if you hadn't.

Don't talk like that. You'll find somebody.

He shook his head violently. *Never!* "Never!" He squeezed his eyes shut, and tears streamed down his temple. He was exhausted, in body and mind, and he slept.

It seemed only a moment had passed when Bobby awakened him with a hand to his shoulder. "Your turn, cowboy," Bobby said.

Will rolled on his back, sat up and rubbed his face with both hands. "Right." He shook his head, pulled on his boots and stood.

"Right," Will said again. He stretched. "I'll try not to disturb your sleep with Old Paint."

Bobby pulled the saddle and blanket from his horse, carried them near Will's blanket and dropped them. "You won't disturb me. Maybe you'll lull me to sleep." He hobbled his horse and removed the bridle, looked up at Will. "Just don't scare my horse."

Will walked to the sage and peed, facing away from Bobby. After a minute, he turned back, buttoning his pants. He looked around. Bobby was not there. A moment later, Bobby emerged from behind a large sage, tucking shirttails in his pants. He turned aside when he saw Will and worked on his bed, spreading the blanket beside his saddle.

"I'm off," Will said, smiling. He saddled his horse, removed the hobbles and mounted. He rode to the cattle that were bunched up, some lying down, others walking about slowly, circling.

What are you smiling about? Bobby can't see you in the dark, you know.

That's okay. We're getting acquainted pretty well. It's not necessary for good friends to always be talking to understand each other.

Oh, is that so . . . You know, sometimes you're not the sharpest knife in the drawer.

He pulled up, frowned. *Where did that come from? What do you mean?*

Silence. He glanced right and left, as if searching.
Ellie?

"Ellie?"

No response. He frowned, moved off at a slow walk.

My foot's in the stirrup, my pony won't stand.
Goodbye, old paint, I'm a-leave'n Cheyenne.
Goodbye, old paint. I'm a-leave'n Cheyenne.
I'm a-leave'n Cheyenne, I'm off for Montan.

High noon. Will and Bobby pushed their cattle toward the main herd that was grazing in a meadow beside a narrow creek. The banks of the stream were lined with mountain laurel that was covered with purple, grape-scented flower clusters.

Will and Bobby's cattle joined other bunches of a few hundred head each that moved slowly toward the herd. The cows in all these strings smelled the water and ran the last half-mile or so to the creek. They pushed through the laurel and into the stream where they stood in the shallows and drank.

"Cookie, you got something to eat in that wagon?" Will called as they approached the encampment.

"Come on in, Will, Bobby, I'll see if I can come up with something. Hell, yes, I got something! I been servin' breakfast all morning."

A half dozen cowboys sat around the campfire and beside the chuck wagon, holding plates, eating their late breakfast. They looked up at Will and Bobby, nodded and waved as they dismounted and tied reins to wagon wheels.

Teddy handed plates of steak and potatoes, beans and cornbread to the newcomers. They sat on the ground beside the wagon. Kirk, sitting at the fire, frowning, stared at Bobby.

Bobby noticed. She forked a chunk of steak to her mouth and chewed. She looked up and saw Kirk still staring. She lowered her fork to the plate. "Spit it out, Kirk."

"You gotta stop riding that mare," Kirk said. "Mares ain't suitable for a cattle drive."

Now it was Bonnie's turn to frown. "What the hell you talking about, Kirk?"

"Geldings are what you need for a cattle drive where there's lots of horses workin' together."

"Have you noticed that all the other animals in my string are geldings?"

"Then why do you ride a mare?"

"Because I've become attached to my mare. I like her. Have you noticed that Rod rides a mare, and he knows a lot more about horses then you and me, put together?"

Everybody turned to look at Rod, bent over his plate. He didn't look up.

"Well, I wondered about that, too," said Kirk. "What do you think, Rod?"

Rod took another bite. "Geldings are best suited on a cattle drive, where there's lots of horses working together."

"Then why do you ride a mare?"

Rod set his fork down, looked at Kirk, unsmiling. "Because I choose to. I've become attached to her."

Kirk pulled a face, shrugged his shoulders.

The hands had followed the exchange and now returned to their plates. All except Fred. Fred looked back and forth from Bobby to Will, squinting, his mouth slightly open, grinning from ear to ear.

Will noticed. He lowered his fork slowly to his plate. "You got something you want to say, Fred?"

"No, no," said Fred. He pushed his fork into the

potatoes on his plate and lifted a forkful. "Just happy to see everbody gittin' the critters in and gittin' their break-fast." He glanced at Bobby, grinning. "Everthang's dandy."

Will set his plate on the ground. "If you—"

"Okay, listen up." McBride had walked up and stood near the chuck wagon. "Most everbody is in now, and the herd is pretty well watered. I expect the others will show up before supper. Win, take a count after everbody's in. If we've only lost a few, I want to get back on the trail tomorrow. We can't waste any more time. We're already behind schedule, and we need to make up some time."

Win stood, walked to the wagon and handed his plate to Cookie. He strode toward the stream where the herd was grazing. He called over his shoulder, "Bobby, Will, let's do a count now, then we'll count the other bunches as they come in."

The two scrambled up, walked slowly toward the chuck wagon, forking hasty bites to their mouths. They handed their plates to Cookie and hurried after the re-treating Win.

Fred looked up at them as they passed, cocked his head, grinned and bent over his plate.

Mack, sitting across the firepit, empty plate in his lap, glared at Fred.

Yesterday's final count revealed that not only had they not lost cattle, they had picked up sixteen head. Most of the strays wore brands, probably lost by a herd ahead during a stampede. McBride said they would inquire anytime they came near enough to an outfit to ask. A few cows were not branded, wild cattle that had wandered off from a herd or home ranch before branding. The hands were always happy to pick up unbranded cattle. These were the beasts that would be slaughtered for supper.

This morning, the herd was lined out and moving in good order. After watering the previous evening, they had grazed until bedding down nicely at dusk. The cowboys had watered them again this morning, pushed them across the small stream with no difficulty, and the column now was in motion, headed north.

Will was a swing rider today. McBride had hailed him this morning when he was saddling up. He said he was satisfied with Will's performance in the drag and flank positions and moved him to swing. Placed a third of the way from the front, the swing rider was charged with keeping the cattle bunched and moving. He would remain here until he was ready to move up to point, the most responsible post. The point rider determined the direction and pace for the herd.

Will looked across the backs of the cattle to see Bobby on the other side of the column, also riding swing. Bobby was looking at him. Their eyes met for a moment, and Bobby turned away.

You two seem to always be on the same track.

Yeah, coincidence, I suppose, but both of us have about the same experience in trail driving.

You like Bobby, don't you?

Yeah, seems a nice kid, sensitive. Still don't under-stand why he would choose the life. Seems always to be thinking about something else.

Will looked across the backs of the cattle to see Bobby, looking straight ahead. As if he sensed the eyes, he turned Will's way, watched him a moment, somber, almost sad, then turned back to the front.

Bobby drove the hoodlum wagon over what appeared almost to be a road. At least, the worn surface gave evidence that wagons had come this way. But for Bobby's wagon, the road was empty this morning. Will rode alongside, whistling.

Bobby looked over. "I know that song."

Will stopped whistling, glanced at Bobby. "I 'spose you do. I told you it's the only song I know."

"Well, I'm going to have to teach you one or two more. You'll drive me crazy before we reach Cheyenne."

"Wouldn't want to do that. Be happy to learn something else." He turned back to the front, patted his horse's neck. And began whistling "I'm A-leavin' Cheyenne." Bobby looked down, grimaced. He shook the lines.

They were headed toward Brady, a settlement that called itself a town where trail bosses replenished provisions. Brady was little more than a crossroads with a blacksmith, a small Baptist church, a large saloon and two general stores that serviced the small population of farmers, a few dozen townspeople, and passing trail drivers. A corner of one of the general stores was designated the town post office.

Every cattle outfit that passed this way sent one or two hands into town in a wagon. Will had volunteered to help with the provisions and collect the mail. He had thought he would be riding with Cookie and was surprised when he saw Bobby hitching up the hoodlum to go in his place.

"Yeah, he said this is the first time he's had two wagons, and why should he drive to town when I can go," said Bobby. "Fine with me. Better'n scrubbing pots and collecting cow chips." He looked over at Will. "Expecting any letters?"

Will looked at his horse's ears. "No." After a moment, he turned to Bobby. "You?"

"No . . . I got nobody who . . ." He shook the lines.

They rode in silence, each struggling with memory.

In town, Bobby and Will helped the clerk load supplies in the wagon. Will laid the canvas bag containing three letters under the wagon seat. "Two letters for Mister McBride and one for Cookie," he said. "I suppose that shows how little the rest of us are connected outside this little cow community."

"Sure fooled me," said McBride. "Thought this was going to be an easy crossing."

McBride and four others, holding their reins, stood on the bank of a placid stream about thirty yards wide. They looked at twenty or so cows that stood rigid up to their bellies in the shallows as if they were statues. These leaders had entered the water without hesitation, stopped and dropped their heads to drink as they sank into the quicksand. Now they were locked tightly and could not pull out. Cowboys held the bulk of the herd away from the stream, a difficult task since the cattle smelled the water.

"They're standing on hard bed," said McBride, "so they're not sinking any deeper, but the quicksand on that hard bed has got 'em good. We'll have to pull 'em out, one at a time. And we gotta find a firm crossing place. He looked in both directions, up and down the stream. "Let's get at it."

They mounted and rode to the herd where McBride spoke to the men. Leaving four to watch the herd, the others rode in both directions along the bank searching for a firm crossing.

After an hour, the riders returned. Those who rode upstream reported no success. The stream in that direction was wide and shallow with what appeared to be a quicksand bottom. Those who rode downstream reported that they had found a likely crossing place. Narrower, with more current, probably swimming in places, but with a firm bottom.

McBride selected six cowboys, including Will and Bobby, with Mack in charge of the lot, to work on extracting the cows from the quicksand, then instructed the others to drive the herd downstream to the intended crossing.

Mack described how they would extract the mired cows. He had faced this same chore more than once on previous drives. The six worked together on one steer at a time. They looped a rope over the animal's horns and wrapped it around a stout tree trunk on the bank. While one man kept the rope taut, the others waded in, stepping softly and often to avoid the quicksand's pull. They dug around the cow's legs, releasing the quicksand's hold. The muck was not heavy and once the four legs were freed, two or three of the men scrambled up on the bank and pulled the rope while the others continued to dig around the legs.

Once on the bank, the ropes were removed from the cow, and the cowboys ran for cover since the beast, now free, quickly turned from captive to belligerent. As soon as the cow calmed, the men turned to the next mired animal.

Finally, the last captive was freed and, after threatening to charge his saviors, the steer joined the herd that grazed placidly on a patch of almost-green grass at water's edge. The men mounted and drove the bunch downriver to join the last cows in the herd that were just entering the water for the crossing. The freed cows were nervous at this second baptism, but they followed the cattle ahead, swimming briefly.

Bobby and Will sat their horses on the south bank,

watching the end of the column leave the water on the other side. The stream was empty now, flowing free, rippling gently.

McBride and four others rode their mounts down the bank and into the stream, heading for the south bank. The horses swam most of the way and lunged up the bank. Will and Bobby rode to them.

"Okay, now for the wagons," said McBride. "We got less than three hours of daylight, and we've got two wagons to get across. Win and I did it last year, so listen up. We have two axes. Look for dead cottonwoods. The wood will be dry and pretty light. Cut out the trunks and big limbs and drag them up there on the bank near the wagons." He pointed. Cookie leaned against his chuck wagon, smoking.

"We'll raft the hoodlum first," McBride said. "If we're going to lose a wagon in this confounded crossing, it'll be that one. Sure don't want to lose the chuck wagon. Okay, three riders upstream and three downstream. Not a minute to lose; I want to be on the other side before dark. Late supper tonight. Let's get on it."

For the next two hours, the six men did the sort of work they detested. On horseback, nobody could best a Texan. But any task that had to be performed afoot was a test for the best cowboy. They passed the ax around and competed in cutting cottonwood timbers that soon looked like beavers had gnawed on them.

Next they moved the logs to the hoodlum wagon, a less onerous task since they were horseback. Wrapping a lariat around the log, the cowboy tied the rope to the saddle horn, mounted and dragged it. The logs were light, and the task was a respite from swinging an ax.

McBride finally decided that the supply of logs was sufficient. He had Cookie drive the hoodlum wagon into the two-foot deep shallows that mercifully had a gravel bottom. Cookie unhitched the mules, climbed up on a lead mule and swam them to the north bank.

Meanwhile, the men floated logs under the wagon and lashed them to the underside, creating a raft. When this was finished, two stout ropes were tied to the wagon's front. Win took the other ends of the ropes and rode to the north bank, the ropes floating behind him, and passed them to Jimmy and Cowboy Mack. In the meantime, other cowboys had crossed the stream, dismounted quickly and joined Jimmy and Mack at the ropes.

Will and Bobby stood with McBride and Fred in the shallows beside the wagon. "Are you ready?" shouted McBride.

"Yep!" said Win.

McBride and the three others in the shallows waded to the back of the wagon. "Okay, go!" McBride shouted. The four pushed on the back of the wagon-raft while the others on the north bank pulled on the ropes. The wagon was soon off the gravel bottom and floating.

The raft was quickly at the mercy of the current

and drifted downstream, dragging the rope-pullers until the lead two men on each rope were standing knee-deep in the stream.

"Pull, you duffers, pull!" shouted Win. They pulled, digging their heels into the gravel of the shallows and those on the bank struggling to avoid being dragged into the stream. Gradually, they checked the drift of the raft and pulled it upstream to the landing where Cookie waited with the team. The mules were hitched and held the wagon in place while the logs were removed from the bottom of the wagon. The timbers were then lashed together, and Win swam his horse to the south bank, holding the ends of the ropes.

The process for converting the chuck wagon to a raft was performed in shorter order than the transformation of the hoodlum. The crossing was also faster and with less effort. McBride and Fred waded from the shallows, found their horses and swam over, reaching the north bank just after the chuck wagon was pulled out. In short order, the two wagons were pulled from the bank by their teams.

Only Bobby and Will remained on the south bank, sitting their horses and watching the activity on the other bank.

"C'mon, you need an invitation?" shouted Win.

Bobby waved. They were in no hurry. "That was some day," Bobby said. "The quicksand was a first. Not something I would like to do again any time soon. First time I've seen wagons floated too."

"Learn something new every day," Will said. They pushed their horses into the shallows and were soon swimming.

When they had almost reached the north bank, Will suddenly tensed. He saw gentle V-shaped ripples pointing toward Bobby's horse.

"Bobby!" Will leaned forward, slashing his quirt repeatedly in the water that churned from the quirt striking the surface and the snake's thrashing. Bobby's horse plunged aside to escape the frenzied splashing, and Bobby gripped the horn to keep his seat. The snake wriggled past as the horses found the bottom and lunged up the bank.

Will and Bobby dismounted quickly as cowboys crowded around them.

"What was it?" said Jimmy.

"Moccasin," Will said. "You okay, Bobby?"

"He didn't get me. What about my horse?"

"Seems okay," said Rod. He rubbed the mare's chest and shoulder, then her neck and sides. "I think she would be telling us by now if she got bit."

Bobby inhaled heavily, exhaled. "Whoo. That was scary. I didn't see him till you yelled."

The cowboys walked toward the chuck wagon, chatting. Fred turned toward Win. "What the hell is a duffer?"

Win chuckled. "Hell, I dunno. I crossed paths a few years ago in Wyoming with an Englishman who was hunting with a bunch of people. An expedition, he called it. Anybody he thought was too slow in doing his job he called a duffer. 'You duffer! Do this, do that,' he said. I just like the sound of the word. 'You duffer!' " He chuckled again.

Will and Bobby, leading their horses behind the group, looked at each other, smiling.

"We were lucky there was only one snake," said Will, "and he was in a hurry." They paused at a line of a dozen graves at the edge of a cottonwood grove. "Some of these boys might not have been so lucky. Most of them probably drowned, but I've heard some nasty stories about water moccasins."

Most of the graves were covered with grass, the wooden crosses weathered and leaning. Will bent, straightened a cross and pushed it into the ground. He pointed at a fresh grave. "This one is new, this season, for sure." The rounded soil of the site was almost free of grass, only a few weeds just beginning to sprout.

"Sad," said Bobby. "Might have been a newer one, if you hadn't seen that snake coming for me. Never did thank you." He reached over and took Will's arm, squeezed it. Will turned, smiled. Bobby ducked his head, withdrew the hand and walked on, Will following.

A passel of cowboys at the new campfire silently watched them come.

CHAPTER THREE

Days and then weeks passed in regular order. Everything had fallen into place, and everyone knew what he had to do, and he did it. They made twelve to fifteen miles a day, depending on grass and water, weather, threats from renegades who attempted to cut off a few head and buffalo that seemed to have a penchant for running smack into a peaceful herd of cattle.

There was also the problem with slow herds. All drovers were familiar with the unwritten law, which said that a herd didn't pass the herd ahead. So how should a trail boss respond when the herd ahead lagged, and there was no obvious reason for the delay? McBride fumed and argued and threatened a couple of trail bosses ahead that slowed his progress, but they managed to settle the problems without any violent altercations.

Evenings, supper around the campfire was accompanied and followed by yarning, telling and repeating real stories and outrageously creative tales that resulted in leg-slapping laughter or shouts of disbelief. Card games, seven-up or poker mostly, could become so intense that players risked the wrath of those who wanted to sleep at the campfire, or the players crept away with a lantern to finish a game.

Most evenings, Jimmy collected his guitar from the hoodlum and played and sang at the campfire. He was a pleasant fellow, quick to smile and tell stories. But casual banter was a chore for him. He was actually shy and had some difficulty with idle conversation. He tried hard to make contact, but often was ignored.

It was then that he turned to his music. His songs were a mix, mostly raucous cowboy and dance hall tunes, but sometimes he played a soft plaintive ballad, often his own composition, that aroused sweet memory, or painful regret. On these occasions, more than one cowboy turned away and wiped a tear.

Will soon moved up from swing rider to point man, the most important assignment among the drovers. From the first day at point, he worried constantly that he would have to deal with all sorts of problems, but all went smoothly. After McBride was satisfied that he knew all of the positions, he moved, as expected, back to drag. Though McBride now judged him fit to occupy every position, he was still the greenest man in the outfit. Therefore, he rode drag.

He didn't mind, actually. Bobby had been moving through the various positions on the other side of the column, so he returned to drag only a few days after Will found himself there. Bobby was his best friend in the outfit, so Will was content to share drag with him.

A number of cowboys had noted offhandedly how often Will and Bobby worked together. At first, Will thought nothing of the comments and grins and replied that since McBride had paired them early on in night riding, they often worked together and got on well. Lately, Will had become a bit irritated at the attention, but decided he would ignore it.

The usual routine was broken one afternoon in a fashion most unwelcome. The herd had watered that morning at a shallow creek and was driven across to good grass on the north side. The hands let the herd graze for a time, then threw them on the trail at a good pace in a broad valley.

After a brief stop at noon for dinner, the cowboys had hardly put the cows in motion when they heard a soft rumbling and pulled up. They looked up into a soft blue sky with not a cloud in sight. Looking around, they searched for the source of the sound, glanced at each other and shook their heads.

Then they saw it.

At the head of the valley, they saw a gentle dusty swirling at ground level. The swirling increased, expanded and became a churning gray cloud hugging the ground, moving in their direction. A black line emerged at the base of the cloud, expanded and became a tightly packed herd of stampeding buffalo.

Win, riding point, jaw hanging and wide-eyed, was mesmerized, but only for a moment. He turned in the saddle and shouted down the column. "Buffalo!

Stampede! Comin' this way! Draw your six-shooters! When they are close enough, fire at the leaders! Wait for my shot! Swing, turn the herd to the right all th' way around, and let 'em run! Now! Do it now!"

The two swing cowboys shouted and quirted cows and shot their pistols at the feet of the leaders to turn them and set them moving down the back trail. Then the swing riders and the other hands rode up beside McBride. They drew their pistols and stared, some open-mouthed, others with clenched jaws.

Beyond the oncoming buffalo, forked lightning shot toward the ground. A rumble of thunder followed, faintly heard over the sounds of hundreds of stampeding hooves.

"Shoot at the leaders!" said McBride. "Keep shooting till your gun is empty. Then get outta the way, and stay away. Don't stand your ground. If you do, they'll run right over you. Nothing more you can do at that point but get run down."

The cowboys were bunched up, as horses shied and trembled at the approach of the buffalo, the sounds of hooves growing in intensity.

McBride looked back at the herd. It had been turned and now moved on the back trail. Some cows walked while others had begun to run, a slow gait that quickened as the sounds of the oncoming buffalo increased.

Bobby rode up beside Will who sat his horse apart from the others. Will, holding his pistol at his side, glanced at him.

"Ready for this?" said Will. "Bit more excitement than I wanted today." He frowned when he saw the gun shaking in Bobby's hand. "Are you okay, buddy?"

"Yeah . . . no. I've heard too many stories. Will . . ." He looked at the line of buffalo, drawing closer. The shaggy heads, lolling tongues and twitching tails were clearly visible.

"Hang on, Bobby. This'll be over real quick."

Bobby stared at the surging buffalo, his hand shaking. "Will . . . I don't feel good about this. In case I don't make it through, I need to say—"

"Ready, Bobby!" Will watched the buffalo, now almost on them. "Here we go!" Will urged his horse toward McBride and the others, and Bobby followed.

"Remember," said McBride, "get a few shots off at the leaders, then hightail it, and run with 'em! Stay away from 'em!"

Bobby pulled his horse alongside Will. "Will," he said, looking over at him.

Will heard the tremor in his voice. "It's okay, buddy," he said softly. "We'll make it. Stick by me when—"

Will flinched at McBride's shot. Immediately a fusillade of shots exploded. A half dozen buffalos in the lead stumbled. Two went down, tumbling as followers veered around the rolling bodies. Others that were hit slowed, shook their heads, recovered and continued charging straight toward the line of cowboys.

The barrage of shots had little effect on the stampede as fallen or wounded leaders were replaced by those behind.

While the shots did not slow the charging buffalo, they did turn the leaders aside enough so the buffalo no longer pointed directly for cowboys or cattle, now running south on the back trail and scattering in all directions.

Will and Bobby sat their horses with the others, watching quietly for what seemed an eternity as the huge buffalo herd passed and flowed over a rise, disappearing from view, the sound of hooves fading.

Cowboys looked down the back trail and saw no cattle. Not a single beast. The prairie was empty of animals but for their own horses. And empty of sound except for the sharp chirp-whistle of an unseen cowbird.

Fred broke the silence. "Well, that was no fun." He looked around for a response and received none. Fred generally was not taken too seriously. Some thought him a bit slow, but for the most part, he was tolerated. He was a good hand.

McBride searched the faces. "Where's Kirk?" The others looked around. "Anybody seen him?" The cowboys looked at each other, shook heads.

"Ah, boss," said Lester. "Just about when we started shooting, he pulled his horse back from the bunch of us and rode right into the middle of the buffalo, kicking his pony hard and whipping him with the quirt. Looked like he was yelling his head off, though I couldn't hear 'im."

McBride inhaled deeply, exhaled. "Well, let's have a look. We'll find him soon enough."

The cowboys spread out and rode over the trampled ground where the stampeding buffalo had passed. Sharp hooves had crushed grass, sage, cacti and vegetation of all sorts.

"Charlie," Brad called. McBride and the others rode over to where Brad looked down at the mangled remains of what had been Kirk. Now he was but a layer of cloth and crushed flesh and splintered bones. The trampled grass was colored with his blood.

The outfit dismounted and walked slowly to the body. Some pulled hats off and stood quietly, in awe, hats and reins in hand. Some had never seen a dead body. None had seen a body reduced to a colored, grisly mass like this. Bobby stared, jaw hanging. He looked at Will, who glanced at him, his jaw clenched.

"Let's get him buried," McBride said. He looked around. "Anybody has a knife you can use to dig, get on it. Maybe we can find some sticks or rocks to help dig." He looked at the corpse, shook his head. "Let's get it done. We got some cows to find."

A few men pulled knives from saddlebags and boot sheaths; other searched for anything they could use to dig, a sharp stick, a flat rock with a sharp edge. All set to work digging beside the body.

In a half hour, they had opened a two-foot deep

cavity, just long and wide enough to accommodate the body. The remains were lifted gingerly, as one would lift a wet blanket, and placed it in the grave. A couple of cowboys began to push soil over the body when Rod touched the shoulder of one of the men.

"Hang on," Rod said. He pulled off his jacket, stooped and placed it on the body's head. "Don't like to see dirt on his face." He stood upright, looked into the grave. "Seems we oughta say something." He looked around. "Anybody know the Lord's Prayer?" They looked at each other, solemn. Some shook their heads.

Cowboy Mack stepped up, removed his hat and knelt beside the grave. He closed his eyes and lowered his head. He spoke in a deep, strong voice.

> Our Father who's in heaven, hallowed be thy name.
> Your kingdom come, your will be done, on earth like it is in heaven.
> Give us this day our daily bread;
> And forgive us our trespass, as we forgive them that trespass against us;
> And lead us not into temptation, but deliver us from th' devil.
> For your kingdom and power and glory, forever. Amen.

The men looked sheepishly at each other as

Cowboy Mack stood, still looking at the body, and backed away from the grave.

"Amen," said McBride. He stepped back, spoke to the group. "After filling it up, pile a load of rocks on top. That'll keep the critters away for a while." He shook his head and turned aside, spoke under his breath. "They'll get it soon enough."

McBride looked westward where the sun hung low over the horizon. "We've got an hour or so of daylight. We need to find as many beasts as we can before dark. You decide whether to bring in what you find this evening. If you're a good ways from camp when you finish, you might bed your bunch and come in tomorrow. We won't be in no hurry to get on the trail."

He shook his head. "This is bad business. We lose a good man, and I'm afraid we're going to lose a bunch of cows." He walked toward his horse, turned back. "Cowboy Mack. You come with me. Win, send out pairs in all directions." Win nodded.

Will still held his reins. He started to walk toward Win when he noticed Bobby standing nearby. He stopped, waited.

Bobby walked over to him. "I'm sorry," he said.

"Nothing to be sorry about," said Will. "Everything worked out fine. Except for poor Kirk." He looked toward the grave that was now covered with a pile of rocks. He looked back at Bobby. "What was it you wanted to say back there before we started shooting?"

Bobby looked down, shook his head. "Nothing, nothing really. C'mon, we need to find some cows." He took Will's shirtsleeve and tugged him toward Win who was giving instructions to the others. He looked up at Will. "We're still a pair, aren't we?"

Will raised up on elbows, opened his eyes and saw the top of the sun disc that shone above the eastern horizon. He rubbed his eyes and scratched his head vigorously with both hands.

"Goddammit," said Bobby, softly.

Will saw Bobby standing beside his, Will's, horse. He sat up. "What's this? Never heard you cuss before."

Bobby looked back over his shoulder. "Never lost a horse before to stupidity."

Will pulled his boots on, stood and tightened his belt. He walked over to Bobby. "What happened?"

"My mare is gone, and the hobbles as well. I must not have tied 'em right. She's nowhere in sight."

"Well, that does pose a problem." He looked aside, frowning. He relaxed, cocked his head. "We'll be okay. Let's collect our cows and head back to camp. If we need to, we'll get a horse for you and set out again. Charlie's going to be happy with our bunch."

Will and Bobby had happened last evening on a couple of hundred head that had found their way to a swale where a shallow pool fed by a small spring nourished a patch of good grass. The cows had grazed, watered and bedded down as if this were the proper thing for a bunch of cows to do on their own. The sun had just touched the horizon, and Will and Bobby had decided to bed down as well.

"We'll ride double," Will said. "We could look for your horse, but if the looking wore out my horse, we'd have to walk that bunch to camp. I sure don't want to do that. So we'll push 'em to camp now and see what Charlie has in mind for us. That sound okay?"

"Fine with me. Without a horse, I'm pretty dependent, ain't I?"

Will smiled, gently slapped Bobby's back. He saddled his horse, pulled Bobby up behind him, and they rode to the swale just a hundred yards away. Most of the cattle were still bedded down, a few were grazing, and some stood in the shallow pool fed by the spring.

They collected the cattle with no difficulty and pushed them from the swale up the slope to the prairie in the direction they agreed was the likely way to camp. Fed, rested and watered, the cows were docile and herded with no problem.

They rode silently, Will humming the "Cheyenne" melody. Bobby occasionally bumped Will's back with the gait of the horse.

Well, that worked out fine, didn't it?

Will straightened. *Ellie! Yeah, if the others had the same luck we did, everything's going to be dandy.*

That's not exactly what I meant.

"Look." Bobby pointed at a thin, wispy, almost perfectly vertical smoke spiral in the distance. "I hope that's Cookie's fire. I don't think I've ever missed breakfast and dinner before in the same day."

Will was not thinking about his belly. He had said little this morning. He was still trying to understand why Ellie had shown up after a long absence and then spoken in riddles.

He reined aside to push some cows back to the bunch. On the treeless prairie with a scattering of acanthus shrubs, none taller than a few feet, he could see for miles in all directions. He and Bobby had already spotted a few bunches of cattle moving toward the smoke spiral. As they neared the camp, other bunches appeared and converged, driven by others in the outfit.

"Looks good," said Bobby. He had ridden for the most part with arms dangling, except once when the horse shied from a meadowlark that had burst from a sage and almost collided with the bay. Jostled abruptly, Bobby threw his arms around Will's waist to keep from falling and as quickly withdrew them.

"Pesky bird," said Will.

They were approaching camp now and could make out wagons, the herd and cowboys walking about, unsaddling horses, tending them. Will hummed *Cheyenne*.

Bobby smiled. "I like that song, even if I have heard it a thousand times."

"You said you would teach me some other songs."

"I will, beginning tonight. I'll teach you."

Bobby hooked a thumb in Will's belt and leaned

forward, gently resting his head against Will's back.

Will stiffened and adjusted his seat. Bobby abruptly straightened and withdrew his hand.

They rode silently until they reached camp. Bobby slid off, and Will dismounted stiffly, stretched. He tied the reins to a rope corral. They waved to others, some seated at the campfire, others wandering about, smoking and chatting.

"Let's see if Cookie has anything in that wagon worth eating," Will said. Bobby nodded and followed him to the chuck wagon.

The herd grazed in a patch of dry grass. A few head stood nearby in what had been a shallow pool left from a recent rain. The lead cows had waded into the water and drank their fill, and now the pool was reduced to a layer of sandy mud.

McBride and half a dozen cowboys stood beside the chuck wagon, silently watching two galloping riders, headed their way from the north. Win and Brad pulled up and dismounted.

Win handed his reins to Brad who walked the horses to the hoodlum wagon where he tied the reins to wheels. "It's Cy Oldman," said Win to McBride. "He's stopped at a stream that he expected to have got over by now, but he's still on the south bank. The men he sent ahead this morning to look for a crossing reached the stream just as it was beginning to rise. Seems there's been heavy rains upcountry, and now this little crick is thirty yards wide, swimming all the way with a strong current.

"He said he expects it will go down as fast it came up. Figures he can cross tomorrow morning. He told me to tell you to keep your damn cows—that's what he said—well back from his herd. He smiled when he said it."

"Yeah, I know Cy," said McBride. "He's a good man. I'll ride up this evening and have a smoke with him. And a shot. Old Cy always has good whiskey in his chuck wagon.

"We'll bed the herd here and get back on the trail tomorrow 'bout mid-morning. That should give Cy time to get his herd across. If he's right about the stream going down. We're on respectable grass right now, but I would like to water our bunch before setting out. That way, the herd won't need to water at the crossing. Win, send some of the boys out to see if we can find water."

"Bobby and I saw a pool yesterday fed by a little spring," Will said. "If the spring is still flowing, it might be enough. We could ride out and see if it's still there. Bit off the trail, but not far."

"Okay, sounds good," Win said. He named three other pairs to search for water in other directions.

Will and Bobby walked to their horses at the back of the hoodlum. Bobby gathered his reins, reached up for the horn, then stopped and turned to Will. "You know what Charlie said when I told him about my horse wandering off?" Will shook his head. "He said, 'well, that leaves you with four mounts, don't it? Good thing you got backup driving the hoodlum.' He wasn't smiling."

"Well, it is . . . was . . . his horse." He mounted, looked down at Bobby. "If that's the worst thing that happens to Charlie on this drive, he's not going to worry about a lost horse. C'mon." He set out at a lope. Bobby mounted and kicked his horse to a gallop to catch up.

After riding a good hour, they reined up atop a low rise and looked down at the clear pool they had seen the day before. The small rivulet from the spring flowed in a meandering course to the pool.

"What do you think? Can this little bit water the herd?" said Will.

"Should be enough. It's a good spring."

"Right. Let's get back."

"Uh, Will? Can we sit a while to rest? There's plenty of time. McBride said we wouldn't get the herd moving till mid-morning tomorrow."

Will frowned. He wasn't tired and didn't need to rest. Bobby had already dismounted and waited, looking up at him. Will cocked his head in a why-not motion and dismounted. He followed Bobby to a mesquite where they tied reins to the trunk.

Will walked to the rise that overlooked the pool and sat down, grunting. He watched yellow butterflies fluttering among wildflowers on the bank.

He looked back at Bobby who stood by his horse, his back to Will, stuffing something into the saddlebag. Bobby looked over his shoulder at Will, smiled, closed the saddlebag and walked to the pool where he sat beside Will.

They sat silently, searching the prairie. "Pretty, if you stop to look at it," said Bobby.

"Yeah, 'spose so. I guess we're mostly too busy to notice. But you're right. It's pretty country when we slow down and look."

They lapsed into silence. Looking, listening, searching the land, looking up into the clear blue sky, marked only by a scattering of wispy white clouds. They watched a meadowlark, its yellow breast flashing, fly low across the flat and alight at the edge of the pool. It drank in a head-bobbing motion, then burst into flight and disappeared over the rise.

Will leaned forward and put a hand on the ground to push himself up. "We better get moving."

Bobby touched his arm to stop him.

"Will?"

Will leaned back, turned to him. "Yeah?"

They looked at each other. Will waited, frowning.

"Will?"

"What is it, Bobby?"

Bobby reached and took Will's hand.

"Whoa, hold on, Bobby." Will straightened and made to withdraw his hand, but Bobby held it.

"Bobby, don't do this."

Bobby locked his eyes on Will's and pulled Will's hand to him, pressing the hand to his chest.

Will jerked backward, frowned, started to pull his hand away, then stopped and pushed against Bobby's chest.

"Bobby, what th' hell?"

Bobby unbuttoned his shirt with his free hand and pushed Will's hand through the opening. Will let the hand slide inside and rest on Bobby's chest.

"Bobby, that feels like . . ."

"That's what it is, Will. And my name's not Bobby. It's Bonnie."

Will pulled his hand back slowly and straightened. He squeezed his eyes hard, opened them and shook his head.

"Whoa. Bonnie? You're . . . you're . . ."

"Yeah. I'm a girl."

"But . . . but . . . wait a minute. You're a girl? How could I have been so . . . so . . ."

"Well, I tried to sound like a boy," she said in the voice that had always been Bobby, a bit low, strong and assertive. "No more of that now, at least not with you." Now she spoke in a softer voice, an octave higher, in the voice that was Bonnie.

"Why didn't I see your . . . uh, your—"

"I had them wrapped. I took off the cloth just a minute ago."

She took his hand again. "I have wanted to talk with you from the first time I saw you. I wanted to talk with you as Bonnie." She lowered her head, and her hands went to her face as tears trickled through her fingers. "I've been so lonely."

Will reached for her, pulled back, then reached again, stopped and lowered his hands to his lap. "Whoo, Bobby, uh, Bonnie, give me time to get my head around this. You know I've always liked you as a pard. And you know that some of the boys wondered about the two of us, you know, two fellas."

She leaned back, wiping her eyes with both hands.

"Yeah," she said, forcing a thin smile. She looked aside. "I didn't know whether to laugh or cry. I was hurting inside so much. Hurting 'cause I couldn't tell you, and 'cause I wanted you to like me as Bonnie. I don't care what they think now, but I s'pose it's better if I'm still Bobby in camp. At least, for now. Is that okay?"

"Okay with me. But why? Why Bobby?"

"Nothing to tell. I needed . . . I needed to get away. And I figured they wouldn't take a girl. So I became a boy."

"That doesn't explain—"

"We better get back to camp now. Charlie needs to know about this pool."

They walked to their horses, untied the reins and mounted. She quirted her horse into a gallop, her hat held by a cord flopping about on her back, her hair flying. He had never noticed that her hair was a bit longer than most of the hands. In fact, he could not recall ever seeing her without a hat during the day. Will shook his head and galloped after her, his head spinning.

The days that followed were ordinary trail-slogging days. The weather was mild, streams passable, cattle fed and watered on schedule. Meals were on time, adequate and appreciated. Cowboys still yarned around the evening campfire, listened to Jimmy's guitar and his songs, played serious card games. Some talked about getting a real job when this drive was finished, then guffawed, saying there was nowhere on God's Earth they would rather be than right here. They talked increasingly about what they intended to do in Dodge.

Will and Bobby shared little in the campfire banter, rather helping Cookie at the chuck wagon and passing the time. At dusk sometimes they strolled from the camp, stopping to look at the sky or bending to inspect a lone wildflower. The boys at the fire often watched them, shaking heads and commenting softly. They noticed when Bobby pulled Will's sleeve to show him something he had picked up.

The cowboys were especially anxious to reach Dodge since McBride had forbade anyone going into town at Abilene, the Texas Abilene. That is, anyone except Cookie and Bobby to pick up supplies, and Mack and Rod to be sure they and the supplies returned intact. Abilene had acquired a reputation of late for relieving visitors of their cash and virtue, often accompanied by brawls and occasional bloodletting. Since the boys had been denied the pleasures of Abilene, their expectations for Dodge had intensified.

Not so Will. Since Bonnie's revelation, he had gotten his head around this, this transformation, and his world was right here in this camp. He looked forward to seeing Dodge as a vestige of civilization on the prairie, but his curiosity ended there. He could think only of Bonnie.

She was still a mystery to him. She had told him little of herself, and he had not pushed her to explain. He decided that she would tell him everything when she was ready. Her silence was not a barrier, rather an enticement.

They still rode night herd as a pair, and she had to insist he ride in a different direction when he wanted to ride alongside her. But I want to be beside you, he had said. I want to talk with you and touch you. She had laughed and touched his cheek, leaned over and kissed him. Go, she had said. He turned and rode in the other direction.

As a night herd pair, they still slept beside each other. A few nights after Bonnie's revelation to Will, they moved their blankets on the other side of the hoodlum, out of sight and hearing of the others that slept near the fire circle. When questioned by the others about the move, Will replied that he was a light sleeper and was often awakened by the snoring and coming and going of the others. Some accepted the explanation without question; others exchanged doubtful looks.

Now Will understood why Bonnie, when she was still Bobby, had seemed uncomfortable on rainy days when they shared a small tent. She had pushed against the canvas as far away from him as possible. He glanced at her more than once to see her wide-eyed, staring at him, before turning over to face the tent wall.

Bonnie had wanted to continue as Bobby in camp, but working together and sleeping beside each other wore on their nerves. On the first night they moved their beds, Bonnie raised Will's blanket and crept underneath. They loosened their clothing and explored each other's bodies. Will had to put a hand lightly on her mouth to quiet her moans. At the finish, he kissed her, then withdrew. She held his face, kissed him softly and scooted away to her blankets.

On his back, Will stared up into a sky filled with more brilliant, sparkling stars than he had ever seen. He sat up, then stood and walked away from camp to relieve himself. He peered into the darkness, at peace, marveling at his good fortune.

I been watchin' you, cowboy.

Ellie!

Things moving right along. I told you a long time ago that I liked Bobby.

Yes, you did. I think you knew before I did.

I saw a softness that you didn't even suspect. Remember when I said you weren't the sharpest knife in the drawer?

Yeah. That confused me. Not now.

I think it's time for me to go.

Ellie! Wait! Don't . . . I . . .

She's a fine woman, Will. I told you you'd find someone.

Wait, Ellie. I don't . . . I can't lose you. What can I do? Ellie . . .

Time doesn't stand still, Will. You have a new life. Grab it and live it. I loved you, Will. Remember me. Goodbye, sweetheart.

Ellie! "Ellie!" Leaning forward, he sobbed into his hands. He looked up into the black void that had lost its stars. He lowered his head, wiped a cheek.

"Will, what's wrong?" Bonnie stood behind him, her hand on his back. She wore only shirt and underpants.

He turned, took her in his arms and held her. She wiped the tears on his cheek.

"What is it, honey? Who's Ellie?"

He inhaled deeply, exhaled. He leaned back, raised her chin and kissed her softly. Pulling her to him, he rested his cheek on her head. "I'll explain. Not now. Back to bed."

CHAPTER FOUR

No one in camp had openly questioned Will's explanation for the move beyond the hoodlum until Lester, who came to wake them for night herding a few nights later, saw a sleeping Bobby cuddled against Will's backside. He spread the word to the others, who responded with nods, grins and a few snickers.

When Will and Bobby, carrying breakfast plates that same morning, walked from the chuck wagon to the fire circle, all conversation ended abruptly as the cowboys seated on the ground watched them come. All held forks on plates or suspended in midair, staring at Will and Bobby. Waiting.

Fred grinned and snorted. "Got something going there with Bobby-boy, Will?" The others looked at Fred, then at Will and Bobby, standing beside each other, holding their plates.

Will stared at Fred. He shook his head.

"Will?" said Win.

Will had not taken his eyes from Fred. "I'm trying to decide whether to beat hell outta this fool or feel sorry for him."

"That ain't what we need to hear, Will," said Lester.

"Shut up, Lester," said Cowboy Mack. He looked at Bobby and Will, still standing with their plates in hand. "Will, I don't give a damn how you're goin' to explain this, but whatever you say, I'll back you, and the hell with anybody who don't like it."

The others frowned at Mack, looked back at Will and Bobby, still waiting.

"Thanks, Mack. I appreciate that," said Will.

A long moment passed as the cowboys waited.

Bobby turned to Will. "You think I need to?" she said, softly.

Will looked aside at Bobby, said nothing, then looked up, his eyes closed. He opened his eyes, turned to Bobby. "I hate it, but maybe you do."

Bobby handed her plate to Will. She tugged at her shirttails, pulling them from pants. When they were free, she rolled up the cloth, jerked the roll to her chin, then pushed them down quickly, giggling.

Jaws dropped, and eyes opened wide. "Hey, what th' hell! Them's tits!" shouted Jimmy. The others stared at Bobby, then at each other.

"And my name's not Bobby. It's Bonnie." She spoke in her Bonnie voice, softer and higher, while tucking in shirttails.

"Bonnie! You're . . . a girl?" said Win.

"All right! Entertainment's over," said McBride who had stood behind the circle, watching and listening. "No more jawing. Finish your breakfast, and we'll get moving. We're late."

"Hey," said Lester, looking up at McBride. "Will ain't finished telling us what's going on."

McBride glared at Lester. "Am I speaking Chinese this morning, Lester, or do you understand what I'm saying?"

The others laughed, turned back to their plates, still watching Will and Bonnie. Some stared wide-eyed, some grinning and shaking heads.

"Will, Bobby, uh, Bonnie, we need to talk." McBride walked toward the chuck wagon. Will and Bonnie followed, carrying their untouched breakfast plates. Cookie, standing at the back of the wagon, sprinkled flour on a cutting board. He had watched the morning's spectacle without any noticeable surprise or interest. Now he ignored the others and concentrated on his biscuit dough.

McBride looked back to the campfire, confirmed that the men seated there were paying attention to their breakfast and each other. He turned to Bonnie and Will.

"Bobby, uh, Bonnie, I'm floored, flabbergasted. You sure had me fooled." He straightened. "Now. You've put me in a real pickle. Girls don't go on cattle drives. A cattle outfit is all men. A woman can be the cause of all sorts of problems."

"You said Bobby was the smartest hand in the lot," said Will, "a good worker that went out of his way to help. That same person is standing right in front of you."

McBride squirmed. "Yeah, I know what I said, but . . . it just ain't *done*. When the men in a cattle outfit ain't had a woman in months—sorry—or even *seen* a woman in months, there can be problems." He looked aside, back to Bonnie. "Sorry, missy—damn, am I really saying that—but you're gonna have to go, soon as we reach a town that has transportation. Before Dodge, I hope."

"She can't just . . . go," said Will. "She'd not be safe. Besides, I'm getting sort of used to having her around." He smiled at her, and she ducked her head.

"See, that's what I mean. You're a cowboy, a good cowboy doing a good job. If you had a girlfriend tagging along, you'd be distracted."

"She wouldn't be tagging along, Charlie. She'd be doing her job, just like she's been doing for months."

McBride looked down, shook his head. "Sorry, but it won't work. We'll be sure she's let go at someplace safe."

Will stared at McBride, grim, silent. He looked aside a full minute, frowning, while McBride waited. Then he turned back to McBride, straightened. "If she goes, I go."

"Be damned." McBride drooped. He rubbed his face with both hands. "Well, I'll hate to lose two of my best hands, but if that's the way it is, I'll just have to work it out. Should be able hire on a couple of cowboys at Dodge, if not before. Shouldn't be too hard." He grimaced. "Damn, Will."

Cookie looked up from the bread dough, stared into the wagon interior a long moment. He straightened, turned to McBride, wiped his hands slowly on his apron. "You gonna find a cook in Dodge as well, Charlie? If Bonnie goes, I go."

"What!" McBride squinted, glared. "What th' hell's—"

"You see, Charlie, Bonnie's my granddaughter."

McBride's jaw dropped. He lowered his chin, put a hand to his forehead, sighed. "Teddy, you got some coffee in that pot? I need to sit down."

Cookie reached inside the wagon, put four cups on the tailgate board. He pulled on a glove, walked to the cooking fire and picked up the coffee pot. Returning to the wagon, he poured coffee into the cups and set the pot on the tailgate. He took the plates from Bonnie and Will, poured the contents into a bucket beside a rear wheel.

"Hope the coffee's still warm enough for you." He handed a cup to McBride, took one for himself and motioned to Will and Bonnie. They took cups. Cookie leaned against the tailgate, sipping his coffee as if this were a normal morning. The other three sat down slowly on the ground.

"Bonnie never had a mama," said Teddy. "My sweet daughter died giving birth to Bonnie. Her daddy passed on to his reward two years ago. She's been staying with me and my wife since then. We love her like our own child. When I'm on a drive, she and my wife get on real good. But that didn't work this year.

"You see, Bonnie had a boyfriend. He was a good fella until he got kicked in the head last fall by a horse he was shooing. He's a blacksmith. He seemed to recover, but he was never the same. He yelled a lot, wanted to be with Bonnie all the time, but wasn't the kind person he was before."

Bonnie listened, alternately looking up at Cookie and at the prairie beyond the chuck wagon.

"Then he hit her, and that was it. I told him to stay away from her. I told him I'd shoot him if he came close to her. He threatened me, said he would have his way when I left on the next drive. I couldn't leave her with my wife, so I asked my brother. My brother is older than me and is afraid of the fella. She wouldn't have been safe with my wife or him. So here we are."

Bonnie looked aside at Will who had watched her during Cookie's explanation. He sipped from his cup, lowered it and leaned toward Bonnie. "Sorry," he whispered.

McBride stared at the ground in front of him. The others watched him, waiting.

Finally, he looked up, raised his cup and emptied it. "Okay. I understand. You did what you had to do. Now here's what *we* gotta do. Bobby—damn it, *Bonnie*—in camp, you're Bonnie, and you'll carry on as you always have, doing the same work. Yeah, I did say you're a good hand, and I meant it. Nothing's changed there. You'll keep on being a good hand.

"But hear me on this. Any time we come into

75

contact with anybody other than the cowboys in this outfit, you're *Bobby* until you're out of sight of those people."

He looked around at the three who had listened silently. "Are all of you okay with everything I said?"

"Yep," said Cookie. He spooned out hot beans and beef on two plates and handed them to Will and Bonnie. He turned back to his bread dough, signaling that the conversation, as far as he was concerned, was over.

McBride had watched all this, waiting. "Bobby? *Bonnie*! Will? You're okay with this?" They nodded.

McBride stood, walked slowly to the campfire, Bonnie and Will close behind, carrying their plates. The cowboys sitting at the fire and standing nearby looked up, and all talk stopped. McBride recounted the conversation he just had with Will, Bonnie and Cookie. The men listened without a sound, some jaws hanging, some wry smiles and shaking heads, and not a few low be-damns and hard frowns.

Bonnie smiled, and this seemed to break the tension.

"Hell, Will," said Fred, "I guess I'm the only one here that knew what was goin' on. I figured you was gettin' sweet on Bobby, but you was gettin' sweet on *Bonnie*. I knowed it!" He looked around the group, as if asking for affirmation. No one responded.

Will and Bonnie sat down at the fire circle. They turned to their breakfast, ate with little comment, as they did every morning. The others were quieter than usual, conversing in low tones, glancing often at Bonnie, smiling and shaking heads.

Bonnie stopped her fork in midair, looked around, lowered the fork to her plate. "Would you lot get over it? I'm still a better hand than any man here, and I'll prove it." She glanced around with a stern look. The others stared at her, frowning, still unsure how to respond to this transformation. Jimmy pulled a face, looked aside at Lester who snickered.

Bonnie smiled, and the tension evaporated. The cowboys grinned, laughed, accompanied by a few claps on backs, and the usual chattering returned.

"Okay, Bonnie Bobby," said Rod, "we're watchin'. My mama would be real proud of you, and so am I."

The top of the setting sun was a luminous crescent just above the horizon. The sky above the orb glowed golden while the higher sky was teaspoon silver.

Bonnie and Will strolled from the campfire toward darkness, sipping from coffee cups. A passel of cowboys sitting around the fire, empty supper plates on the ground beside them, watched the pair. More than one hand leaned over to a compatriot, whispering, grinning, shaking heads. A cowboy slapped his neighbor on the back and laughed out loud.

Will looked back, saw the faces turned their way, smiling faces that asked questions. He walked with Bonnie to the edge of firelight and stopped, looked up at a sky that was slowly populating with new stars. He sipped from his cup, turned to her.

She took his hand, held it to her cheek. "I'm sorry I didn't tell you about myself, why I'm here. I was going to tell you, just waiting for the right time. I'm sorry you heard it from Grandpa."

He smiled, raised her chin and kissed her lips. "It's okay. I can understand that you might find it hard to talk about something unpleasant like that. I can also understand why the boyfriend was so unhappy about losing you."

She put an arm around his waist and leaned against him, resting her head on his chest.

"On that point," he said. She leaned back, looked up at him. "There's not a man in this outfit that wouldn't like to bed you. I been watching 'em lookin' at you. You be careful, especially when they find some liquor. If I'm not around, you make yourself scarce."

She stopped, frowned. "You think they'd be mean to me, knowing me as a friend and a hand in this outfit?"

He took her face in his hands, leaned down and kissed her. "These fellas hadn't had liquor in weeks. They hadn't had a woman longer than that. Liquor on a stomach that hadn't seen liquor in a long time can make a man do things he would never do sober. You just watch yourself."

She put her arms around his waist and pulled him close. "You gonna take care of me?" she said softly.

"If I'm around, I'll take care of you."

She tightened her hold, reached up and pulled his head down, kissed him. She whispered in his ear. "You're around right now. Take care of me."

He took her cup, and they walked past the fire circle toward the chuck wagon, passing four cowboys who still sat at the dying campfire, talking softly. Will nodded to them, and they silently returned the nod. Will decided that someone was telling a thoughtful story, which always sobered impressionable listeners.

Will placed the cups in the tub on the ground beside the chuck wagon and retrieved their bedrolls from the hoodlum. They spread the bedrolls on the ground on the far side of the wagon. Now in a hurry, they removed boots, loosened clothing and crawled into his bedroll where they struggled out of pants. Their lovemaking was intense, prolonged, each putting a hand gently to the other's mouth to stifle groans and gasps.

Afterwards, they fell apart and lay quietly on their backs, inhaling deeply, exhaling slowly. After a minute, he rolled over to face her and whispered in her ear. "You make enough noise to cause a stampede."

She turned on her side, almost nose to nose with him, and spoke softly. "You sound like a bull in heat. You're going to wake up the whole outfit here and the camp up north at the river as well."

He kissed her mouth, her nose, her forehead. He lay on his back, looked up into the clear sky, now filled with sparkling stars.

She rose on an elbow, studied his face, dimly illuminated in the weak moonlight. A minute passed, or an hour.

"Tell me about Ellie," she said.

He stared up into a black void, a sky that had lost its stars. He said nothing, and she wondered whether he would.

"You don't have to if you don't want to," she said.

"I've been meaning to, and I want to."

She waited.

"We grew up together. Her family had the farm next to ours. Both families ran a few beef cows, and Ellie and I tended them as kids. We went to school together. We were pals. When we were old enough to know the difference between boys and girls, we became sweethearts. She was my dear friend and my sweetheart."

He choked back a sob. Bonnie wiped a tear from his cheek. He took her hand and held it to his cheek.

She waited.

"The sickness took her," he said. "Two years back, it was. It took her and her mama and her little brother. Samuel, a sweet boy. And it took my daddy." He turned on his side to face her. "I had nobody, Bonnie, nobody. I'd already lost my mama to the Comanches. I wanted to die. The preacher and some neighbors helped me bury our dead, and I left what had been my home, our homes. That's when I started wandering.

"I was on the road two years, not knowing where

I was going, and not caring. I went to south Texas, to Mexico, to Louisiana. I was a dirty, worthless bum. I did odd jobs, working cattle mostly, but didn't stay long anywhere. I'm sorry to say that I became pretty good with a six-shooter.

"I remembered that my brother was a trail boss on cattle drives. I hadn't thought about him for years. He left home just before the sickness, and I lost touch with him. I decided that I would try to find him. Maybe I'd join a drive. Just for something to do. I had to get away from Texas."

He rolled on his back, exhausted, staring into a void.

"Ellie went with you, didn't she?"

He looked at her, then looked overhead again. "Yes, she was the reason I'm still sane." He turned to her. "Am I still sane?"

She touched his cheek, leaned over and kissed him. "You're still sane, honey. A little crazy sometimes, but I like you anyway."

"She likes you, you know. She told me that I'm lucky I found you." He turned away. "That's when she said it was time for her to go." He rolled over and took Bonnie in his arms. Her head rested on his shoulder. "She's gone, Bonnie." He shook his head, choked back a sob. She put a hand on his cheek. He cleared his throat. "And it's okay. She's at peace. So am I. If you'll help me."

She spoke softly into his ear. "We're gonna help

each other, cowboy. We've both had our troubles, and we've whipped 'em." She pulled back, patted his cheek, ending in a soft slap. "Now let's get some sleep, or we're both gonna be blubbering." She kissed him and pulled up the covers, snuggling against him.

"There it is," Bonnie said. She and Will sat their horses, looking across a flat sagebrush plain at the distant pond bordered by a line of tall trees. Rising heat waves on the plain blurred the view of the pond and woods.

"We'll see." He pushed his horse to a lope, and she followed. As they approached the pond, it seemed to shimmer, recede and break up. Then it vanished. Only the empty sagebrush plain remained. They reined up.

"Damn mirage," he said. "That must be what Jimmy and Cowboy Mack saw this morning."

McBride had sent out pairs of riders at first light to search for water. The herd had not been watered for two days now, and the thirsty cows were becoming restless and difficult to control. Jimmy and Cowboy Mack had returned early to report the sighting of the pond ahead. McBride was not convinced and sent Will and Bonnie to confirm before setting the herd in motion toward the pond, which was a half mile off the main trail.

"We better get back. I hate to report this bad news. Charlie won't be happy." They set out at a lope. After riding a good stretch, the herd came in sight, and Will pulled up abruptly. Bonnie reined up.

"What is it?" she said.

Will stared. "Look over there on the left at that shallow cut at the base of the rise, the one with the little juniper on top. Isn't that a horse's head in the cut? Yeah, and it looks like a man laying on the back slope of the rise. Seems to be looking at the herd."

"I see it."

"This may be the same man the others have reported seeing, somebody all by himself, watching the herd. Charlie thinks he's likely scouting for rustlers who're looking for a chance to stampede the herd and pick up a bunch of cows in the confusion. He said he's seen this happen before.

"Let's mosey over and see if we can have a talk with this fella." They rode off at a lope toward the rise. The figure there sat up, looking their way. He stood and ran to his horse, mounted quickly and galloped down the cut toward open country.

Will and Bobby pulled up and watched the rider disappear. "Sure would like to go after him and have a little talk, but we need to report to Charley."

They rode toward the herd and pulled up where McBride talked with half a dozen cowboys. McBride was not surprised at Will's water report. "Pretty much what I expected. Didn't think there was any water in that direction, not a pond anyway. Just as well. Lester and Brad found a pretty good crick up ahead, almost on the trail. Must have rained up that way. We're moving out right now." McBride waved the cowboys toward the herd. He motioned Will and Bonnie to stay.

"Now, about this fella watching us," McBride said. "I don't suppose you got close to him."

"No, he got away on a fast horse," Will said, "and we needed to report the pretty pond we saw." He smiled.

"Well, we're in good shape with the crick, if it is a crick and not another damn mirage. Lester said he got a drink from it, but you know Lester. The old boy's beginning to wander a bit." He straightened, stretched. "Let's get this herd moving."

The creek was real, after all. It was running full, a good twenty feet wide, no doubt from good rains upcountry. Well before sunset, the herd had been watered on a sandy bottom and was grazing on a decent patch of grass that bordered the stream.

Cowboys sat around the campfire, supper plates in laps, coffee cups on the ground beside them. Conversation was subdued as they listened to Jimmy's song and guitar. Instead of his usual wild western songs, tonight it was a soft Irish ballad. When he finished, and conversation resumed, all agreed that it had been a good day after the worry about water.

Will had finished his supper and returned his plate to the chuck wagon. Now he held Cookie's binocular trained on a distant thick patch of sagebrush. It was dusk, but still light enough to make out shapes.

"See him?" said Cookie.

"Yeah," Will said, still looking through the binocular. "Can't make out much. White man, reddish face color, like he's spent lots of time in the sun."

"What's he doing?"

"Just looking this way. I think that's his horse behind him, like he's down in a gully."

"Should we send somebody out?"

"Well, Charlie has tried that already a couple of times, but the guy's got a fast horse, and he's always able to get away. I'll tell Charlie. I suppose we'll just keep watching. Fred said we should just shoot him and get it over with."

Cookie chuckled. "That's Fred for you."

While cowboys lingered over breakfast, McBride and Will and Bonnie stood on the banks of the creek, looking down at the placid flow.

"Too bad we didn't have time to cross yesterday. The crick was deeper and faster, but it was swimming, and we could've got the herd across. Now we got a crick that ain't swimmin,' and we got quicksand. I suspected that last evening. Cowboy Mack and Lester tried to cross an hour ago to look for trail on the other side, and they had to turn back when their horses started to bog down. They rode up and down the bank on this side and didn't see anything that looked like a firm crossing." He turned to Will and Bonnie. "You know the name of this crick? Little Boggy, they call it. For good reason." He shook his head.

"How 'bout bridging it?" said Will. "I saw it done on a creek about the same size near Fort Worth. There's timber down there." He pointed downstream at a line of cottonwoods on the bank. "Looks like there's some down stuff as well. It's a short span, and we should find plenty of wood and brush. We could make the bridge bed wide enough for the wagons."

McBride frowned, still looking at the flow. He turned to Will. "By damn. Let's do it. Hell, we can do it. I crossed a herd last year on a bridge built by young Pete Slaughter. His outfit and the cowboys from the herd behind them built it and left it for anybody following that wanted to use it."

He hitched up his pants. "Let's git on it. Bobby—*damn it!*—Bonnie, ride back and tell the boys. Bring Cookie's ax and hatchet. We need to finish this thing before dark so we can cross at first light tomorrow. Will, let's find the best spot to build."

McBride and Will rode the bank and settled on a narrow channel about twenty feet wide and mostly two feet deep. Cowboys rode up slowly, reined up and dismounted, some grumbling about having to perform manual labor that couldn't be done on horseback.

"Turn to, boys," said McBride. "Sooner we get this done, the sooner you'll be back in the saddle."

For the rest of the morning, cowboys passed the ax and hatchet around, chopping down trees, removing limbs from trunks and downed logs, dragging brush and logs to the selected crossing. Cookie and Bonnie had brought the chuck wagon to the work site, and everyone stopped for a brief cold dinner.

Then it was back to work. A foundation of brush was laid in the stream, about twelve feet wide and four feet high from streambed to top. In some spots, brush sank into the sandy bottom, and more brush was piled on top. When the line of brush reached the other bank, some cowboys struggled across the foundation and worked on trees on the north bank. One cowboy slipped off the leafy causeway to the streambed and quickly climbed back on the line of brush. Everyone had been warned about the quicksand bottom.

Now logs were laid and lashed over the brush foundation. That done, cowboys used three spades provided by Cookie to spread a layer of soil on the log bed. They walked back and forth, stomping on the dirt until it had the appearance of a natural roadbed.

Will and a half dozen others stood in the middle of the span, looking about at their handiwork.

"That's it?" said Brad. "Sure don't look like any bridge I ever saw." He stomped, planted his spread-eagled feet and swayed side to side. The bridge moved ever so slightly. He frowned, looked at the others.

Will shrugged his shoulders. "This sort of bridge seems to have worked before. We'll see." The cowboy bridge builders looked at McBride on the south bank where he stood with Win.

McBride looked westward, upstream, at a dark cloud on the horizon. "I figured we would cross tomorrow, but I sure don't like the looks of that sky." He looked back at the bridge. "That bridge bed is just two feet above water level. It's shallow here, and the slack current is flowing nicely through the brush foundation, but if we get a lot of rain upcountry, we could be in trouble. I think we should cross right now. We got three hours of daylight." He turned to Win. "What do you think?"

"Sounds good to me."

"Okay, get the herd ready."

McBride shouted to the men on the bridge. "Get your horses. We're crossing today." The cowboys hustled toward the south bank, smiling at each other, happy to be finished with manual labor on two feet.

McBride went to the chuck wagon where Cookie and Bonnie had watched the bridge building. "Bonnie, tell Rod to walk the remuda across the bridge half a dozen times. That'll pack the sod. Cookie, when that's done, take the chuck wagon across. Supper on the north bank." Cookie acknowledged with a wave.

McBride called to Will who was walking with the others toward the horses. "Will, wait for me. Might need you." Will nodded and walked to him. McBride looked westward, frowned, lowered his head. "Sure don't like that cloud." He walked toward the bridge.

Will tarried a moment, cocked his head at Bonnie. She looked over her shoulder to verify that her grandpa was not watching, smiled, unbuttoned the top two buttons of her shirt and opened the front, her eyes fixed on Will's. He grinned, clenched his jaw and frowned, turned and hurried to catch up with McBride. Bonnie went in the other direction toward the remuda, buttoning up. She laughed out loud.

Cowboys mounted, rode to the herd, preparing them for the crossing. They watched Rod and Bonnie push the remuda across the bridge with no difficulty. On the other side, they turned the horses and walked them back across the bridge. And again. And again.

"Okay, enough," McBride shouted to Rod on the north bank who was in the process of turning the horses for another pass on the bridge.

McBride waved to Cookie who sat on the chuck wagon seat. Cookie shook the lines, and the mules moved onto the bridge without hesitation. Brad followed in the hoodlum, still mumbling under his breath because he didn't fancy himself a muleskinner. He looked over the side of the bridge, wide-eyed, nervous, at the stream flowing through the porous brush foundation. He cracked the whip over the team's backs.

"Now, let's see what the cows think of our bridge," McBride mumbled to himself. He waved to Win to bring the herd to the bridge.

Win had the cowboys cut out a bunch of about a hundred and move them toward the bridge. Riders close herded the leaders in a file of two or three abreast toward the bridge, but there they balked and turned aside. The cowboys quirted and cussed the leaders and pushed them toward the bridge where they balked, heads hanging. They would not step on the bridge sod.

"Okay," McBride shouted. "Pull 'em back. We'll try something else." He pondered and finally decided to try to push a smaller number across. At his instruction, Win had twenty head cut from the herd and walked them around a bit to demonstrate that they were a cohesive, compact bunch. At least, he hoped they would think themselves something special.

Win and three others walked the twenty cows slowly toward the bridge. Before reaching it, they turned them and close herded the bunch along the bank away from the bridge. Then they turned and walked them slowly to the bridge where the cows absolutely refused to step onto the span.

McBride cussed under his breath, motioned Win to return the balky cows to the herd. He frowned, stared at the bridge.

"How 'bout the calf?" Bonnie shouted from the north bank.

McBride looked up. His eyes opened wide. "By damn, Bonnie," he said softly to himself. He waved to Bonnie, turned and strode to his horse. "C'mon, Will." McBride mounted as Will ran to his horse. McBride and Will arrived at the herd at the same time.

"Win, remember the calf that's running with its

mother?" McBride said. Win nodded. McBride turned to Will. "Will, put a rope around that calf's neck, and parade it slowly around in the middle of the herd. You might tighten the rope a bit so the calf will bawl out loud. After you've roused the ire of every animal in the herd, pull the calf slowly to the bridge. Stop there a while, maybe tighten the rope a little more, then pull it across the bridge."

Will rode around the perimeter of the herd, looking for the calf. He pulled up beside Cowboy Mack and asked him if he had seen the calf. Mack beckoned him to follow and rode into the herd. They pulled up near the calf and its mother. Will dismounted and handed his reins to Mack. He untied his rope from the saddle and walked toward the calf.

"You won't hurt the little critter, Will."

Will responded without looking at him. "I won't hurt him if he cooperates." He loosened the coil as he approached the calf.

"I don't want to see the little critter hurt, Will."

Will looked over his shoulder at Mack. "I'll be careful." *What th' hell, Mack, it's a calf.*

The calf backed away at Will's approach, and he tossed the loop over his head, pulled the noose snug. The calf bawled, and the mother became agitated. Will walked back to his horse, pulling the calf with some difficulty as the calf balked and pulled on the noose which tightened with the pulling. The mother cow followed.

Will took his reins from a glaring Mack and mounted. He rode back into the midst of the herd, pulling the reluctant calf that now bellowed and cried. The mother followed the calf, and other cows became agitated, tossing their heads and following along behind the calf and mother.

After he had collected a sizable entourage, Will rode slowly toward the stream. Arriving at the entrance to the bridge, he paused as the calf bawled, and excited cows milled around behind the calf and mother. McBride and a half dozen cowboys sitting their horses nearby watched all this.

McBride looked to the west. The dark cloud at the horizon had enlarged, and a silver-gray sheen below the cloud signaled rain. A cool breeze from the west quickened as he watched.

"I don't like this at all," McBride said. "That bridge is steady enough in this light flow, but we don't need no wind or current." He shouted, "Move it, Will! Weather coming."

Will rode onto the bridge, pulling the balking, stumbling calf. The mother and a few sympathetic cows followed. He stopped in the middle of the bridge, pulled the noose tighter, and the calf bellowed louder. The mother nudged the calf, and more cows moved onto the bridge. Will rode slowly across the span to the north bank, pulling the crying calf that fought the rope, tossing its head and bawling. The following cows crossed and bunched up on the bank around the calf.

Will looked back and saw the entire herd moving slowly toward the bridge. Riders on the bank controlled the movement at the entrance, trying to keep the line no more than two or three at a time. Mack sat his horse on the south bank, just off the bridge, staring at Will, scowling,

The breeze from the west picked up, rustling the dry leaves of the dead brush in the bridge foundation.

"Move, move, move," McBride mumbled.

The cows now moved steadily across the span. The herd bunched up at the entrance, as if anxious to join the others on the north bank.

The breeze became a brisk humid wind, and the current increased. The bridge shuddered, causing some cows to jerk sideways before recovering and continuing across the span. Some of the cows at the south bank entrance hesitated at the movement of the bridge, but were moved ahead by the quirts and shouts of cowboys.

A gust of wind, accompanied by a gentle surge in the current visibly moved the bridge on its brush foundation. Just a few inches, then settled ever so slightly tilted to the right. After the slight jolting, cows recovered footing and continued to move at a good pace across the span.

Most of the cows were across now, only a hundred or so bunched up on the south bank, still moving steadily onto the bridge. All cowboys were on the north bank or on the bridge but Brad and Lester who pushed the last bunch onto the span. McBride sat his horse at the bridge entrance, scowling, looking west.

Cowboy Mack rode off the bridge on the north bank, looked around, pulled up beside Will. He wasn't smiling.

"Calf's fine, Mack. He's with his mama. Other there." Will pointed to a knot of cows that milled about the calf, still curious and concerned about the little critter. Mack looked, turned back to Will, nodded, unsmiling, and rode on.

Still on the south bank, McBride watched the bridge, gritting his teeth. The wind and current increased noticeably, and large raindrops began falling. The bridge slid a few inches more on the foundation.

"Move 'em, boys!" he shouted to Brad and Lester at the end of the column. McBride rode up alongside the two as they pushed the last dozen cows onto the span. "Good job, boys." The three riders were halfway across the span when the bridge shuddered slightly, and McBride looked upstream.

CHAPTER FIVE

McBride stiffened. He watched the two-foot high wall of water roll around a bend in the stream and move rapidly toward the bridge.

"Watch out! Water coming!" he shouted.

The surge crashed into the side of the span and pushed it across the brush foundation. Soil sprayed from the bed as logs twisted and plunged, lashings broke, and the logs rolled off the foundation into the raging current. Cows and cowboys were thrown about on the disintegrating bridge and slid into the water.

Everyone on the north side rushed to the bank and gaped as cows bobbed and thrashed, struggling to swim amid the debris in the surging stream. Brad, Lester and McBride lost their seats before hitting the water and now flailed about in a desperate effort to keep heads above water. Their horses, eyes bulging, swam through debris toward banks.

Will ran to his horse, untied the reins, mounted and kicked the horse to a low point on the bank and into the water. He reined the swimming horse toward Brad, who had just broken the surface after sinking from sight. Brad flailed about, eyes bulging and mouth agape.

Will leaned over and grabbed a handful of Brad's shirt, pulling him toward the horse. "Grab my leg, hold on!" Brad gasped, coughed and held Will's leg, encircling it with both arms. Will turned the horse and swam toward the bank, avoiding floating logs, making headway slowly against the current.

Cowboys lined the bank, frenzied, uncertain, moving downstream, searching the water. Some held ropes, ready to throw a line to a struggling cowboy or put a loop around a swimming cow's head and horns.

Bonnie was not in the line at the bank. She had seen the wall of water rolling toward the bridge and gasped. Before the surge hit the bridge, she was running downstream. As she ran, she looked back over her shoulder at the tumult, the bridge breaking apart, throwing men and beasts into the current.

She rounded a bend in the stream, crashed through a thicket of Blue brush, oblivious of thorns tearing at her clothes, to a low bank on the stream. She hurriedly pulled her boots off and waded from the sandy landing into the shallows, into the stream to her waist, searching.

Then she saw him. A cowboy in midstream, his arms flailing, his weak cries for help. She pushed off and swam toward him. He sank, then broke the surface, flailing, gasping.

"Hold on!" she yelled.

The stricken cowboy saw her. "Help me! . . . help me." He sank slowly from sight, his long hair spreading in the water. She reached below the surface and grabbed his shirt, pulling him up. His eyes popped open, and he gasped. It was McBride.

He reached for Bonnie, struggling, gasping, reached again, gripped her arm with one hand and her hair with the other, pushing her head under.

She surfaced, sputtering. "Stop it, let me go! I'll help!" She struggled against his grip, sinking, gasping, trying to break his hold. Wild-eyed, he tightened his grip. She broke her arm away, pulled it back and smashed him hard in the face with a fist, almost submerging with the effort. His eyes rolled as blood oozed from his nose, his head fell back, and his arms became limp.

Bonnie tightened her hold on his shirt, twisted him on his back and stroked for the shore. After ten feet of frantic swimming, her feet found bottom. She pushed toward the bank, stepping lightly and quickly when she felt the suction of quicksand on her feet.

She stepped onto the sandy shore, pulled McBride on his back until he lay still on the bank, his legs still in the water. She fell to her knees and collapsed on her back, gasping. She rolled on her side, raised up on an elbow and put a hand on McBride's chest to see if he was breathing.

He suddenly wheezed, coughed, turned his head and saw her. "What th' hell?" he said weakly.

She struggled to stand, leaned down, grasped McBride's hands and pulled him to a sitting position. "Think you can walk? I sure as hell can't carry you."

"Gimme a minute." He breathed evenly, deeply.

She sat down and pulled on her boots, watching him.

"Okay," he said.

She stood up and offered her hands. He took the hands in his, and she helped him stand, straining, grunting. "You weigh a ton, Charlie, you been eatin' too much fat and not enough beans."

He wavered a bit, stamped to find his balance. "Okay, I can walk." He frowned, sniffed, put a hand to his nose. "What's this?" His hand was smeared with blood.

"That's where I tapped you when you tried to drown us both."

He frowned, wiped his nose on a sleeve, lightly pressed on the sides of the nose. They walked slowly upstream, Bonnie supporting him with an arm around his waist.

He walked with his head hanging, studying the path. Then he stopped, looked over at her. "You saved my life out there, Bonnie. I was a dead man, and you saved me."

"Just did what I could. You'd do the same for me."

"Hell I would! I can't swim a stroke." She smiled, pulled him ahead holding his belt at his back. "If I could swim, I'd have saved my little sister that I watched drown in a crick when I was just a sprout. I swore I'd learn to swim after that, but I never did." He shook his head. "I won't forget it, Bonnie. I owe you."

"No, you don't, Charlie. Well, you owe me three meals a day, a string of horses to use, and a payday in Montana. That's what you owe me."

"We'll see." He stumbled, and she tightened her grip on his belt as he regained his balance.

McBride looked down at her, smiled, then looked up at the cloudless cobalt sky, closed his eyes and inhaled deeply. "Be damned." He opened his eyes, stepped off, almost sprightly. "Be damned. I feel born again!"

Cowboys sat around the campfire at dusk, relishing the beef steaks cut from the carcass of one of the three cows that had drowned. Half a dozen other cows had made it to the shallows where they bogged down in the light quicksand. They had been pulled out easily enough. All were rescued but the three dead that washed up on the bank half a mile downstream.

Will and Bonnie sat together, inseparable now that all had accepted Bonnie's revelation and her attachment to Will. There was still an occasional grin or headshake, but it was done openly and without malice. And Bonnie particularly enjoyed the quizzical looks. Will was not so sure the boys always looked at Bonnie now simply as one of the hands.

"We'll look for Lester again before settin' out tomorrow," said Win. The cowboys had looked on both banks, but saw no sign of the body.

"Poor old Lester," said McBride. "He was an

ornery cuss, but a good ole boy anyway. We'll miss him." McBride stared into the fire. "Damn. Lost two good men on this drive. Never done that before.

"Damn if I didn't think I was gonna be one of the lost uns. If I was a believer, I'd a thought out there in the water I was standing at the pearly gates. But who did I see at that point? Not Saint Peter, but Bonnie! She's some kind of angel." He looked sideways at her. She concentrated on her plate, ignoring the attention and stares.

Fred grinned. "Was it that angel that did th' job on your nose, Charlie?" He guffawed. The others looked at the large bandage on Charlie's nose, then at each other, waiting for Charlie's reaction.

McBride glared at Fred, then relaxed and smiled. "Yes, Fred, in fact it was that angel that busted me. And saved my life doin' it." He touched the bandage. "Damn, she's got a pretty good right hook." Fred hooted, and the others laughed.

"If that's the case, we gotta recognize that we got a boy angel in the camp as well," said Brad. "Will saved my life sure as shootin'. I was just about to go down for the last time when ol' Will grabbed me. I owe him a big favor."

Everybody looked at Will who ducked his head, then looked up. "It happened so fast, I didn't have time to remember that I can't swim a lick. Good thing you didn't pull me off my horse, Brad—you sure tried to— or we woulda both ended up over there, both of us."

He gestured with a nod of his head toward the line of a half dozen graves at the edge of firelight. The graves were covered with grass and withered wildflowers, weathered crosses askew, all but the one at the end with a tight cross at the head of the bare, mounded soil.

"The fellow in that new grave belonged to an outfit a few days ahead of us," McBride said. "I know the name. Talked with him and his boss just before they set out from the Rio Grande. Sad case. Old fellow said he had been up the trail a dozen times. This was going to be his last drive. He planned to settle with his daughter and her husband on a nice little spread at Jacksboro, north of Fort Worth. He had saved most of his money from the drives to buy some cows to put on the place. Sad."

McBride stirred the embers with a stick, tossed it on the low flames. "Live life to the fullest, boys. You never know when your time's up." He stood with a grunt, flexed his back and walked to the chuck wagon, empty plate in hand.

The cowboys were quiet, pensive, staring at the flickering red and yellow flames of the dying campfire.

"Anybody for a few poker hands?" said Fred. He looked around the circle. Some shook heads; others ignored him. Cowboys got up, carried plates to the chuck wagon and either walked to the edge of firelight to relieve themselves or fetched bedrolls from the hoodlum. Only Bonnie and Will remained at the fire that had died to embers.

"I guess we better mosey off too since we're

sitting in the boys' bedroom," said Will." He put an arm around her shoulders, leaned over and kissed her cheek, nipped her ear.

"You better save that, cowboy, or I might not wait till we get to our bedroom."

"The boys would enjoy that. You know, maybe I don't need to worry so much about you, not after you showed what a wicked punch you've got. Hope you don't ever use it on me."

She leaned over to whisper in his ear. "You get me excited enough, no telling what I might do to you." She stood and took his plate. "C'mon, let's continue this talk over there." She motioned with her head toward the hoodlum wagon where they laid out their bedrolls each night. He stood, wrapped an arm around her waist, and they walked toward the wagon.

Will and Cowboy Mack rode at a lope in the middle of the trail. They left camp at first light in the daily search for water just as the other hands had begun leaving their bedrolls. That is, those that weren't up all night.

By the time they rode from camp, some of the hands were already out looking for Lester's body. Will and Mack agreed they were glad to be looking for water rather than a body. No disrespect to Lester, Mack had added.

The rest of the outfit would be out looking for cows. A brief storm about midnight accompanied by soft claps of thunder and sheet lightning had unsettled the herd, and some cows had bolted before the night herders and others who jumped out of bedrolls could control them. Will and Mack figured that the errant bovines would not all be collected by the time they returned to camp, and they would be put to searching for stray cattle.

"Let's give 'em a little exercise," Mack said. He set out at a gallop, and Will followed. After about ten minutes, they slowed to a walk.

"That looks like a crick up ahead at that line of trees," Will said. "Or a pretty mirage. We'll see." They rode on, silent, the trees becoming more distinct, taking on the appearance of reality.

Will turned toward Mack. "What was all that about the calf back at the bridge, Mack?"

Mack looked straight ahead, frowning. "I seen too much suffering, Will. I don't like to see any suffering, man or beast."

"It was a calf."

"Man or beast. I seen too much suffering. I won't have it."

They rode silently. After five minutes, Will looked aside at Mack. "Mack, were you a . . . uh . . ."

"Slave?" Mack looked a long moment at his horse's ears. "Yeah, I was a slave. My mama and daddy were slaves, and their mamas and daddies before them."

They rode in silence, Mack studying his horse's mane. Will waited, unsure whether he dared say more.

"I can't imagine what you went through," said Will. "I can only guess what you mean by the suffering you've seen."

Mack looked away, as if studying the meadow, searching. He turned back to Will. "Did I know suffering? Yeah, I did. My mama was an angel, a pretty angel. Master and his boy and the overseer all shamed my mama. They beat my daddy over and over with a whip when he tried to protect her. We run away, and they caught us. They killed both of 'em, my mama and my daddy, right before my eyes. I was the only one alive, and they beat hell out of me, taking it all out on me. Almost killed me. I was twelve years old then. That was in '63. I swore to myself and God that I would kill master and those that helped him.

"On the day two years later I heard I was a free man, I killed the overseer with my bare hands, and me and three others killed master and his boy. I went to the stable that very day, saddled master's favorite horse with his best saddle, made up a sack of food from master's kitchen and headed west. And here I am. Been out here ever since."

"Sorry, Mack, I didn't mean to—"

"It's okay, Will. I don't mind telling about myself to friends. It was hard. I miss my mama and daddy ever' day, but they're in Heaven, and I'll see 'em again. I don't mind taking some pride in knowing that those people that did those bad things to us is roastin' in hell. If I have to join 'em in hell for what I did, that's okay."

Mack inhaled deeply, looked up at a clear blue sky, turned back to Will. "I seen too much suffering." Will looked down, turned to look uneasily at Mack.

Mack laughed. "It's okay, pard. I'm past all that now. I ain't forgettin', mind you, but I've moved on. Life's good to me now. What about you?"

Will smiled. "Well, I think you know 'bout me. Never been happier."

"She is a purty little thing."

Will nodded. "Let's get on up there, and see if this crick has water in it." He pushed his horse into a lope, and Mack followed.

After a hurried breakfast, a few cowboys not otherwise occupied had searched both banks a few miles downstream for Lester's body, but they found nothing. They decided that either it had not surfaced, or it was buried in the mass of logs that had drifted from the bridge site and piled up on a sandbar in the middle of the stream.

The hands rounding up strayed cows had pushed all they found onto what had been the bed ground. Two cowboys were left to watch the herd while the others rode to the campground where they joined the other hands at the cold fire circle, all awaiting McBride's next move. They looked up to see Will and Mack ride in and dismount.

McBride listened impatiently to Will's report on the creek they found. "That's good news." He looked back at the river. "I hate to leave without finding Lester,"

McBride said, "but we can't delay no more. Mack, would you say the Lord's Prayer again, like you did before?"

Cowboy Mack nodded. He walked to the graves nearby, removed his hat and kneeled. The others walked over and lined out behind him. They took off their hats and bowed their heads. Mack recited his version of the prayer, said amen. He stood, replaced his hat and looked at McBride.

"Thanks, Mack. Hope that's the last time on this drive you have to do that." McBride and the others replaced hats and walked to the chuck wagon.

"Get you some breakfast quick," McBride said to Will and Mack, "and listen up while you're doing it." Will and Mack hurried to the chuck wagon where Cookie was already loading a couple of plates and pouring coffee.

McBride spoke to the group, loud enough for Will and Mack to hear. "Okay, back to business. We should hit the crick Mack and Will found by mid-afternoon or so. We'll wait to cross till next morning. Shouldn't have any problem with that, if it's still shallow then.

"Win, throw the herd on the trail. You're going to be real short-handed." He pointed to five cowboys, one by one. "You five come with me. Be sure your six-shooters are loaded, and you have reloads. We're gonna find us some cows and some cow thieves."

He turned to Bonnie. "Bonnie, some of the boys know what you found, but some don't. Tell it again."

Bonnie and Jimmy were among the hands who

had ridden out at first light to collect strays. They were heading back to camp with a few dozen head when she noticed a trail of compact hoof prints that led away from the bed ground. Telling Jimmy to go on with the cows, she turned around and rode a hundred yards or so back along the trail, then stopped and dismounted.

In the middle of the trail, she picked up a glove. She studied it, pushed it into a pocket. Mounting, she rode to the camp where Cookie was still filling breakfast plates held by waiting cowboys. She dismounted, tied her reins to a wheel and walked among the cowboys, showing the glove. They looked at the glove, shook heads and returned to their breakfast. She had gone to McBride, told him her story and showed him the glove. "Nobody in the outfit claims it," she said.

"Based on Bonnie's description," McBride said to the hands, "I'm guessing a hundred head or more wandered off in that direction, or, more likely, been driven off. So you see what we're about this morning." McBride frowned, looked up. "I wonder whether the fella shadowing us is part of this outfit."

Will and Mack bolted their breakfast since they were among the five that McBride named to ride. Bonnie was miffed that she was not included, but she would be driving the hoodlum wagon, as usual.

Will and Bonnie stood alone beside the hoodlum as he buckled on his pistol belt. "You be careful, Will Bishop," she said, holding him close with a grip on his shirtfront. "I won't be there to look out for you."

He leaned down and kissed her. "I'll do my best." He pulled his hat snug. "You take care of yourself and Cookie and the wagons, and watch out for bad guys and good guys with bad ideas."

She put her arms around his waist and hugged, leaning into his chest. "I mean it," she said. "I can't lose you." She looked up at him, her eyes glistening.

"Hey, hey." He took her face in both hands and kissed her softly. "Nothing's gonna happen, sweetheart. I'm riding with some tough cowboys, and, besides, bad guys are not very smart. We'll meet you at the crick, and we'll eat supper together."

She released him, wiped her face. "Okay, you say so, cowboy. Now, git on your horse before I start blubbering." Leading his horse, he walked to the knot of cowboys waiting for McBride.

McBride stood apart from the others with Cowboy Mack who held his reins. McBride spoke softly, leaning toward Mack. He pointed to the northwest, and Mack nodded. Mack mounted and spurred his horse to a gallop. McBride watched a moment, then strode to the waiting cowboys.

"Okay, boys, just need to tell you something. This area has seen a number of cases of rustling this year, more than usual. Ned Bundy, head of the outfit ahead of us, sent back word yesterday. That's why I doubled night herd. We can't blame the rustlers for the storm, but you can bet they were real happy to benefit by running off cattle that scattered in the confusion. Bonnie's find confirms that some strangers were about last night.

"So that's what we're dealing with. Ned's warning means they're professionals, not just some hare-brained small-time rancher who wants to build up his herd at other people's expense, or some amateur who wants to sell a few head of stolen cattle. They'll have loaded six-shooters. Anybody who doesn't want to ride today is okay to withdraw, and no hard feelings."

The cowboys looked at each other, some grim, but most grinning.

"Nobody?"

"Hell, boss, I wouldn't miss this for double pay," said Jimmy. "I just might write a song about it." He grinned, and Brad clapped him on the back, laughing.

"Let's get on it," said McBride, and they walked to the tethered horses.

"There's our cows," said McBride softly. "Looks like it could be a couple hundred." He and Will lay on the side of a low bluff, looking over the top at the line of cattle being close herded by a dozen men in the bed of the narrow arroyo. "You see that opening 'bout a mile ahead where the ravine opens up to the flat?" Will nodded. "That's where we'll meet 'em." He slid backwards down the slope. Will inched down. At the bottom, they stood and walked to their horses.

McBride spoke softly to the hands. "They're down

there, and we don't want to spook 'em. The arroyo opens up a couple of miles ahead. We're going to make a wide circle to where it ends and meet 'em there. They're slow moving, so we should get there in good time. Go lightly, if your horse can tippy toe. We don't want 'em to hear us." This was received with scowls and grins.

McBride and Will mounted, and the outfit set out at a lope on a loop leftward, out of sight, hopefully out of hearing, down a gentle slope toward the distant opening of the arroyo.

After a half hour's ride, McBride held up an arm, and they pulled up on the flat just short of the mouth of the ravine. Ten minutes passed, and they saw dust rising from the unseen herd.

"Follow me, and be ready," said McBride, softly. "No gun play, dammit, hear me? Unless they start something."

He walked his horse toward the opening, and the others followed. Hardly had they begun moving when the first cows appeared. A cowboy at the head of the column saw them, turned in the saddle and shouted over his shoulder.

Immediately a man rode at a gallop from the arroyo and pulled up beside the lead cows. He looked at McBride's bunch.

"Who are you?" he shouted.

McBride, Will and the others reined up. "Who are you?" said McBride.

"It's obvious, ain't it? I'm a rancher, moving a little herd to grass. Who are you?"

"I happen to be the owner of that little herd, and I didn't give you permission to move those cows anywhere."

The rustler captain leaned back in surprise, backing his horse, and drew his pistol in the same movement. His men who had ridden to the mouth of the arroyo saw their captain with gun drawn, and they quickly pulled their pistols from holsters.

McBride and his cowboys quickly drew six-shooters and leveled on the rustlers.

"Whoa, what have we here!" It was a rider at the head of a dozen others who approached at a gallop from the north and reined up sharply, horses coming to a sliding stop near the head of the cattle column. Cowboy Mack sat his horse behind the speaker. Every man in the group, including Mack, had his six-shooter leveled on the rustlers.

The head rustler, frowning, looked at the riders. "Who in hell are you?"

"Well, nobody particular you'd care to know, but officially, I'm Corporal Johnny D. Biggs of the Texas Rangers. And you are? . . . I'll be damned." His eyes opened wide, and he smiled. "And you are none other than Ned Brother, the biggest, dumbest cattle thief in west Texas. Now use whatever brains you might have, Ned, and all you rustlers back there, drop your six-shooters to the ground, right now, or you're fixin' to have every man in the Texas Rangers descending on you like a frog-stranglin' rainstorm."

Brother lowered his pistol, dropped it, and the cowboys around him followed his lead. All but one.

"Hey, Ned, don't let him do that!" It was a young cowboy behind Brother, young enough that his scanty blond whiskers had not seen a razor blade.

"Shut up, Davey," said Brother, without looking at the speaker. "Do what the man says."

"By damn, I won't." The kid brought his six-shooter up and pointed it at Biggs. Suddenly his head jerked backward with a bullet hole in the forehead, and he slid from his horse.

Biggs turned around to see Mack lowering his smoking pistol. "Fine shot, Mack. Appreciate it."

Mack nodded, grim, pushed the six-shooter into its holster.

Corporal Biggs rode toward McBride while the Rangers herded the captives into a manageable group. Two of Brother's men dismounted, lifted Davey's limp body, hefted it across his saddle and tied it on. The Rangers escorted the rustlers from the arroyo. One of the rangers dismounted and collected the six-shooters the rustlers had dropped when challenged.

Will looked closely at the captives as they passed.

McBride and the cowboys holstered their six-shooters. As Will and the other cowboys rode to the cattle, McBride, Biggs and Cowboy Mack dismounted.

McBride extended his hand, and Biggs took it.

112

"Johnny, good to see you again," said McBride, "especially under such fortunate circumstances."

"Fortunate indeed. I've been after this bunch since the beginning of the season. This must be the tenth herd they've hit."

"Lucky for us that Ned Bundy with the herd up ahead sent word to me about 'em. Double lucky that he said you were in the area. Glad Mack found you so quickly. He's a good tracker. Pretty good shot too."

"Indeed he is, on both counts. Uh, probably shouldn't tell you this, but I want to persuade him to join the Rangers. He said he would think on it, though he also said he had always had some reservations about the law." He looked at Mack who displayed the rarest hint of a smile.

"I want the best for Mack, but I'll try to persuade him that he's a good cowboy, and I'd hate to lose him, and this is where he belongs, with us." Mack ducked his head, walked to his horse, mounted and rode toward the other cowboys at the herd.

Biggs put a hand on McBride's shoulder. "We'll take this lot off your hands, Charlie, and be on our way." He took his reins from the Ranger who held them, mounted, turned and shouted. "Mack, you think on it!" He looked at McBride, smiled. Riding off at the head of the Rangers and their forlorn rustler captives, he waved over his shoulder, and McBride returned the wave.

The cowboys moved the cattle from the arroyo

and pointed them northward toward the creek where they expected to rejoin the herd before supper. McBride and Will rode side by side.

"Will, did any of those desperadoes look like the fella who's been spying on the herd?"

"I don't think so. I've never got a really good look at him, but what I've seen through Cookie's binocular, none of this lot looked like him. Maybe he's a lone wolf. But what's his game?"

"Hmm. Dunno, he must have something else on his mind." He stared ahead, shifted in the saddle. "My, I'm hungry enough to eat a mule. Hope Cookie remembers to save us a plate. It's gonna be dark before we join the herd." He glanced aside at Will. "You anxious to get back?"

Will looked at him, smiled.

"You keep a close eye on her, Will. I've heard the mutterings of some of the boys."

Bonnie stood beside the chuck wagon, staring at the back trail, searching. The sun had just slipped below the horizon, and the western sky was colored with churning balls of gold and orange and azure.

"When you're done with the dishes," said Cookie, "we'll have us another cup of hot coffee." She nodded. When Will was away in the evening, she usually volunteered to help her grandpa with the supper cleanup. He grinned and said he wished Will were away more often in the evenings. She frowned, and he smiled. She looked again at the sunset.

Why is it taking so long? If the cows were just wandering, they wouldn't have gone far. If rustlers have them, they couldn't move cattle fast, even a little bunch.

She watched the changing display at the horizon as sunset turned to twilight to dusk. Picking up three plates from the ground, she spooned the leavings into the slop bucket beside the wagon wheel. Dropping the heavy spoon into the bucket, she hefted the bucket and walked into a stand of sage. She leaned forward, tilted the bucket and emptied it.

She was seized suddenly from behind. A hand was hard on her mouth, and the other hand was wrapped around her chest. The hand found a breast and squeezed. Bonnie struggled, but strong hands held her. She tried to shout, but almost gagged from the hand over her mouth.

Bonnie wriggled, and her assailant's hold on her loosened. She jerked an elbow hard backwards, catching him in the belly.

"Oof!"

He doubled over, and his arms fell away. Bonnie grabbed the heavy spoon from the bucket and swung it, landing a hard blow to the jaw. He stumbled backward and fell on his butt. His hands went to his face.

"Damn, Bonnie . . . I think you broke my jaw."

"You sumbitch, you . . . Brad? Is that you, Brad?" She bent over, trying to recognize him in the soft light. She stood upright, frowning.

"What in hell got into you, Brad?"

Brad rubbed his cheek. "Well, now that you ask, a couple of shots of bad whiskey got into me. Somethin' I'd saved. Made me a little frisky. You sure cured me of that . . . Damn, that *hurt,* Bonnie."

He looked up at her. "I'm real sorry. That wasn't me done that. I'm not like that."

She dropped the spoon into the bucket, extended her hands to Brad. He took them, and she helped him stand.

He rubbed his jaw. "Damn, that hurts. I think it might be broken."

She picked up the bucket, and they walked slowly toward camp. He staggered slightly, and she took his arm. "Have Cookie look at the jaw tomorrow," she said. "He's done a little trail medicine in his time."

"What do I tell him?"

"That's your problem, pard."

They emerged from the sage and walked toward the campfire.

"You gonna tell the boys?" said Brad.

"Not unless you want me to. But you might be thinking about how to explain that swollen jaw. Already looks big as a watermelon."

"Wonder what Will's going to think about all this?" she said.

He stopped, eyes bulging. "Don't, Bonnie! You don't have to tell Will. He'll kill me! I know it."

Bonnie turned away. Her smile quickly turned to a frown. She was enjoying this too much.

They stopped at the edge of the circle of light cast

by the campfire. The three cowboys sitting there looked up at them.

"Night, Brad," she said softly. She waved to the three at the firepit, and they returned the wave. She turned aside, restraining an urge to laugh out loud. She started to walk away, then stopped at a shout from the darkness.

"Halloo, the camp, coming in with the stolen cows!" McBride shouted. All at the fire stood, and everyone in camp looked toward the shout. The cowboys pushed the cows to the main herd where they mingled, circled and began bedding down. McBride and the other cowboys rode into the circle of light from the campfire.

Brad looked anxiously at Bonnie, then at Will. Brad strode from the campfire toward the hoodlum. She smiled to herself, looking for Will.

"Come on over, boys," said Cookie, "saved supper for you." The cowboys dismounted, removed saddles, and sent the horses to the remuda. They spoke to the men at the fire circle and walked to the chuck wagon.

Bonnie took Will's arm as he passed. "I want to hear all about your day," she said, "but not tonight."

"How was your day?" said Will. "Boys at the fire said we didn't miss nothing."

"You didn't miss nothing."

CHAPTER SIX

The full sun ball rested on the eastern horizon, changing tint and intensity, coloring the cloud layers above, as if it were a living part of the landscape. Cowboys dropped empty breakfast plates in the tub at the chuck wagon and sauntered toward the remuda. Some paused long enough to look briefly at the sunrise, roll and light a cigarette, then walk on.

Cookie stood beside the wagon, hands on hips, scowling, calling to their backs. "If anything breaks or dents, it's yours till Montana!" The cowboys waved over their shoulders without turning. They had heard the warning before. They figured it was Cookie's way of saying good morning and have a nice day.

Will stood at the back of the wagon, holding Cookie's binocular to his eyes, trained on a stand of cottonwood downstream. McBride walked up, bent and put his plate and cup in the tub.

"He still there?"

"Yeah," said Will, still looking through the binocular. "He's been there since I first saw him before breakfast. He's hardly moved. Strange fellow." He lowered the binocular and turned to McBride. "Okay if

I go have a look? Maybe I can run him down before he gets a chance to cross the crick."

"Yeah, okay. We're getting the herd on the trail right now. Maybe that'll distract him some. Be careful. You'll join us at the crick before we're over." McBride headed for the remuda where others were already saddling up.

Will went to the hoodlum where Bonnie was helping cowboys collect their tack. She reached into the wagon for Will's bridle, handed it to him, smiled and kissed him. He pulled out his saddle.

"I'm going to pay a visit with our mystery man," he said. "This has gone on too long. I'm dying to find out what's going on."

"Don't say it like that."

"Well, you know."

"Okay, but you be careful. He must have a good reason for hanging on us this long. I don't like it."

He cupped her chin in a hand and kissed her. "Won't be long. I'll need a cup of coffee when I catch up." He walked away, hefting the saddle and dragging the bridle. She watched him a moment, then headed for the remuda to collect her mules.

Will rode in the bottom of an arroyo, shallow but deep enough that his head was not visible from the plain. Nor could he see anything but the sides of the cut. He pulled up, dismounted and tied the reins to a stunted cedar. He dug the binocular from the saddlebag and knelt to lie on the side of the arroyo. Slowly he crawled up until he could just see over the top. Looking through the binocular, he confirmed that the mystery man was still in the brush under the streamside cottonwoods.

Man, what is it with you?

Will scooted down the slope, stood and mounted. He pushed his horse to a fast walk. He decided that he would stay out of sight as long as possible, but when the cut would no longer hide him, he would head downstream at a gallop, knowing he would likely be seen, but the spooked mystery man would have to ride upstream to get away from him. Directly toward the outfit and the herd.

After a mile or so in the arroyo, the land flattened to a plain. The cottonwoods were in plain sight, and he kicked his horse into a hard gallop downstream from the copse. Coming up on the creek, he rode at a lope upstream on the bank, searching the meadow and the stream.

He pulled up at the cottonwoods, looked down at the hiding place. It was trampled and littered with cigarette butts. But no mystery man.

Damn. He saw me.

Will dismounted and looked for hoof prints, expecting to see them heading upstream toward the herd, but the only prints he saw led upstream to the hiding place, then fresher, more deeply etched prints downstream from the hiding place. He scanned the bank and the plain and saw no sign of man or beast.

He suddenly felt an unease, slightly lightheaded, his back prickling. He looked rapidly around in all directions.

He mounted hurriedly and kicked his horse into a gallop upstream along the bank, looking back over his shoulder. He soon veered off to the right and slowed to a lope. The shallow stream had a firm bed, and the herd was already across. The outfit was moving north on the trail.

Dusk. Cowboys lounged around the campfire. Supper was finished, plates deposited at the chuck wagon. Some hands smoked, Jimmy strummed softly on his guitar, others silently looked into the flames. All leaned back or scooted away from the firepit when Fred dropped short lengths of dry limbs on the fire, causing a scattering of hot cinders in the light drafts.

"Damn it, Fred," said Win, "how many times do I need to tell you to *lay* wood on the fire, not *toss* it.

Fred looked at him and grinned. He sat down heavily, close to the fire, closed his eyes.

Will and Bonnie sat behind the circle of cowboys at the fire, whispering, smiling, ignoring the glances from the loungers at the fire.

All agreed that the day had been better than usual on a number of counts. It had been pleasant all day, almost cool under a light overcast. The herd was on good grass at day's end yesterday, and they had been watered before setting out this morning. The cattle had moved along steadily all day. No problems at all.

"Must of made twenty miles today," said Fred.

Jimmy stopped strumming, his hand poised over the strings. "Not likely. Not on the best of days, unless you're on wheels. We might've made fifteen miles, more likely twelve or so." A few of the cowboys murmured agreement.

Bonnie pulled her jacket tight around her shoulders. "I'm headin' for the barn. I'm cold, and that twenty-mile day was really tiring."

"Me too," said Rod. "I'm plumb wore out." A scattering of soft laughter.

Bonnie stood, took Will's hands and pulled him up.

"Go ahead," said Will. "I need to check my horse. Looked like he had a little sore on his neck." He walked toward the remuda.

Brad jumped up from his place at the fire, watched Will a moment, then hurried to Bonnie. He looked over his shoulder at Will. Leaning toward her, he spoke softly.

"Did you tell him?"

She cocked her head. "No, just waiting for the right time, when he's in a good mood, you know, 'cause this is gonna make him real mad."

He grimaced. "Bonnie, you know what Charlie says, that we gotta git along in the outfit, with no arguments and no fightin' and cussin' each other. We gotta have peace inside the outfit, he says. If you tell Will, there ain't gonna be peace, and Charlie is gonna be mad."

Bonnie frowned, as if pondering. "That makes good sense, Brad." She turned to go. "I'll think on it," she threw back over her shoulder, smiling now that he couldn't see her face.

She and Will reached the hoodlum at the same time. They collected their bedrolls and dropped them on the far side in their usual place. The outfit respected their choice, and nobody interfered, though there were mutterings every evening about what went on over there on the other side of the wagon.

Will and Bonnie walked past the chuck wagon to the edge of the circle of firelight. When Will followed her, she turned to him and frowned.

"Go on," she said.

"I'm watching."

"You are not! Go on over there." She pointed to a clump of sage bushes. He smiled, kissed her cheek and watched her walk into the darkness.

He walked behind the sage, unbuttoned his pants, looked up at the sky, now full of sparkling stars since the overcast had lifted. The bright moonlight made clumps and shadows of the sage bushes.

He stepped back, buttoning up, and waited. He looked back at the camp, the fire almost gone, still faintly outlining the wagons, cowboys in their bedrolls scattered about the campground.

He waited, staring at the dark sage bushes where Bonnie had gone. He frowned, annoyed.

"Bonnie?" softly. Nothing.

Then, a muffled sound, not a sound he had heard before.

"Bonnie? You okay?"

A soft, sharp cry.

Bonnie!

He waded into the sage. She was not where she likely would have stopped to relieve herself.

"Bonnie!" he called. He walked on, rounded a thick stunted cedar.

And saw them. The man stood behind Bonnie, holding her tightly with an arm around her neck. His other hand held a six-shooter with the muzzle pushed hard into her cheek. She squinted, her mouth open, inhaling in sharp gasps, her eyes, wide open, locked on Will's. The man's face was strangely calm. His mouth twitched on one side, almost a hint of a smile.

"You've been watching us," Will said softly. "What do you want?"

The man smiled, his eyes slits. "I got what I want, don't I?"

"Think about it, man. We've got twenty guns in this camp."

"I got the only gun that means anything right now, don't I?" He smiled. Bonnie whimpered when he pushed the muzzle into her cheek.

Will stepped toward the man.

"Don't do nothin' foolish. I'll kill her before I give her up. She's mine, or she's nobody's. Back off, or she's dead. And you'll be next." Will stood his ground. "Back off, goddammit!" He pushed the muzzle harder against Bonnie's cheek, and she gasped.

Will backed up a step, then another. *Bonnie, what can I do?*

The man stepped backward, dragging Bonnie with him, the six-shooter still pushed hard into her cheek. They vanished around a stand of sage. Will started to follow, stopped, uncertain.

Then, a muffled grunt, a sharp cry!

Will crashed through the dense sage and saw her, illuminated in the bright moonlight. She was rigid, looking down, her hands on her cheeks. She looked up at Will, then back to the ground at her feet. She stepped back, and Will saw the man lying there. He knelt and saw in the moonlight the knife in the side of the man's neck. Bonnie stared at the face, relaxed now, serene in death.

Will stood and wrapped his arms around Bonnie, her hands still on her face.

"I need to talk to Grandpa," she said, almost a whisper.

He frowned. "Now?" She nodded.

He released her, put an arm around her waist and guided her from the sage to the chuck wagon. Will stooped, crawled under the wagon and roused Cookie.

Cookie sat up, rubbed his eyes, and saw Will, a

shadow in the gloom. Cookie frowned. "What th' hell you doin' out this time uh night?"

On his knees beside Cookie's bedroll, Will told him what had happened while Bonnie watched them, her arms folded across her chest.

"Oh, my," said Cookie. He sat up and wrapped a blanket around his shoulders. Crawling from underneath the wagon, he stood, flexed his back. He went to Bonnie and put his arms around her. Her arms hung limply, her head resting on his chest.

They remained still a long minute as Will looked on, his mind racing. Finally, she raised her head and looked at her grandfather. "It's Grant."

Cookie recoiled, grimacing, then recovered. "You two, go to bed." Will raised a hand to protest. Cookie was grim. "I said go to bed, hear me? I'll take care of this, and we'll talk in the morning. It'll have to be after breakfast. Now go."

Will hesitated, looking at Bonnie.

"Go, dammit." He spoke softly, sternly.

Bonnie nodded, kissed her grandpa on the cheek, took Will's arm and guided him to their bedrolls. She bent to lay out the beds. He took her arm and gently pulled her up.

"Bonnie?"

She took his cheeks in her hands and kissed him. "We'll talk in the morning with Grandpa. I'm exhausted, and I'm going to pass out unless I get some sleep."

*****

The eastern sky was marked by lacy cloud layers of pastel pink and purple. Long shadows of mesquite and cedars cast by the morning sun across the flat receded slowly as the sun climbed above the horizon.

Cookie, McBride, Bonnie and Will stood at the back of the chuck wagon, watching the cowboys strolling toward the remuda. They carried and dragged saddles, blankets and bridles, chatting, laughing softly. Fred belly laughed, doubled over at his own joke and clapped Jimmy on the shoulder.

McBride turned back to the others. "Okay. Teddy, you say you know this fella." He gestured with a nod toward the small pile of sacks and boxes under the wagon. The seeming debris covered a stretched-out canvas, which in turn covered the body that Cookie had dragged from the sagebrush last night after dismissing Bonnie and Will.

Cookie glanced at Bonnie who looked down. "Yeah, I know him. His name is . . . was . . . Grant. I told you about him. Grant was Bonnie's boyfriend."

"So that's who's been shadowing us," said Will. "Not some rustler lookout."

"Yep. I told you he was a little crazy in the head after he got kicked by the horse."

McBride looked at Bonnie. He shook his head, wrinkled his forehead, smiled thinly. "You're somethin' else, little lady. You knock hell outta me with a punch back in the river, now this." He held the knife that Teddy had pulled from Grant's neck.

"When Grandpa gave it to me, he said he hoped I would never have a chance to use it. It's just in case, he said. He showed me how to handle it and made a little scabbard inside my boot." She leaned on Will, and he put his arm around her shoulders.

"Now what do we do?" said Will.

McBride looked at the sky, his lips pursed, turned to Will. "Good question. Should report this to the authorities, but I don't see no authorities in the neighborhood, do you?" He looked at the others in turn, and they shook their heads. "The boys don't know nothin' about this, right?"

"Not so far as I know," said Cookie. McBride looked at Will and Bonnie who shook their heads again.

"Well, his carcass would get a little ripe if we try to transport him to Dodge," said McBride, "and I don't much want to do that. And some of the boys have a loose jaw when they've even smelled liquor. So we'll bury the body right here and keep it between the four of us. That okay with you?" The three nodded.

"Teddy, you and Will stay here with the chuck wagon when the herd leaves. I'll think of somethin' to tell the boys. Bonnie, you drive the hoodlum on ahead as usual so it looks like a regular day." He turned to go, stopped and turned back. "Don't be too long, Teddy, I don't like a late dinner." His grimace almost became a smile, and he turned to walk toward the remuda.

Cookie picked up the tub of soiled breakfast

dishes and hefted it into the back of the chuck wagon and fussed around inside. Will turned to Bonnie who stared blankly at the herd. Cowboys had just begun the usual process of starting, hallooing and waving hats at sluggish cows.

Will put an arm around Bonnie's waist and walked her toward the hoodlum. "Are you okay?" he said.

She ducked her head, studying the ground at her feet. "Yeah. I s'pose." She looked up at him. "He was a good boy, a good man. Before the accident."

"Did you love him?"

She looked down, aside. "Love? I don't know. We were kids, played together, grew up together, laughed together. Then we weren't kids any more. I cared for him, and . . . and then he had the accident. Then . . . then I killed him." She turned to Will and buried her face on his chest. He put his arms around her shoulders and held her as she sobbed.

She leaned back, wiped her face with both hands. She pulled away from his arms. "Okay, got that done. Now I'll get my mules."

"I'll help."

She held up a hand and shook her head. "No, you won't. This is the same as any day, like Charlie said." She pulled his head down and kissed him. "Except what you have to do when I'm gone. Catch up fast as you can. I'm gonna need holding."

He watched her pull the mule harness from the gear wagon and walk toward the remuda.

"She'll be okay." Will turned and saw Cookie standing at the back of the chuck wagon. "She's had a shock," Cookie said, "but I think she'll soon come to be relieved, knowing it's all settled and behind her. We've had some talks, her and me, about Grant, what happened to him and all, her wondering whether he recovered and was back to his old self. She'll get over it and put it all behind her. She'll be okay. She's soft in a way, but she's also a tough 'un in a way. You've seen that."

"Yes, I have."

Cookie lifted a shovel and ax from the hooks on the side of the wagon. He handed the shovel to Will, and they walked a few feet from the wagon. They watched the end of the herd moving away, the two drag riders with bandannas tied across their faces under their eyes riding back and forth to push the stragglers ahead. One of the riders pulled up and looked toward the chuck wagon.

Cookie chuckled. "Hear what he's thinking?"

"Yeah. 'What th' hell's going on over there?' "

"Well, they know the wagons usually pull out before the herd is thrown on the trail. Anything happens different gets their attention. Wonder what Charlie told 'em? I s'pose we'll find out soon enough." He sobered, walked a few steps from the wagon, hefted the ax. "This looks like as good a place as any. Let me loosen this ground a bit before you start shoveling." He swung the ax and drove it into the soil. "My, this ground's hard."

Cookie and Will set to work, alternating between Cookie chopping with the ax and Will shoveling soil. After a half hour of hard labor, they had a trench three feet deep, just long enough and wide enough to receive the body.

Will stood upright beside the grave, wiped his forehead with a sleeve. "Should be deeper, but that's as far as we're gonna go. The bottom is like rock. Feels like it hasn't rained here in ten years."

"It'll have to do," Cookie said, walking to the wagon. He bent and reached under the wagon. Throwing the canvas sheet aside, he pulled the body from underneath the wagon and dragged it to the edge of the pit. Will stepped down into the grave and gripped the body's shoulders while Cookie lifted the legs. They eased what had been Grant down into the trench, and Will climbed out.

Cookie stared at the corpse, the face soft, eyes closed, seemingly sleeping. "That's the Grant I knew, Will," Cookie said, without looking up. Will started to say something, but held back. Cookie was in another place, staring at the corpse.

Cookie shook his head. "Grant, you were a good boy, a good man," Cookie said softly. "Good blacksmith, too. Damn horse changed all that, changed the whole story." He shook his head again, looked up at Will, sober. He retrieved the canvas sheet from under the wagon and laid it over the body.

"Will, if you'll do the shovel work, I'll see if I can

find some rocks. After you fill it in, saddle up and walk your horse all over the grave. Make it look like regular ground. When you finish, I'll scatter my rocks around. Won't find many in this pasture."

Will fetched his saddle, blanket and bridle from the pile beside the wagon where Bonnie had left them. He walked to his horse carrying the tack, dropped it on the ground and removed the hobbles that Charlie had fitted on the horse when the remuda left with the cattle.

He saddled the bay, mounted and rode back to the grave, walked the horse back and forth on the mounded loose soil till it was packed and level. Charlie had found only a half dozen small stones, which he dropped randomly on the grave. Will dismounted and pulled handfuls of dry grass which he sprinkled over the bare earth between stones. He kicked it around till it looked natural.

They looked down at their handiwork. "How's that?" said Cookie. "Looks like nothing out of the ordinary. Hope it fools the coyotes." He pulled off his dusty gloves, slapped them against his thigh and strode to the wagon. "Now, we gotta get hoppin.' "

Will helped Cookie harness the mules, then mounted, and they set out on the herd's track. The outfit was out of sight, but their trail of hoof prints and cow patties was easy enough to follow.

The chuck wagon, Will riding alongside, had hardly passed the head of the cow column when McBride called the noon halt. Cookie pulled up, climbed down and walked around to the back of the wagon and began fussing inside.

Will tied his reins to spokes on a front wheel and walked over to Bonnie who had just pulled up in the hoodlum wagon. She had been ahead of the herd and turned around when McBride sent Jimmy to fetch her. Now she set the brake and wrapped the lines around the brake handle. She jumped down and fell into Will's arms.

He raised her chin and kissed her lightly. "How you doin'?"

"I'm all right. Did you take care of . . . everything?"

"We did. Your grandpa will tell you all about it."

She pulled back, looked aside. "When he grabbed me out there, he looked like nobody I ever knew. Wild. But the face I saw on the ground after . . . that was the Grant I knew. Soft, sweet." She shook her head vigorously. "The knife. I still see it in his neck." She put her arms around Will's waist, trembled, her face soft against his chest.

She pulled away from him and wiped her face with a hand. "Okay, I'm done." She grasped his sleeve and pulled him toward the back of the chuck wagon. "And I'm hungry."

They saw Brad strolling over to the wagon. He waved to them, peered underneath the wagon. He looked at Cookie, frowning. "What was you doin' back there? Charlie said you had a broken axle, and I wondered how you two was gonna change it all by yourselves. But I see your spare axle is still hanging under the wagon." His frown was a question.

Cookie looked up. He grimaced, glanced briefly aside at Will. "Ah, broken axle. Uh, well—"

"We thought it was broken," said Will. "I heard a snapping sound just before we stopped last evening. Sounded like the two pieces of a broken axle popping against each other. Turned out it was just a limb that was caught in the spokes of a wheel."

Brad frowned. "Uh limb. Funny you didn't see that limb last night. Uh limb? I didn't see no trees that big on yesterday's drive."

Cookie brightened. "Well, I guess you ain't too observant, Brad. There was a sizable cottonwood at the seep we passed. You didn't see that? If you want to go back and have a look, I can tell you right where it is." Cookie grinned, knowing he had the upper hand.

Brad scowled. "I ain't going back nowhere. I'll stay for dinner, if it's all the same to you."

"Won't be long now." Cookie waited until Brad showed him his back. He turned to Will and Bonnie, nodded, smiling.

"I heard that," said McBride who had just walked up. "That's good. Quick as you can, Teddy. We need to reach the Red before sundown. I've told Win to water the herd anywhere he can before reaching the river. The Red's too salty for drinking, for cows or people.

There's usually good grass on the south bank, so we should be in good shape for bedding the herd. I want to cross tomorrow at first light."

The Red River had been the principal topic of conversation for days. It marked the boundary that put Texas behind them and Indian country ahead. Only about half of the outfit had ridden on drives through the territory before. Around the campfire, these old hands told stories of battles with Indians, torture and lingering death for any who happened to fall into the savages' hands.

Just last evening after supper, Jimmy, who had been plucking his guitar softly during the lurid tales of Indian cruelty, stopped and leaned forward, looking around the fire circle.

"It ain't a pretty sight. They strip off your clothes and tie you down spread-eagled on your back in the boilin' sun. Then they skin yuh alive, a little thin strip at a time." He brightened. "I wrote a song about it. You want to hear it?" He grinned, looking expectantly at the gathering, his pick poised at the guitar strings.

"Jimmy, you're so full of horse hockey," said Win, "you should write one of them dime novels. I saw a couple in San Antonio last year. They told about Daniel Boone and Kit Carson fightin' Indians and Mexicans and always coming out on top. You could write about the exploits of the legendary Charlie McBride. Or how 'bout the story of Will and Bobby-Bonnie? There's a story for you." He grinned, looking around at the cowboys who appeared unimpressed with or ignorant of dime novels.

Jimmy frowned at Win, leaned back, looked down at his guitar and gently plucked the strings. He hummed softly, ignoring Win, in his own space now.

"Don't believe what you hear about Indians and Indian Territory," said McBride. "I've been in the country half a dozen times, and you'll notice I still got my skin and scalp. We'll see Indians soon enough."

McBride, Cowboy Mack and Will rode ahead to scout out the best crossing on the Red. They didn't have to search. Before they reached the stream, they saw a herd crossing at a point that was nowhere near belly deep. The river was about a hundred yards wide at the crossing. Another herd was grazing on good grass nearby on the south bank, and still another was in dry grass on the slope of a nearby low hill.

The three riders pulled up. They watched the herd moving steadily through the water with little coaxing by the cowboys that rode alongside and behind the column. It was strangely quiet. Only an occasional bellow from a cow or shout from a cowboy broke the stillness.

Cottonwoods and pecans lined the banks, shading the shallows. Willow thickets grew at streamside, some with roots in the shallows. Shrubs, sumac and buckeye crowded access to the stream except at the crossing.

"Damn," said McBride. "We'll have two herds

ahead of us tomorrow morning. We won't likely get across till afternoon, if then." He pointed westward where a layer of dark gray clouds hung low over the horizon.

They turned to see a rider galloping toward them. The horseman pulled up, wild-eyed. "That your herd back there?" He pointed toward the back trail. The herd was barely visible.

"It is," said McBride.

"Keep 'em well back! That's my outfit up on the hill. We've already had some mixing with two herds. I'm done with stupid people who don't know nothin' about cattle driving. Happens again, and there'll be trouble!" Perspiration streamed down the man's red face and dripped from his chin.

McBride simply stared at the man, then spoke softly, slowly. "I know a little something about cattle driving. I was driving herds when you was still shovelin' shit on your daddy's farm."

The man spluttered, reached for his holster, stopped when Will rode between him and McBride. "We'll wait our turn. Who's first, you or the outfit on the river bank?"

"He was here before me, but if the river starts rising, I'll be damned if I wait for anybody."

"My, my," said McBride. "I'll keep my herd back. Wouldn't want to see any of my cows get hit by stray lead." He spoke to Will and Mack, ignoring the man. "We'll put the herd on grass downstream from this outfit." He pointed toward the herd on the grass at the bank.

"You're getting too close to the crossing! I'm ahead of you!"

McBride sighed. He spoke softly. "You're beginning to annoy me. Will here said we would wait our turn, and we'll wait our turn. Unless you keep annoying me."

The man fumed, his face reddening. He spun his horse around and galloped toward his herd on the hillside.

McBride shook his head. "That man's a heart attack about to happen. Never seen him before. Will, I'm delegating you to keep a watch on that yahoo. Be sure nothin' happens with him or his animals that puts our herd in jeopardy." Will nodded.

"Mack," said McBride, "ride back to the herd and tell Win what's happened here. Stay with him, and when the herd gets here, show him that good patch of grass downstream near the stand of cottonwoods yonder." He pointed. "We need to be real careful. Our herd will be the third here on the south side, and we don't want no mingling. All three herds will cross tomorrow. We're third."

McBride stared silently at the river. "Shallow and nice and peaceful right now, and dry as a bone on the banks. But damn, I've seen peaceful rivers in the evening that was raging deep and swift the next morning 'cause of rains upcountry." He shook his head. "We just have to hope that God, or the rain gods, are good to us.

"How much further, Cookie?" Cowboy Mack sat his horse beside the hoodlum that was stopped in the middle of the road. He removed his hat and wiped his face and the top of his head with a sweat-stained neckerchief. From his perch on the wagon seat, Cookie looked down at the mule team.

"Few more miles, I s'pose. Be there before long."

McBride had dispatched them after an early hasty breakfast to ride to Eagle Springs for supplies, the last chance before crossing the Red into Indian territory. There wasn't much to say about Eagle Springs, but it had one general store where drovers might get supplies. At least, that's what McBride had heard. He had never sent a wagon to the crossroads settlement, always stocking up earlier down the trail. That there was a wagon road here instead of simply a trail suggested that there was something in the town that required a wagon to transport it.

The road lay in a broad meadow of green grass, bordered on each side by scattered oaks, cedars and pecans. Vibrant wildflowers and the remnants of blooms colored the flat. Flashy Indian Blankets and Mexican Hats with their knobby tops, Texas bluebells and fading bluebonnets, new yellow sunflowers pushing up through the green carpet.

"Pretty place," said Cookie. "How'd you like a little ranch right here, Mack?"

Mack looked over at Cookie, turned back to the meadow. "Pretty place, all right. It would do for me, if folks would leave me alone. Figure I'd likely have to kill a few people to get 'em to leave me alone. Unless I had a white man for a partner." He looked over at Cookie. "You want to be my partner, Teddy, kill a few mean fellows for me?"

Cookie smiled thinly. "I'll pass, Cowboy. I'm too old to get into any wars of that sort."

Mack smiled, turned back to the meadow. After a moment: "Somebody comin'." Cookie looked at Mack who nodded toward two horsemen who rode in the meadow toward the road.

"Not coming from Eagle Springs." Cookie frowned. "I don't like meeting strangers in this country. Got a bad reputation."

Cookie looked toward the clump of juniper and sage just off the road. He fidgeted, staring at the mule team, grasping and loosening his hold on the lines. He glanced again at the clump.

The two horsemen reached the road ahead and came on at a slow walk toward the wagon. They pulled up in front of the mules.

One of the riders smiled. "Well, well, well, if it ain't Grandpa Teddy. Wondered whether we might find you somewhere in this big country." The speaker glanced at Mack who stared at him, his face grim.

Cookie frowned. "Buster. Hank. What're you boys doing so far from home?"

"Well, Grandpa Teddy," said Buster, "we thought you might be able to help us. You see, Grant found out that Bonnie was with you, and since we ain't seen our brother in a long time, we come looking for him. If anythang's happened to him, it has somethin' to do with Bonnie and you. And we intend to find out and do somethin' about it."

"Who said Bonnie was with me?"

Buster grinned. "Well, now, that'd be tellin,' wouldn't it."

Cookie glared. "You son-of-a-bitch, if you've hurt any of my kin, I'll kill you!"

Mack, his face hard, pushed his horse up beside the mules.

Buster moved a hand toward his holster. "You stay right where you are, nig—"

Buster was violently pulled from the saddle and sprawled on his back. "What th—" He looked up, open-mouthed, into the muzzle of Will's six-shooter.

Hank went for his pistol and had hardly cleared the holster when Mack spurred his horse, colliding with Hank's mount that lunged, whirled and bucked Hank from the saddle. Hank lost his pistol in mid-air. Mack walked his horse a few steps forward and leveled on the prostrate Hank with his six-shooter.

"Pick it up," said Mack, softly. "There it is, right beside your head." Mack gestured with his pistol. "Pick it up so I can blow your brains out."

Hank, on his back and wide-eyed, scooted

sideways, stretching his arms wide, showing he had no intention of reaching for the gun. Buster sat up slowly, watching Will who took a step backward, his six-shooter still pointing at his head.

Cookie sighed. "Git on your feet, boys. You always were worthless troublemakers, even as little kids. Looks like you never growed up." The brothers stood and brushed themselves off. Hank looked around, dazed. Buster glared at Cookie.

"You had a long ride for nothing," said Cookie. "Bonnie ain't with us. She's somewhere you'll never find her. We ain't seen Grant. He probably got lost or decided to go to Mexico. Or California. Maybe he went home, and you missed him on the road."

Cookie looked at Will, then Mack. "What do you say, boys? Do we shoot 'em right here, or do we let 'em go home?"

Hank and Buster gaped at each other, wide-eyed and jaws hanging.

Mack looked up at Cookie, then glared at the brothers. After a long pause: "I say we shoot 'em right here."

"Wait a minute," said Buster, jerking his head back and forth among his captors. "We, we don't want, we won't—"

"Will?" said Cookie.

Will simply stared at the brothers. Then: "Hell, Teddy, if we kill 'em here right now, then we gotta bury 'em, and that's hard work. Hell, we don't even have a shovel."

Will, Cookie and Mack, all stone-faced, looked at each other, seemingly pondering. "I can go back for a shovel," Mack said.

The brothers leaned against each other, their faces contorted. Hank gripped Buster's sleeve, looked up at Cookie. "Please," said Hank, "we're not bad people. Please let us go. We didn't hurt your brother, Teddy." He looked anxiously, terrified, at Buster, then back at Cookie. "Well, we scared hell out of him, but we didn't touch him. Honest!"

Cookie glanced at Will and Mack. "Whatta you say, boys?"

"Please, Teddy," said Hank, "we're your neighbors, our families are friends! We didn't hurt nobody!" He fell to his knees, his head lowered, sobbing.

Buster slapped Hank on the back of his head. "Shut up, Hank!"

"Leave him be, Buster. He's got more sense than you do," said Cookie. "Now, git up and find your horses and git on your way. If I ever see you again in this life, you're not gettin' off so easy."

Buster grabbed Hank's shirt and pulled him up roughly. They walked into the meadow toward Hank's horse that stood a hundred yards away in the shade of a huge pecan tree. Buster's mount was nowhere in sight. Buster's shouts berating his brother were audible for a time, then were carried away by the wind.

Cookie, Will and Mack silently watched the brothers

come up to Hank's horse that promptly whirled and galloped into the stand of pecans.

The brothers stopped, looked around, then walked into the copse where the horse had disappeared.

The three at the wagon glanced at each other and erupted in laughter. Cookie, still holding the lines, slapped his leg, causing the mules to jerk in the harness.

"Well," said Cookie, "that broke the monotony, didn't it?" He looked aside. "Bonnie! Come on, we need to get moving!"

Bonnie emerged from behind the juniper. She walked to them, smiling sheepishly, then sobered. "I feel sorry for them. Now they'll never know, will they?"

Cookie extended a hand and helped her climb up to the wagon seat. He hugged her around the shoulders, shook the lines and the mules moved off. "Good thing they rode up while we was stopped for a pee-stop. If they'd seen us on the road, they would've seen you, and all this might've come off differently." He shook the lines. "Maybe we'll find some way to tell 'em someday. Maybe." He shook the lines as Bonnie took his arm and leaned against his shoulder. Will and Mack rode quietly alongside.

CHAPTER SEVEN

McBride sat his horse on the banks of the Red with Will, Win, Mack and Bonnie watching a passel of cowboys pushing a column of longhorns into the shallows. The cowboys hallooed and waved arms at stragglers, shouting at each other and the cattle that didn't particularly want to enter the stream.

McBride looked eastward at the orange sun ball that had just cleared the horizon. He turned to Will. "Didn't get a chance to talk with you last evening. Find everything at Eagle Springs okay?"

"Yep. No drovers had called in some time, so we stocked up. Cookie was pleased. Had a little problem we hadn't anticipated." He recounted the meeting with Grant's brothers on the road.

McBride listened, head lowered, staring at the ground. He grunted, said "Hmm," but nothing more.

He turned to Will, saw he was finished. He looked at the western horizon. "You see that sky out west? That's trouble."

The sky at the horizon was dark. Below the heavy cloud, a silver sheen of falling rain ended, evaporating, before reaching the ground.

"I figure that cloud is going to empty right soon," said McBride, "and the Red is going to be swimming before night. Damn. Twice on the same drive, and we're not even out of Texas yet. That outfit," he pointed at the herd in the water, "is the first of the day. They got a late start, and they won't finish crossing for another hour.

"There's the second outfit." He pointed toward the hillside where the herd of the cantankerous drover from yesterday moved slowly down the slope toward the flat. "That yahoo sees the same cloud we see, and he's fixing to put his herd in the water, and I'll betcha we're gonna see some fireworks when the cowboys at the ford see him coming."

They looked at their own herd, downstream, some cows grazing, others still bedded down and chewing their cuds. A few cowboys sat their horses around the herd, lolling in the saddle. Brad dozed, his head drooping, then jerking up with a start; Renfro sang for his own entertainment, softly, offkey; Jimmy, his leg hooked across the saddle horn, stared at the river.

McBride and Will looked again at the crossing. The cows in the first herd continued moving into the stream without coaxing, following the animals ahead. The four cowboys at the end of the column mostly paid close attention to their own cows, but each occasionally glanced anxiously at the herd moving down the hillside toward them. McBride and Will silently watched what increasingly appeared to be the opening stages of a confrontation.

A breeze came up from the west, bearing the subtle scent of sage. Will faced westward, closed his eyes, enjoying the cool caress of the wind on his face. He opened his eyes and looked at McBride who stared at the crossing, his face blank.

"Do you ever get tired of it?" said Will.

McBride glanced at him, turned back to the river, said nothing. Then: "If you mean, do I get tired of big open country, pretty sunsets, birdsong and wildflowers, working with the best people in the world"—he looked at Will, smiled—"and Teddy's cooking, no, I don't get tired of it."

Will made a face, surprised. "Well, I just thought—"

"I know what you thought. You thought I was all cows, cowboys and horse shit. No, son, there's no place in the world I'd rather be than right here. And that's a fact."

Will smiled. "Well said, Charlie. Can't say that I disagree with you, though I couldn't say it as well as you."

Both looked back at the river. The four cowboys at the tail of the crossing herd watched the cows flowing down the hill toward them. Then they turned to see a rider from the other bank galloping across the shallow stream, sending up cascades of water.

The rider quirted his horse as it struggled up the bank, then galloped straight toward the oncoming herd.

"Look at this, Will. This is gonna be fun," said a smiling McBride.

A man from the herd on the hillside rode out to meet the approaching rider. The men were too far away for Will and Charlie to hear, but the arm waving and snatches of shouts demonstrated that the meeting was not cordial. The riders' horses danced and shied and whirled at the furor, and the men had trouble holding them in check.

"See the rider in the red shirt?" said McBride. "That's the yahoo from yesterday that I had the set-to with. I still say he's going to make trouble pushing his herd too close to the bunch crossing now."

"Whoa!" said McBride. Red Shirt had drawn his six-shooter and leveled on the other. The rider backed his horse, shouted something, pointed at the gunman, then wheeled his horse and galloped toward his herd, the tail of the column not yet in the water.

"I wager the rider is the boss of the herd that's crossing now," McBride said. "If the yahoo moves his cows much closer to the crossing, we need to be a good distance away to avoid some stray lead.

"Let's move downstream to our herd. I don't want no part of this. Might think different if I knew either of the bosses, but I don't know 'em, so best not to get involved."

They rode down the bank toward their herd. McBride pulled up, stared at the shallow water that lapped softly against the bank. Will reined up and followed his gaze. The surface of the bank, dry and almost flat at water's edge, was darkening, a wet line in the soil that crept slowly from streamside.

"Trouble," said McBride, turning to Will. "You see that?"

"It's rising."

They looked toward the western horizon. The cloud there had expanded and darkened. The thin silver sheen of rain that previously had stopped in midair, evaporating, had thickened and now reached the ground.

"Damn," said McBride. "That does it. We won't even try to cross today. We'll just hope the surge will pass during the night or early tomorrow." He turned his horse from the river. "Let's pass the word to the boys. We need to pull the herd back from the river and get 'em on good grass and a good bed ground early. Let's see if we can find a flat with some high ground between us and the crossing. That should absorb all the lead that might be spraying about."

Cookie laid on an early supper since they had camped early and planned to bed cows and themselves before sundown in preparation for what they hoped would be a start at first light tomorrow. The hands sat around the campfire, plates in laps, listening to the same tall tales they had already heard a dozen times since leaving the Rio Grande.

Heads came up sharply at the muffled pop-pop-pop of gunfire from the direction of the crossing. Fred, Brad and Jimmy grabbed gun belts on the ground behind them and stood hurriedly, buckling belts, looking at each other, grinning.

"Hold it right there, boys," said McBride who stood beside the chuck wagon. He held the coffee cup that Cookie had just filled. "This ain't your fight, and you're not gonna be a part of it." The three drooped, stared at McBride. "It's probably over anyway. There's nothing that cools hot blood more than seeing your pard standing beside you get shot up."

Another flurry of shots: pop-pop-pop. The three cowboys looked excitedly at each other, touching six-shooters in their holsters.

"Settle down," said McBride. "That's the end of it. We'll know the result when we cross tomorrow. I don't doubt we'll see two or three new graves at the crossing. Bad business."

The three hot bloods looked at each other, picked up their plates from the ground and walked to the chuck wagon where they placed the plates and forks in the bucket. They walked together around the chuck wagon toward the hoodlum. They leaned together, talking softly, grinning, glancing back over their shoulders toward the fire circle as they passed behind the chuck wagon.

Dawn. The sun had not yet appeared as figures and shapes emerged from the darkness. McBride stood beside the fire circle with Win, Mack, Will and Bonnie. They looked somberly at the dancing flames of the new fire.

"They didn't get back till everybody was sleeping

but them ridin' night herd," McBride said. "They were waiting for me when I rolled out this morning. Seems they were just too curious for their own good. Dammit, I warned 'em.

"They were just settin' their horses back from the bank, watching the two outfits throwing insults at each other. Then some hothead in Red Shirt's bunch started throwing lead. That started it. Jimmy said they saw two cowboys get shot, one on the near bank and one in the water. It looked like it was over at that point, but then two riders on the near shore decided it wasn't over and shot at some cowboys in the water. Those in the water returned fire, and that's when Fred was hit. Jimmy said he was dead before he hit the ground. Boys in the water probably thought our three was part of the bunch shooting at 'em."

"What about Fred?" said Bonnie.

"They laid him out over there," McBride said. He pointed at a stand of pecans near the remuda. They walked to the trees where they saw Jimmy and Brad standing beside Fred's tethered horse. Jimmy looked at McBride, bowed his head and stared at the ground. Brad looked aside, his mouth twitching.

McBride stared at the body. "Dumb sonsabitches," softly. He looked up at Jimmy and Brad. "You satisfied now? Christ! You two ride drag till I tell you otherwise. And don't speak to me unless you're answering me. Now git!" Brad and Jimmy, heads down, shuffled away.

McBride shook his head, turned to the others. "We'll bury him at the crossing. There'll be other new graves. I don't suppose many drown in the Red, but he'll have company. Will, take charge of this, will you?"

"I'll help," said Bonnie.

"You don't need to do that," McBride said.

"Yes, I do."

McBride frowned, touched her arm and walked toward the fire.

McBride, Will and Bonnie sat their horses on the near bank, watching their herd that was strung out a mile moving steadily across the wide, almost belly-deep stream. The brisk current sometimes forced a careless cow to step sideways to gain footing, but the column moved at a steady pace toward the north shore.

The last of the two herds yesterday had finished crossing at dusk before the current and depth of the stream cut off passage. As McBride had predicted, the surge passed during the night. This morning, the stream was still deeper and the current stronger than usual, but it was passable.

McBride pushed his horse into the shallows, and Bonnie and Will followed. On the north side, they rode a short distance downstream from the crossing to what appeared to be the makeshift Red River cemetery. Three fresh graves lay in a row with half a dozen grass-covered mounds in the shade of a tall spreading cottonwood.

Two cowboys stood at the new graves and watched them come. One man, his spade in the soil of a new grave, leaned his chin against the handle. The other, his shovel on the ground at his feet, wiped his face with a bandanna.

McBride, Will and Bonnie pulled up at the graves. "Sad business," said McBride. "You from the last herd to cross yesterday? These your pards?"

"No, we're from the outfit that crossed about noon yesterday. Didn't dare show our backs to the bunch that crossed last. Not after the ruckus during the crossing. We lost two men." He gestured toward the graves.

"In that business yesterday, did you happen to see a man wearing a red shirt, the boss of the last herd, I think?"

The grave digger, his hand still on the shovel, straightened, pointed at the third grave.

"Hmm, why am I not surprised?" said McBride. "You know whether he died of a heart attack or lead poisoning?"

The man frowned. "Couldn't say nothin' about a heart problem. He died by a bullet. In the back. Nobody seemed to know whether he was shot by one of our men while he was running away, or by one of his own men. Point is, nobody in that outfit wanted to stay behind and bury him. So I got my suspicions."

"You might be right." McBride looked at the graves, grim, shaking his head. "Sad business."

"I'll get a couple of the boys to help me bury Fred here," said Will.

McBride nodded. "Win found a good patch of grass couple of miles ahead, and we're gonna lay over there till tomorrow morning. We'll come down after supper tonight and pay our respects." McBride touched his hat to the two grave diggers, turned his horse and set out at a lope toward the herd, followed by Will and Bonnie.

The top half of the orange sun disk cast dark shadows of live oaks and pecans and lacy shade of scattered mesquite. The cowboys, heads down and hats in hands, stood at the fresh grave of their old pard, Fred.

McBride asked if anyone would like to say something. They looked aside at each other, nervous, waiting.

"I'll say something," said Jimmy, staring at the grave. "He was an ornery old cuss, but he was a good cowboy, and he'd do anything for you. When he was ornery, I think it was just a game he was playing, 'cause he didn't think anybody liked him. But I liked him, and I'm sorry he's gone." He sniffed. "I liked him." He wiped his arm across his eyes. Rod, standing beside him, patted his shoulder.

The cowboys, heads hanging, looked at the grave, looked at each other, shifting their feet.

"He talked too much and sometimes didn't make much sense," said Rod, staring at the grave, "but he was a good old boy to ride the trail with, a good pard who wouldn't let you down."

The group fell silent. Then: "I wonder if he had kin," Jimmy said. "He never said, and I never asked. Should have asked."

McBride glanced at Jimmy, then turned to look westward at the sun, now showing only the luminous top rim. He turned back to the men. "Mack, would you say the Lord's Prayer?"

Mack lowered his head and closed his eyes. Some of the cowboys closed their eyes; others stared at the grave. Mack recited in a strong, deep voice.

> Our Father who be in heaven, hallowed be
> your name.
> Your kingdom come, your will be done, on
> earth like it is in heaven.
> Give us our daily bread today;
> And forgive us our trespass, like we forgive
> them that trespass against us;
> And lead us not to temptation, but deliver us
> from th' devil.
> For your kingdom and power and glory, for-
> ever. A-men.

McBride put on his hat and turned away. The others walked with him toward the mesquite where the horses were tied.

· Only Bonnie and Will remained. She knelt beside

the mound, straightened the cross made of two stout sticks tied together with a strip of rawhide. She leaned back, looked beyond the graves to the darkening sky above the bankside willow thicket.

"Poor old Fred," said Molly. "I wonder if anybody will remember him after this drive is finished and all these cowboys scatter. Wonder if any family or friends back home will even know he's gone." She stared at the bare mound, ran a hand over the loose soil. Will watched her, waited.

"I wonder if anyone will remember me after Grandpa's gone," she said. "What's to remember? I never did anything worth remembering. I was . . . I was just . . . there. Now I'm a cowhand." She lowered her head, absentmindedly patting the bare soil of the grave. "What's to remember?"

"Hey, hey," Will said. "Where did that come from?" He took her shoulders gently and helped her stand, took her cheeks in his hands and kissed her, a light touch to her lips. He encircled her shoulders and hugged. She wiped her eyes with a sleeve, rested her head on his chest.

He leaned back and raised her chin with a hand. "What's to remember? I remember a pretty girl who pretended to be a boy to be near her grandpa and get away from a bum who wanted to hurt her. I remember that girl was a top hand in a tough outfit driving cattle hundreds of miles from the Rio Grande to Montana.

"Hell, Bonnie, you're somebody out of the

ordinary. You know what? Your story is so different, I'm going to find somebody to write a dime novel about you!"

She smiled thinly, head down. "Stop it," softly.

"Yeah, we're gonna make money on your story. We're gonna——"

She looked up, frowning. "We?"

He smiled, leaned into her face, almost nose to nose. "Yes, we, sweetheart. You're not going anywhere without me."

She pulled his head down and kissed him. Then she pushed him away and hit him on his arm. "C'mon, you're talking silly. We need to catch up." She stepped off briskly toward the horses.

He smiled and shook his head. Then he ran after her. She heard him coming, looked over her shoulder, and saw him. She ran hard, tossing her head and laughing, her hair billowing in the breeze. He stopped, watched her, *this woman, this moonbeam*, then dropped his chin and walked slowly after her.

Every cowboy, doing his duty at his assigned place at the herd, was tense. Hardly three hours since leaving the bed ground just north of the Red, they saw their first Indians.

A band of a hundred or so rode parallel to the herd a couple of hundred yards away on the right. They were angling toward the trail, so it was apparent to all that they intended to intersect the trail ahead.

From her position at swing on the right side, Bonnie rode up beside Win, who was riding point.

"They seem to be coming our way," she said. "What do you think?"

"Well, there appears to be women with 'em, so they're not hostile, I think. I suspect they want to beg a beef or two. Or three."

"They need a band that size to beg a cow?"

"If just four or five bucks asked the average trail boss for a couple of cows, you think he would pay any attention?'

"I see what you mean."

The Indians rode at a walk toward an intersecting ahead, moving gradually closer to the herd. Every cowboy stared at the band while the Indians seemed oblivious of the presence of the herd and herders. It was as if they were alone on the prairie.

The Indians stopped short of an intersection with the trail. They sat their horses quietly, most with eyes fixed on their horses' ears, but some stole a glance at the oncoming herd. An old man and two young men rode forward and stopped at the trail, watching the approaching herd. They dismounted and waited, holding their reins.

McBride rode up beside Win. "Let's stop here for an early dinner," McBride said. He gestured with a nod ahead on the left. "Looks like passable grass. Put the herd there and come back here. We'll have a little parley with the local landlords. Bring Cowboy Mack and Will."

Win waved back down the column. "Noon stop!"

he shouted. "Let's throw 'em off the trail to graze!" He turned the head of the column toward the grassy flat. A line of cottonwoods and elms beyond the meadow suggested a stream where they could water the herd before setting out after dinner.

Cookie and Bonnie pulled the wagons off the trail and stopped. Bonnie set the brake and jumped down. She saw Win, Mack and Will riding toward McBride. She spoke hurriedly to Cookie and ran to intercept the riders. She called to Will, and he reined up and pulled her up behind his saddle.

McBride and the others rode to the three Indians, arms raised in greeting. They pulled up and dismounted. McBride, Will and Win handed reins to Mack who walked the horses to a mesquite and tied them on low branches. He came back to stand with the others behind McBride.

The three Indians were dressed in breechcloths, buckskin shirts and leggings. All wore feathered caps finished with hawk quills and beadwork. Their long hair hung in two braids down their chests. The cap of one young warrior featured vertical eagle feathers and ermine tails hanging behind.

McBride looked aside at his companions, smiled faintly, looked back at the Indians. He extended his hand to the old man who stood a step in front of the others in his entourage and appeared to be the leader, a chief perhaps. The Indian's expression did not change. He took the hand, and they shook.

"Have you come a long way?" said McBride. "Where is your village?"

The chief replied in Comanche. "Speak a language I understand. Speak Comanche. Or Spanish." He glanced aside at his companions who smiled.

"Mack," said McBride, without taking his eyes off the speaker. "I think this dandy is making fun of me. Talk to him and help me decide whether to shoot him or listen to him beg." McBride smiled at the Indians.

Mack stepped up beside McBride and spoke to the chief in Spanish. "We are taking these cows to Montana where we will give them to the Crow People. Why did you ride to meet us?"

The Indian had listened closely to Mack. He frowned and replied in Spanish. "How did you learn Spanish? You are the first black man I have talked with."

Mack ignored the question and replied in Spanish. "Why did you ride to meet us?"

The chief removed the blanket from his shoulders, handed it to the young man behind him and turned back to Mack. He began a discourse in Spanish that Mack, and even McBride, immediately recognized since they had heard it before. But they listened without interruption.

Mack translated for McBride and the others as the chief spoke. "All this country is the hunting grounds of the Kiowa Apache and Comanche people." The chief waved his arm to encompass the country around them. "The white people have come to our country and killed the buffalo and deer and left us nothing to hunt and eat. This is not good. Now we are poor, and we are hungry.

"Some of our people want to fight the whites. They want to punish the whites for killing the animals and chasing them away from our country. I have always counseled peace with the whites, but some of our angry young men do not agree; they want war with the whites."

"Why did you ride to meet us?" said Mack. He knew the answer before the old chief replied.

"Since we cannot hunt the buffalo and deer because the whites have killed them or chased them away, and since you are passing through the land of the Kiowa Apache and Comanche, we will let you cross our land, but you must pay us."

McBride nodded occasionally as Mac translated. The chief, stony-faced, listened without changing his expression which displayed both disdain and boredom.

By this time, half a dozen cowboys had ambled over from the herd that was now stationary, grazing on good grass, lush and green from recent rains. McBride looked aside, spoke casually to the newcomers.

Will and Bonnie retreated a few steps to the shade of a redbud tree. While Will leaned against the trunk, Bonnie touched the wispy remnants of pink petals on the low limbs.

"Bet this tree was pretty a while back," said Bonnie. Will studied her profile, touched her hand, and she looked at him, frowning, questioning.

McBride and Mack sat down slowly on the ground, McBride grunting with the effort, and pulled tobacco pouches from pockets. They methodically poured tobacco on papers, tapping the pouch lightly. That done, they closed the bags, licked the edge of the paper and rolled cigarettes.

McBride reached up, offering his pouch to the old chief. The Indian and his companions sat down easily before McBride. The old man nodded, took the pouch, reached in and took a pinch of tobacco, pulled off a paper. McBride gestured toward the two warriors behind him, and the old man offered the pouch to them. After they had taken tobacco and papers, the chief returned the pouch to McBride, nodding to him.

McBride examined his handiwork, rolling the cigarette in his fingers, then lit it with a match. He offered the burning match to the chief, who leaned forward, lit his cigarette and inhaled deeply, his eyes closed. He exhaled, opened his eyes, turned and lit the cigarettes of the other two men from his own. Cowboys and Indians alike puffed, nodded, studied each other without embarrassment and stared blankly at the land and animals.

Thus began the practiced routine of wasting time. McBride had considerable experience in south Texas dealing with Mexicans, who he believed had no concept whatever of the value of time. Since he began driving cattle years ago through Indian country and encountering the inhabitants, he found them even more skilled in passing time doing nothing. With the experience gained from these exchanges, McBride had become adept at the Indian practice of negotiating without saying a word.

Will leaned over and spoke softly in Bonnie's ear. "I'll bet some of these bucks understand more English than they let on. Let's see." He straightened and spoke loudly. "That cap with the feathers is something, ain't it? Wonder what kind of feathers they are."

The old chief looked abruptly at his young companion with the feathered cap. He turned back and stared a moment at Will.

Will smiled. "Thought so," softly. Will motioned to Bonnie with a nod, and they strolled over to stand behind McBride.

The chief frowned and studied the ground at his knees. After a half hour of silence and finishing his third cigarette, the chief addressed McBride in Spanish. "You may pass through our country by paying us ten cows." He watched as Mack translated.

McBride smiled at the Indian. He looked the chief in the eyes as he spoke in English. "I'll be damned if I give these thieves ten cows."

Will frowned. "You won't?" McBride looked up at him. "Have you noticed that there are about sixty bucks in that bunch?" Will said. He gestured with a nod toward the knot of Indians. "And most of 'em seem to have rifles."

McBride frowned, still looking at Will. "Tell me

again how many times you been up this trail?" Will looked aside. "Yeah, I know. This is your first drive. These people know the army is not too many days away. They know they live here because they were moved here by the army. They'll not likely give us any trouble. We'll . . ."

McBride stopped, staring at the group of Indians who sat their horses quietly behind the chief. Except not all were mounted. A dozen or so women had dismounted and now stood beside their horses, crowded around Bonnie. Four of the women carried babies in cradleboards on their backs.

Will looked around. Intent on the quiet spectacle before him, he had not noticed that she had left his side.

"What th' hell's she doing over there?" said McBride.

They watched Bonnie as she appeared to be talking with the women. She touched a baby's cheek in its cradleboard, admired a woman's blouse and another's hair. The women alternately frowned and smiled at this white woman who spoke to them as if she were interested in them, though they likely understood not a word.

When a woman touched the blue neckerchief around her neck, Bonnie pulled it off and tied it around the woman's neck. The woman, at first wide-eyed and open-mouthed, smiled and smoothed the neckerchief as the other women admired it.

Molly walked back to the negotiators, cowboys

and Indians, who had been staring at her. She stopped in front of McBride.

"Charlie, these women are hungry. The babies are hungry. You need to give them the ten head they ask for."

"Wha . . . what the hell you talking about, woman! You don't know *nothin'* about dealing with these thieves. Give 'em what they ask for, and next time—"

"You got a dozen unbranded strays in the herd. And we got a half dozen strays carrying other people's brands. You said yourself that we need do something about the branded strays, eat 'em or run 'em off so we won't be called rustlers. You could find ten cows from that lot, couldn't you? And you did say you needed to get some information from the locals about the country ahead, didn't you? Give 'em the ten cows, and they'll tell you what you want to know"

McBride turned, glared at Will.

Will shrugged his shoulders. "Hey, it's Bonnie, not me."

McBride turned back to Bonnie, frowning. He stared a long moment, then relaxed. He spoke softly. "Dammit, Bonnie, you don't know *nothin'* about trail driving. You're a big pain in the . . ." He stopped, inhaled deeply, exhaled. "Okay, what you say makes some sense."

McBride turned to the knot of cowboys who stood nearby, grinning ear to ear, waiting to see how the encounter was going to play out. "Wipe those silly grins off your faces." The cowboys pulled faces, looked at each other, trying to suppress smiles.

"Win, cut out the branded strays and some of the unbranded cows, ten all told," said McBride, "and deliver them to the chief. Mack, go with him and invite the chief to come over for supper. I want to talk to him about the country up ahead. I suspect the trail's not very well laid out north of here."

McBride turned to Bonnie, frowning. "Satisfied?" She smiled, pulled a face at Will. McBride stepped off to catch up with Win and Mack. "C'mon, Will, let's get back to the herd, if I've got a herd. Might find myself giving it up to that snip of a woman . . ." his voice trailing off.

Bonnie smiled smugly at Will, who had looked back at her over his shoulder.

"Damn, Win," said McBride, "trouble comes in twins, don't it? After I gave the old chief the ten cows, and tobacco, sugar and coffee last night, he tells us there's a big village two days ahead right on the trail that's sure as hell gonna demand a big toll. He said that some outfits have given up a couple dozen head."

"I don't suppose you're going to give anybody a couple dozen head," Win said.

"You're right about that. Just after we cross the Salt Fork, which I expect we'll hit by noon, we're going to turn west off the main trail. I've heard a little about that cutoff, and it sounds like it'll do.

"I suspect the old chief will pass the word to the village that we're coming, and I hope we're out of sight before they come looking for us. On the cutoff, we should pass thirty miles or so west of the village. All this means that we need to move the herd faster than the usual pace. Pass the word to the boys.

"That's one problem. Now we gotta deal with this other problem." He nodded toward Rod who rode toward them. McBride waved, and Rod pulled up.

A light rain during the night, accompanied by rolling thunder and lightning, had rattled the herd. The cows got up from their beds, ready to bolt, but the night herders, reinforced by two additional men, kept them milling until the weather settled.

The loose remuda was not so settled. They had scattered during the nocturnal lightning show. At daybreak, Rod and half a dozen others found a bunch of horses in a nearby swale, grazing placidly, and brought them to camp.

"Good job, Rod. How many we got missing now?" said McBride.

"As best I can figure, eighteen or so," Rod said. "Tracks leading from camp are pretty good, thanks to the rain. Looks like they weren't spooked bad and are pretty much stayin' together. "

"Take four hands, counting you, to bring 'em in. Can't spare any more. We gotta get this herd moving." McBride shook his head. "Damn, we're getting thin in this outfit. Never lost three men in a drive before. And we're barely out of Texas. Maybe I can hire two or three drifters in Dodge."

Will and Bonnie, Jimmy and Rod sat their horses, staring at the tracks in the wet soil.

"They've split in two groups," said Rod. "Will, Bonnie, take the tracks to the left, and Jimmy and I will hunt the bunch to the right." The two pairs rode off on the separate tracks.

Will and Bonnie rode at a lope. The prints were clearly etched in the soggy ground, and they had no trouble following them. The tracks suggested that the horses were walking so should not be far ahead.

Then Will held up a hand and pulled up. "The prints are deeper here and spaced farther apart. They're running. Something spooked 'em. Maybe Indians ran them off after all." They kicked their mounts into a lope.

The trail led up the side of a low rise. Will held a hand out, palm down, signaling caution. They rode slowly up the side of the rise until they were near the top. Dismounting, they tied their reins to a dead sage, got down on all fours and crawled forward until they could just see over the top.

And there they were. A dozen horses stood at the base of the rise, rigid, all looking up the swale, ears tipped forward and stiff, nostrils flared.

"These horses are scared of something," Will

whispered, looking up the swale, following the gaze of the horses.

"Look!" said Bonnie.

CHAPTER EIGHT

A small bunch of buffalo stood near an oak grove at the head of the swale, a half mile or so away. The buffalo moved slowly, dropping their heads to graze, looking up, alert but sensing no threat from the horses that were downwind from them. A huge bull stood at the head of the herd, looking aside, down the swale, nose raised, sniffing.

"Oh, my, my, my," said Will. "I sure would like a buffalo steak, and I bet the boys would like one too." He glanced aside at Bonnie. "What about it?"

"All you got is a six-shooter. That won't kill a buffalo. And what about the horses?"

"Yeah." He frowned, smiled. "The horses won't go far. We'll find 'em. After we get us some buffalo meat." He slid down from the top, grabbed her pant leg and pulled her down. They stood and walked to their mounts.

"Here's what we'll do," he said. "You ride in a wide circle and get upwind, but stay out of sight. They'll smell you and start moving. They won't likely stampede if they don't see you."

"What are you going to do?"

He grinned. "You're right about the six-shooter. That's why I am going to rope me a buffalo."

She frowned. "You can't do that. Rope one of those monsters, and he'll tear you and your horse apart."

"That's why I'm roping a calf. Look." He pointed at the buffalo. "Look at the right side of the bunch. If I'm not mistaken, that critter standing by itself is a calf."

She frowned, pursed her lips. "Are you that good with a rope? Or are you gonna get yourself killed?"

He smiled. "You do your part, and I'll do mine, and we'll have buffalo on the menu tonight."

They mounted and set out slowly along the base of the rise. After a few hundred yards, he reined up and pointed ahead to her. She nodded and kicked her horse into a lope in a circle to the right that would take her eventually back to the swale beyond the buffalo.

Will watched her go a moment, then untied the coiled rope from his saddle and looped it over the horn. He walked his horse up the gentle slope of the rise until he could see over the top.

The buffalo were still there, moving slowly down the swale toward him. Most grazed calmly, their heads buried in the lush green grass in the wet center of the swale. The shaggy old bull at the front was the only animal not grazing. He had turned and now stared fixedly up the swale, behind the bunch. The horses in the swale below Will had not moved, still staring at the buffalo.

Suddenly the buffalo were in motion, trotting at first as they followed the bull, then stampeding when they saw what he had seen.

Bonnie! Damn it, I said let 'em smell you! Bonnie whipped her galloping horse toward the herd.

The horses below Will wheeled and were off like a shot, galloping down the swale.

Will walked his horse over the top of the rise. He moved slowly down the slope, angling slightly to his left to intercept the stampeding buffalo. When the herd was almost on him, he kicked his horse into a gallop alongside the bunch and moved over close to the rushing herd.

A large cow at the edge of the herd charged him, bumping his horse and almost unseating him. He righted himself, pulled away from her and looked for the calf. He saw it behind him and eased up slightly to let it catch up to him. The calf was small, and it was having a hard time keeping up with the stampeding herd.

He moved the galloping horse with his knees until his horse's nose was even with the calf's tail. He lifted the coiled rope from the saddle horn with his left hand, holding it with the reins. With his right hand, he shook out a loop, spun the loop and threw it over the calf's head. He reined up slowly, and the rope, looped around the saddle horn, drew taut. The calf bawled, straining against the rope, as the horse braced against the pull on the rope.

Will dismounted and looked up at Bonnie who had just pulled up, her horse sliding to a stop, heaving. She hurriedly dismounted and held the reins, staring at the struggling calf.

He glared at her. "What in hell possessed you, Bonnie? I said to let 'em smell you. I didn't say to stampede 'em."

"Sorry, I walked my horse toward them, but I guess I got excited. I've heard so many stories about buffalo. Sorry."

He relaxed. "No harm done, I guess. I got our buffalo steaks." He pulled the six-shooter from its holster and felt his way down the stretched rope. The calf, struggling and bawling, suddenly stilled. It stood, spraddle-legged, head hanging and eyes bulging, mouth open, no longer pulling against the noose that was tight around its neck.

"Will!"

He stopped, his hand on the taut rope, and looked back at her over his shoulder.

"I don't like this," softly. "It's so little."

"It's big enough. Everybody in camp will have his fill of buffalo meat tonight." He inched down the rope toward the calf.

"That's not what I mean."

He stopped again, frowned and looked back at her. "What do you mean?"

"It's just a baby."

"It's a wild animal. People eat wild animals."

"I don't like this."

His hand gripping the taut rope, his other hand holding the pistol at his side, he looked down the swale, over the crest of the knoll at the wispy layer of gray cloud hanging over the horizon. He started when a solitary roadrunner flushed from a sage thicket and scooted down the center of the swale. He continued to stare after the bird had disappeared in a mesquite thicket.

He turned slowly to her, spoke softly. "What would you have me do?"

She lowered her head, looked up at him. "Let her go," almost a whisper.

His head hung as he studied the ground at his feet. He turned and looked up, closed his eyes momentarily, opened them. He looked back at her, then inched down the rope till he reached the calf. The little calf pulled away at his touch, tightening the loop. He hesitated a moment, then pushed the six-shooter into its holster. He gripped the loop on the side of the calf's neck, shook it until the rope came free.

The calf stood a moment, head hanging and legs splayed. Then, suddenly, it wheeled and ran down the swale, jumping, throwing its head about, bucking and kicking.

Still holding the loop, Will watched the calf. He walked slowly toward his horse, coiling the rope. Bonnie watched as he meticulously tied the coils to the saddle.

"You mad at me?" she said softly.

He looked at her over his shoulder. "Sure, I'm mad at you. Look there." He pointed down the swale at the little calf, still cavorting, following the trail of the buffalo herd. "There goes some mighty fine eating." She ducked her head and turned aside.

Will studied the leather thong holding the rope to the saddle, tightened the knot. He sighed, walked to her and put his arms around her shoulders.

"My sweet girl, I can't be mad at you. You're a little crazy sometimes, but I love you anyway. Maybe I wouldn't like you so much if you were just an ordinary female who acted like all other ordinary females." He released her and walked to his horse, gathered the reins, stopped and stared at the horn. "Course, I can't speculate on what the boys are going to say when they learn that we turned loose their buffalo steaks."

"You wouldn't!" she said, wide-eyed, tense. Then she relaxed, raised her chin and walked to him. She leaned into his face. "Well, I don't care. Tell 'em."

"No, I won't tell 'em. They'd probably beat hell outta me since they wouldn't raise a hand to you, a defenseless little girl, though you're responsible for them missing their buffalo steaks."

He grinned. "On the other hand, you're a tough customer and could probably whup most of the boys. Maybe I'll tell 'em and see what happens." He jerked away, and her swing caught only air.

*****

175

McBride, Will and Cowboy Mack sat their horses staring at a thin plume of smoke a few miles ahead. They had ridden in advance of the herd this morning, searching for water.

"I don't like this a little bit," said McBride. "The big village is a long way east of here, thirty miles or so, but now we got this." He stared, pondering. "Well, let's have a look." He pushed his horse into a lope, and the others followed.

They slowed before reaching the smoke spiral and walked their horses into what had been a sizable encampment on each side of a shallow creek. Embers in dozens of fire circles still smoldered before as many as a hundred tepee sites and brush shelters.

"They left this camp just last night. Maybe this morning," said Mack. "Could be three or four hundred people."

"There's plenty of horse tracks over there," Will said, pointing. "Looks like some cattle as well. The tracks head west. If we can angle the herd a bit eastward, we might miss them."

"Yeah," said McBride, "unless they got word of us heading this way and are out there hiding in the bushes, waiting for us. Well, we'll just have to stay ahead of 'em. We'll water the herd here, then push hard again till dark. Let's hope that band is heading for the Texas panhandle where they lived 'bout a thousand years before being forced on the reservation."

*****

First light, except there was little light. A low overcast and a light rain dampened spirits and soaked the cowboys that stood by habit around the firepit that held no warming fire. Holding plates of cold beans and biscuits, they tried to divert the water from dripping off hat brims onto their breakfast. There had been hot coffee earlier since Cookie had tied a canvas sheet to the chuck wagon and built a small fire underneath. Now the canvas was gone and the coffee finished as Cookie packed up the wagon for departure.

"C'mon, boys, let's have those plates. Gotta get moving," said Cookie.

The cowboys shuffled to the wagon, raked the sodden remains of their breakfast into the pail and deposited plates in the bucket. They collected their saddles from the hoodlum and walked toward the remuda, grumbling to no one in particular.

During three days since leaving the main trail to bypass the Indian village, rain had fallen continuously. The faint semblance of a trail had disappeared, and the outfit moved through a plain devoid of hoof or foot prints.

Will walked from the wagon to McBride who stood alone, facing north, smoking a cigarette. "Do you know where we are, Charlie?" said Will.

McBride glanced aside at him, turned back to the front, inhaled and exhaled a stream of smoke. "No, no more'n anybody else in this camp. All I know is we're headed that way," he said, pointing ahead. "How do I

know we're going that way when there's no sign of a
trail? Look at the chuck wagon." He nodded toward the
wagon. "Cookie always points the tongue of the chuck
wagon in the direction we were headed when he stops
for any meal."

"Be damned. I didn't know that."

McBride smiled and clapped him on the back.
"There's more to moving a bunch of cows than singin'
to 'em."

Spirits lifted the next morning when early risers looked
up into a blue sky with not a hint of a cloud in sight.
Wisps of steam rose from wet wagon canvas and blankets, even clothing, in the bright sunshine.

Bonnie worked on building a cooking fire with
kindling and boughs she had collected last evening and
stowed under the chuck wagon. A couple of cowboys
nearby complained and cussed while they tried to build
a campfire with wet wood and buffalo chips they had
just collected.

Jimmy straightened and flexed his back. He
looked at the cookfire that was now burning brightly,
yellow flames dancing. He eyed the pile of dry wood
beside the fire.

"Uh, Bonnie?" Jimmy called.

"Nope," Bonnie said, glancing aside at Jimmy.
"We need every piece if you expect to have any breakfast."

"Yeah, but Bonnie—"

Cookie looked up from the pot of beans he was stirring. "Jimmy, if you got nothin' else to do, you can come over here and stand by our fire to dry out. If that's okay with Charlie, there." He gestured with a nod toward McBride who stood nearby with Cowboy Mack, smoking, holding their horses' reins and looking intently northward.

Jimmy looked at McBride only a moment. He knelt and lit another match to the wet tinder. Cookie looked at Bonnie, smiled. He carried the pot of beans to the fire and placed it on the grate.

Everyone in camp looked up at the approach of two galloping horses. Will and Brad pulled up hard and dismounted.

"The trail's straight ahead," Will said, pointing, "some distance beyond that line of oaks and willows there."

"How do you know it's a cattle trail?" said McBride.

"Hell, 'cause there's *cattle* on it!" Brad said, wide-eyed. "They're a few miles off, but it's a pretty good-sized herd."

"There's a little creek in the trees," said Will. "Not much, but it should do for the herd before hitting the trail".

"Sounds good," McBride said. He turned toward the encampment and shouted. "On your toes, everbody! Hurry up and get your breakfast! We're headin' for Dodge!"

*****

Win, riding at the head of the cow column, stopped. He turned in his saddle. "Charlie, come 'ere!" he shouted at McBride who rode beside Cowboy Mack, chatting. McBride and Mack kicked their horses to a trot and pulled up beside Win. They looked ahead where Win pointed.

About two hundred yards away, two horsemen rode at the head of a thin column that was just emerging from behind a low rise. One of the riders carried a flag that fluttered lightly, just enough to reveal the stars and stripes. Behind the two leaders, a line of figures followed. Men, women and children. Some were mounted, but most walked slowly, shuffling, heads bowed.

"What the' hell's goin' on?" said Win. They watched as the column moved slowly from behind the rise.

McBride pulled a spyglass from his saddlebag and focused on the column. "Indians. The riders on each side of the column are soldiers." He lowered the spyglass. "They're coming from the direction of the Texas panhandle. There's been troubles in the panhandle for a couple of years now. I'd take bets that those troubles are finished now, and this band is headed east for a reservation. Or a lockup." He replaced the spyglass in his saddle bag.

"Let's stop the herd here. There's a decent patch of switchgrass over there," gesturing with a nod of his head to the left of the trail. "It's just about dinner time anyway. Look yonder." He pointed at the chuck wagon and hoodlum a hundred yards ahead. "They must've pulled up when they saw the Indians."

Win looked back at the herd, saw Will who was riding point. "Will! Go tell Cookie and hood to get the wagons back here."

Will nodded, kicked his horse to a gallop, reined up at the wagons and relayed Win's message. Cookie and Bonnie climbed up on wagon seats and turned their teams to the back trail.

Will rode beside Bonnie's wagon. "Bonnie. Win told me to tell Cookie and hood to get back there."

Bonnie frowned at him. "Yeah?"

"Hood?"

"Oh. The driver of the hoodlum is called 'hood'."

"Hmm." He stared at his horse's head, frowning.

"What's wrong?"

"I wanted to make a joke about it, but nothing comes to mind." He frowned. "Hmm. Hood."

She watched him a moment. "You're kinda strange sometimes, honey."

He brightened, turned abruptly toward her. "If you're gonna call me 'honey' every time I'm strange, just watch me . . . sweetheart." They both laughed.

Cookie and Bonnie pulled up near the herd that was circling and milling now, settling and grazing.

Bonnie set the brake, hopped down and went to Will who had dismounted, pulled the saddle and bridle off, and turned the horse into the remuda. They walked to the hoodlum wagon where he dropped the horse gear, then went over to stand beside Cowboy Mack who stared at the moving column in the distance.

"Who are they?" Bonnie said.

"Charlie says they are Indians from the panhandle," said Mack. "The last holdouts. The army finally put down the hostiles."

"Hostiles?" Bonnie said. "Didn't the Indians live there?"

Mack frowned, looked aside at Will, who pulled a face. "Time's passed that Indians can live any place that white folks want," Mack said. "Sorry, but that's the way it is. Come to think of it, maybe some black folks fit in there as well, now we have the right to own land."

They watched silently as the Indians and their army escort continued their slow progress eastward across the cattle trail.

Bonnie broke the silence. "It's not right." Will and Mack looked at her, then at each other.

"It's been going on a long time," said Will. "Government has tried to make peace with the tribes, but there's always trouble."

She turned to Will, her face hard. "Well, wouldn't you make trouble if somebody was forcing you from your home?"

"Will's right," said Mack. "The strongest people have always taken what they want from them that are not so strong. Course, that don't make it right. White folks took from my people what they held most dear, their freedom."

Bonnie crossed her arms, stamped a foot. "That's what I mean. It's not right! I don't like it. Just look at them up there! They're being herded like a bunch of cows." She stared, grim.

She turned to Will. "Why do you call them 'bucks'? Do they call each other 'bucks'? Doesn't sound right to me. Why don't you just call them 'men' or 'Indians'?"

Will frowned, pursed his lips. "Well . . ." He looked at Mack.

"The lady's got a point there, Will."

"Guess I never thought about it," Will said. "I just listen to people I'm around all the time and pick up stuff from them."

Bonnie frowned, looked at Mack. He cocked his head, almost smiled. She turned back to the procession ahead crossing the trail.

"Where are they going?" she said.

They watched in silence. "Probably Fort Sill," said Will. "I understand that's where the army is sending Indians that don't seem to be content to go to reservations." He turned to Bonnie. "Since when you been thinking kindly toward Indians? Maybe you never lost any kin to Comanches. They killed my mama and a brother."

She winced. "No, I never lost family to Indians.

I'm sorry about your mama and brother, but it works both ways. I bet every Comanche has lost kin to army and settlers."

"That's probably true. I don't mind telling that I killed a couple of the bunch that hit our farm. They started the fight, and they deserved to die."

Bonnie hung her head, pondering, then took Will's arm. They walked toward the chuck wagon, her head leaning against his shoulder.

Mack watched them go a moment, then turned back to see the end of the column of Indians and soldiers cross the cattle trail and disappear into a mesquite thicket. The prairie was empty, quiet, still, as if no one had passed that way in living memory.

Rod pulled up beside Will who was riding point. They stared across the rolling prairie ahead at the gray-black column of smoke that seemed to be issuing from the earth.

"If I didn't know what it was, I'd say it was the chimney of hell," said Rod. "Maybe it is."

"I sure couldn't say," said Will. "Never saw a train."

"You'll see one soon enough." Rod turned toward Will. "Did you know they're already talking about running railroad tracks into Texas? Yeah! It'll mean the end of the cattle drives. I don't want to even think about it." He inhaled deeply, exhaled. "Raises too many questions." He pulled away and rode toward the remuda, toward Jimmy who sometimes helped him with the horses.

The drive from Indian country into Kansas had been without incident, day following day, monotonous almost, with tolerable rains and moderate temperatures. They sometimes pulled in sight of a large herd ahead, usually losing sight of it the next day. Another herd sometimes came into view on the back trail. So far, herds had been far enough away that nobody feared mixing.

On one notable day, they reached an important way station on the drive. Cowboys stood outside camp staring ahead at a cluster of dark buildings that was Dodge. McBride had called a halt in mid-afternoon a few miles short of the town. All were gathered here but Brad and Jimmy who sat their horses watching the cattle grazing on a patch of green grass. They had watered the herd at noon, and the cows now were placid and easily contained.

The Kansas railhead towns had been the subject of conversation around the campfire the past few days. The talk betrayed both an eagerness and nervousness to revisit past experiences. All in the outfit but Will and Bonnie had been to Wichita or Ellsworth.

Win was particularly anxious to reach Dodge. "I left a considerable deposit last year at Joe Brennan's Saloon in Ellsworth. I intend to make a like withdrawal in Dodge at the Long Branch this year." The cowboys sitting at the campfire that evening looked at each other, skepticism written on every face.

While they were most interested in the prospects at Dodge, the boys enjoyed hearing tales of other railhead towns as well. Only McBride, Win and Mack had seen Abilene and Ellsworth, farther east, when they were the railheads at the end of the Chisholm Trail from Texas. Clustered around campfires, the cowboys had listened without interrupting to McBride's tales of wild nights in Abilene as if they had not heard the stories a dozen times.

McBride told again of his chance meeting with Wild Bill Hickok on one memorable occasion in Abilene. Already a western legend, Hickok was the marshal, charged with keeping the town quiet and orderly. Generally, he was successful, and his duties did not interfere with his spending most of his duty hours at saloon gambling tables.

On this particular night, McBride had played cards with Hickok and others for a couple of hours and more than a couple of whiskeys. He had left with a pounding headache from too much drink after long abstinence, responding to Wild Bill's wave with a brushing-a-fly wave of his own.

McBride learned the next day that Hickok was involved in a confrontation later that night with a rowdy bunch in which he shot and killed an old adversary that Hickok thought was out to assassinate him. Then Hickock mistakenly shot and killed a deputy who had rushed to assist him. He was relieved of his post later that year.

That was 1871, the last time McBride had driven cattle up the Chisholm Trail to Abilene. Abilene town fathers, fearful of a longhorn-borne tick that carried a contagious sickness and tired of the uproar caused by the presence of Texas cowboys, told drovers to move on.

Trail bosses listened and headed west for the new railhead at Ellsworth. Town leaders in Ellsworth soon followed the example of Abilene and, in 1874, drovers headed for Dodge City.

Dodge welcomed the prospect of becoming a cattle town. The railroad had arrived in 1872 when thousands of stinking buffalo hides were regularly stacked at the tracks awaiting loading. That source of income declined as buffalo in the region were killed off. The arrival of Texas cattle was Dodge's salvation.

McBride turned to the cowboys that still stared at Dodge. "Okay, here's what's goin' down." The cowboys crowded around him. "We're laying over here two days. We're off the main trail, so there shouldn't be any mixing of stock with any passing herds. We'll have two nights in Dodge for any who want to go in. I'll work out a schedule of who's watching the herd. Anybody not interested in Dodge and wants to stay in camp the two days?"

The cowboys looked around, smiling sheepishly, pulling silly faces.

"That's what I figured," said McBride. "Bonnie?"

She smiled, leaning against Will. "I'm going to

Dodge with my pard here." She looked up at Will, back to McBride. "Besides, I need a bath. Don't suppose anyone has noticed."

"Oh, yeah?" Brad held his nose, glancing at Bonnie. He jumped aside, laughing, as she aimed a successful kick at his backside.

"Okay, simmer down. I'll work on the schedule, and no complaints. Now, I'm advancing each of you $25. Spend it wisely. Get a good meal or two. Some of you need a bath and haircut so bad that you're in danger of being mistook for a wild animal. Cookie will put up a lighted lantern on a pole to guide you back here. If you can still see at that point."

McBride and some of the other hands had talked about Dodge for weeks, mostly for the benefit of Will and Bonnie, but also to rekindle their own expectations.

Dodge was a town in tumult at its beginning. In the early 1870s, there were two factions, those that wanted a town of free spirits, with little restraint on saloons, gambling and prostitution, and the other group that wanted a town of law and order. The latter won the contest, and Charlie Bassett was elected sheriff.

"Bassett's a good man," said McBride. "Don't get on his bad side. Deposit your six-shooters at his office, and leave it to him to keep order. He's been in Dodge some years. It was Charlie opened the Long Branch Saloon a few years ago, so you see, he's been around and knows the town. You'll spot the law easy. They carry shotguns, and they aren't shy about using 'em.

"Enjoy Dodge, but don't do nothin' dumb. Some of you might bring back an aching head, but that will pass. But think on it. Don't bring back something you don't want that's likely to stay with you." He shot a quick glance at Bonnie.

She frowned, pulled Will's head down and whispered. "What's he—"

Will put a finger to his lips "Later," he said softly.

Will and Bonnie rode at a walk toward Dodge. The horizon was still bright with the memory of day, a horizontal layer of soft gold topped by a charcoal line that merged with the black ceiling above. Ahead, pinpoints of light flickered on in the gloaming as lanterns were lit in the town. The other cowboys from the outfit, except those that McBride had assigned the first watch, rode nearby, laughing, chatting loudly, excited and nervous.

"Okay, it's later," Bonnie said. "What did Charlie mean when he said don't bring back something you don't want to stay with you?"

Will studied his horse's ears a moment before answering. "Hmm. Well. I've not been on a long drive before, but I understand that the hands, after a drive like this, after not being around women for some months, they might, they *likely*, will visit—"

"Okay, I got it." She straightened in the saddle, turned to him. "Are you going to . . . I mean, if I wasn't here, would you . . ."

He grinned. "If you weren't here, I wouldn't know you, would I? So if you weren't here, I would likely do what any other young cowboy would do at this point of a long drive, after not even seeing a woman for months."

She leaned toward him. "Even if you knew you could, you know, get something you didn't want to take back to camp with you?"

He laughed out loud. "Don't worry about it. Don't even talk about it. It's not going to happen." He frowned, turned serious and leaned over in the saddle toward her. "Bonnie, have you given me something I don't want to carry around with me?" He looked anxiously at her, trying to hide a twitching smile.

"Me! You!" She jerked her foot from the stirrup and tried to kick his leg. Her boot bounced off his horse's belly, and the horse shied. He gained control and pulled back beside her.

"Truce," he said. "I know you are as clean as the morning breeze." He raised his nose and sniffed. "Even when you need a bath real bad." He laughed and pounded his horse's flanks with his boot heels. She yelled and raced after him.

The other cowboys watched the galloping pair as they approached the flickering lights ahead.

Will and Bonnie met Mack at the livery just outside the town proper where they left their horses. They walked to the sheriff's office and deposited their six-shooters.

From there they went their separate ways to establishments where they expected to make themselves presentable to polite society. They agreed to meet back at the livery.

Will and Mack, ablutions finished and clean-shaven, sporting new haircuts and new clothes, returned first. They watched Bonnie coming, head down, seemingly embarrassed by her transformation. She wore new jeans and shirt, her just-washed hair invisible under her hat. She looked up sheepishly at her pards.

"My, my," said Mack, smiling, looking down at her. "Pretty new clothes, even got a new hat."

Will raised his chin and sniffed, looked side to side. "Anybody see Bonnie 'round here? I can't smell her." Bonnie punched him softly in the belly. He winced, laughed and grabbed her. He inhaled. "Mack, this'n don't smell like Bonnie, but she'll have to do." He kissed her on the forehead.

They walked in the middle of the street, passing cowboys going in both directions who chatted loudly, guffawing. Most were in various stages of inebriation. The dusty road was dimly illuminated by light from windows and the occasional outside gas lamp attached to a wall or hanging from a pole.

Mack looked around at the shops, saloons, haberdasheries and establishments of all sorts that lined the street. "My, my, this is a pretty new cowtown, but it's catching on real fast. Already looks like Abilene."

They turned a corner and pulled up sharply. Bonnie's eyes opened wide, and her jaw dropped. There, not thirty paces away, stood a massive, towering monster. Outlined by the last weak rays from the dying sun, the huge black machine seemed alive, a low throbbing in its bowels, steam issuing in lacy streams, rising, swirling, dissipating.

"Oh, what . . ." said Bonnie, hands on her cheeks. "I never thought . . ." She turned abruptly to Will. "You ever see a train?"

"Nope," Will said, staring at the engine. "I'm not sure I need to see another one."

"You, Mack? You ever see a train?" said Bonnie.

Mack smiled. "I have seen a train a few times at railheads. That ain't all, missy, I have been *inside* a train. Last year, we sold our herd in Ellsworth, and Charlie paid us off. Me and a pard put our horses on the train when it left Ellsworth and rode east to Abilene. We got off there and headed for Texas. Scared my pard out of his wits. He didn't stop shaking till we reached Red River."

"I'm not sure I want to get on a train," Bonnie said, still staring at the huge locomotive.

"Maybe you will," said Mack. "Word is that the railroad will be in Texas before long. A body will likely be able to go anywhere in the country from there. I bet you can get on the train in Fort Worth and go all the way to Chicago, if you want to."

Bonnie took Will's arm and leaned on his

shoulder. "I don't want to think about that. Things are moving too fast. I didn't start driving a wagon till a couple of years ago."

"This train is pretty impressive," said Will, "but what I'm thinking about now is my stomach." He turned to Mack. "Where's this great place to eat that the sheriff recommended?"

Mack beckoned, and they walked back to the main street, turned the corner and walked between a wall of shops and saloons on each side. Bonnie released her hold on Will and stepped away from him. She pulled her hat down and became Bobby.

Will had been anxious about Bonnie's coming into Dodge. She assured him that nobody would take notice of a slight cowboy named Bobby. Since she had been revealed as a girl, she had let her hair grow a bit, not too much, not so long that she couldn't still be recognized as a careless cowboy who didn't care much about his appearance.

Nevertheless, after washing her hair, she had coiled it, tied it in a knot and pulled her hat low on her forehead. Any notice by passing cowboys was directed at Mack, not her.

McBride had mentioned that in many outfits, a quarter of the cowboys might be black. Since arriving in town, they had seen only a half dozen black cowboys. These nodded to each other in passing, touching their hats, aware that though they worked with white cowboys every day, they still stood out. They also knew that alcohol often aroused prejudices in white cowboys that bubbled just beneath the surface.

"I must say, Bobby, you do smell a mite better after your bath," said Will, smiling.

She sniffed, looked her two pards up and down. "You boys didn't do too bad yourselves. You smell more like soap now than cows. Do you think we're presentable enough to go inside and sit down for some supper?"

"I do think we qualify since we smell like soap and each have $25 in our pockets," said Will. "I see Wright House up there." He pointed a few storefronts ahead. "I hope the sheriff knows what he's talking about." Bassett had told them it was the best eatery in town. Will took Bonnie's arm and stepped off.

She pulled her arm away slowly, looking around. She shook a finger at him. "Will, you're fixin' to get us into trouble."

"Oh, yeah," Will said, "Bobby." She nodded. They started walking, but Will stopped when Mack did not follow. He looked back. "Mack? You coming?"

Cowboy Mack pondered, frowning, then walked up beside them. The three stepped up on the board walkway in front of the restaurant, and Will opened the door. Bonnie walked in. Will held the door open for Mack.

"You go on," Mack said, "got to go around back."

Will went inside and sat at a small table with Bonnie in the crowded dining room. They looked around.

Across the room, a long table accommodated ten cowboys, all freshly shaven, mustaches and beards neatly trimmed, all wearing clean clothes, some apparently new. At the far end of the table, cowboys huddled, joking, laughing, one brandishing a fork for emphasis. At the near end, older men talked in hushed tones, wielding their tableware as if they ate in this fashion every evening.

"Looks like a good outfit," said Bonnie. She looked toward the door. "Where's Mack?"

"Went to the outhouse, I suppose," Will said.

They looked around the restaurant. It was crowded at early evening. They had taken the only unoccupied table in the place. Two middle-aged women and one young man worked the tables, taking orders, clearing dishes and making small talk with patrons.

An aproned waitress came over, smiling. "What'll you have, fellas? Most of the cowboys come in here been herding steaks on the hoof for so long they like to eat one for a change. We got the best steaks in Dodge. What'll it be?" She was still smiling, pencil poised over her pad.

In her best Bobby voice, Bonnie ordered for both. Coffee now, steaks rare with potatoes and beans and biscuits, to be followed by hot apple pie. Will looked at Bonnie, smiling.

She leaned toward him, spoke softly. "Watch out, pard." She leaned back, frowning. He pulled a face, nodded.

The waitress was gone only a moment. She returned with a coffee pot and filled their cups. "Bet this is the first time you've set in a chair in months."

"Yep," Bonnie Bobby said. The waitress walked toward the kitchen.

Bonnie and Will leaned back, still basking in the luxury of being waited on. They sipped coffee, eavesdropping on their neighbors' conversation. Sheriff Bassett had told them that the Wright House was patronized almost exclusively by Texans, all drovers. The talk was mostly of cows and weather, trails and trials. There was also anxious, excited comment by younger patrons on prospects for the rest of the evening, focused on cards, whisky and women.

Bonnie listened with more than casual interest, particularly to a neatly trimmed bewhiskered middle-aged cowboy wearing a new red shirt and a clean hat, probably new, that hung on his chair back. He described in some detail a memorable romantic encounter south of the Rio Grande just before the start of this drive that ended two days ago in Dodge. The three other men at the table leaned toward him, grinning, jaws hanging.

Bonnie turned back to a smiling Will. She shrugged, looked toward the outside door. "Where's Mack? He's been a long time in the outhouse."

"Might have been a lineup," said Will.

The waitress brought their plates and deposited them on the table. She left, returned with a coffee pot and refilled their cups. "Enjoy your supper, fellas."

She walked to a nearby table where three men sat, obviously cowboys recently bathed, shaved and hair cut. She held a pad and pencil, poised. "What'll you have, fellas? Most of the cowboys come in here been herding steaks on the hoof for so long they'd like to eat one for a change. We got the best steaks in Dodge. What'll it be?"

Bonnie looked at Will who pulled a face. He sliced a chunk of steak and forked it to his mouth. He smiled at Bonnie as he chewed, picked up a biscuit.

Bonnie looked toward the door. "I'm gonna check on Mack. He's been an awful long time." She went to the door, opened it and stepped out to the board walk.

And there was Mack. He sat on the edge of the walk, his booted feet in the street, his plate in his lap and coffee cup on the walk beside him. He looked up at her.

CHAPTER NINE

"Mack! What's goin' on? Why you sitting out here?"

"Because I can't sit in there," gesturing with a fork toward the door. "You knew that, didn't you?"

Bonnie grimaced. "Well, I guess I heard," Bonnie said, "but I forgot. Sorry." She paused, frowning. She went back inside, picked up her plate and coffee cup.

Will looked up, frowned. "What're you doing?"

"Mack's sittin' on the walk. I'm sittin' with him. Coming?" She stood there, plate and cup in hand. Patrons at nearby tables who had heard the conversation watched, knives and forks suspended in midair.

"Be damned. I forgot." Will stood, put the utensils on his plate, picked up the plate and cup, and followed Bonnie. Diners at nearby tables watched until the outside door closed.

Bonnie and Will sat down on each side of Mack. He nodded somberly to them, and they ate in silence. A lamp on the wall beside the door dimly illuminated the porch. Restaurant patrons going in and coming out looked at the three with unrestrained curiosity as they passed.

Two cowboys heading for the restaurant stepped

from the street up on the board walk and stopped. One of the men, wearing rumpled clothing and a sweat-stained hat, obviously had visited the saloon instead of the bath house on entering Dodge. He smirked thinly at the trio.

"Enjoying the night air, are yuh? Too bad you ain't up to settin' inside." He snickered to the cowboy beside him.

Will methodically lowered his plate to the plank walk beside him and slowly stood, facing the cowboy. "Now why would we want to sit in the same room with you, asshole?"

The cowboy recoiled and stepped toward Will. His companion grabbed his arm. "C'mon, Benjy. You ain't up to this, and it's not worth it anyway. C'mon."

"Lemme go, Walt! Sumbitch cain't talk to me like that." Benjy tried to pull away, but Walt tightened his hold on the arm, pulling him off the walk and into the street. Benjy looked over his shoulder at Will, mumbled. "I'll see you agin."

Will and the others watched the pair walk away, Benjy stumbling, Walt supporting him with a hand gripping his arm. Will shook his head. The three turned back to their plates and ate in silence.

When they were finished, Will stood, collected plates and cups and walked inside the café. He deposited the dishes on an unoccupied table, smiled and touched his hat to the inquiring faces of patrons, and went back outside.

He stepped off the porch, took Bonnie by the arm, and started to walk.

She didn't move. "Will, would you . . ." as she pulled away from his hand.

Will grimaced, eyes shut, "sorry, sorry."

He stepped aside, and they set out, avoiding cowboys with glazed eyes who had lost the ability to navigate and others who were in a hurry to be somewhere else. A darting glance by some passersby hardly interrupted their haste.

Panels of weak light from windows lay on the dusty road, barely illuminating the horse droppings and occasional discarded or lost bits and pieces of somebody's belongings.

"Will, Mack, c'mere!" They saw a bunch of their pards ahead. Brad waved, pulling Jimmy along with the other hand. Rod and Marley followed. From their gait and grins and familiar, rumpled clothing, it was obvious that they had gone straight to the saloons on entering Dodge rather than to baths or cafes.

"We got somethin' goin' here," said Brad, wide-eyed and excited. "This fella in the saloon says that his outfit has the best guitar player this side of the Mississippi. I naturally disagreed and said that his man probably couldn't carry a tune and likely couldn't tell a guitar from a hay rake. I told him we had a cowboy in our outfit that was the best picker north of the Rio Grande.

"We was just having a good time, you know, joshing and drinkin' and tellin' lies. Then this same cowboy, who could hardly talk by this time, he was that drunk, says he'll put up his player against my player any day of the week or month. I straightened up, turned real serious and asked if he's willing to bet on it. I figured he would hem and haw and go on his way. But he said for me to bring my man to the livery in half an hour, and we'll settle who's got the best git fiddler. I looked him up and down and decided he was serious, and here we are. C'mon. We're goin' to the livery and win us some money." He grinned broadly, heavy lidded and weaving.

Will looked at Bonnie, who pulled a face and shrugged her shoulders. He looked at Mack who simply cocked his head. They hurried to catch up with the others.

Will had not noticed till then that Jimmy carried a guitar case. Will spoke to his back. "Jimmy, you brought your guitar?"

Jimmy didn't turn. "Never leave home, or camp, without it."

Bonnie pulled Will's arm to slow him. She leaned toward him and whispered. "Is Jimmy that good? You gonna bet on him?"

"Sure, he's a pard." He leaned over and whispered in Bonnie's ear. "But I'm not bettin' my poke on him."

They had hardly reached the livery when a half dozen cowboys sauntered toward them, grinning and joking. One of the men, only slightly steadier in his gait than the others, carried a guitar case.

Brad extended a hand to the cowboy he had talked with in the bar. "Andrew, it is, I think? I'm Brad, and this here's our musician, Jimmy."

Jimmy nodded to Andrew. Jimmy raised his chin, frowning, an obvious challenge.

"Brad, Jimmy," said Andrew. "Buddy is our player." He pointed at the cowboy beside him, who touched his hat, grinning. Andrew then gestured toward a man who stood apart from the others. "And this is Mr. Burrows. He has agreed to be judge." Burrows nodded solemnly.

Brad frowned. Burrows looked out of place. He was freshly-shaved, dressed in clean, pressed pants and shirt, and he wore a fine broad-brimmed felt hat. Brad decided that the clothes were new. He looked at the cowboys in the other outfit and realized that they all wore what looked like new clothes.

"Uh, Mister Burrows, are you part of this outfit, or do you have any dealings with them?"

"None whatsoever," Burrows said. "Unless their trail boss decides to do business with me. I'm a cattle buyer, you see. I'll be happy to do business with your boss as well."

"You'll do," said Brad. He looked around, saw a passing young cowboy who looked their way. "Hey, son, come over here. Got something for you." The cowboy stopped, walked over.

"We got some bettin' going on here. I'll pay you five dollars to hold the bets and pay the winners at the end of this here guitar-playing contest. You'll write down the names of the bettors and how much." Brad frowned. "You can write?" The young man nodded. Brad took his arm and led him forward.

"While you've been organizing," said Burrows, "I've been thinking. I've seen contests like this before. Let's say that each performer will play and sing three pieces. Betting will end five minutes after the first piece finishes. Will that work?"

Brad and Andrew looked at each other, and both nodded. By this time, a number of curious passersby had wandered over. A few men in each of the two outfits placed bets, but others said they would wait for the first song. All looked toward the appointed judge.

"For the first piece," said Burrows, "let's have a song that most everybody knows. Do you know 'Streets of Laredo'? It's sometimes called 'Cowboy's Lament'. Do you know it?" Both players nodded.

Burrows pulled a coin from his pocket. He pointed at Jimmy. "You are heads," then pointed at Buddy, "and you are tails." He flipped the coin, bent forward and picked it up. He studied the coin, looked up. "Tails will play first." He stepped back and looked at Buddy.

Buddy strummed his guitar, getting his head and his hand ready. Then he played the opening notes and followed with the song. Spectators quietened, moved closer. A tear rolled down the cheek of an old drunk cowboy who had listened intently.

The song ended to cheers, clapping and raucous comment.

The judge nodded to Jimmy. Like his opponent, Jimmy strummed a bit, twisted a couple of pegs at the head, hesitated.

Bonnie leaned toward Will and whispered. "Is he going to play?"

Jimmy answered her question with a soft chord that set the tone of his song. He played and sang with skill and intensity, with passion and feeling that captivated the onlookers, including his own outfit. At the end, cheers and shouts were followed by a general rush to the young cowboy to place bets.

Burrows waited, frowning. "Let's move on," Burrows said to the cowboys clustered around the bet-holder. "Are you done?" Bets were placed, money collected, and names written down. The last bet was recorded, and the young man waved to Burrows.

Burrows smiled, looked down, pondering. He looked up. "Now, for the second song—"

The judge and onlookers jerked upright at the sound of shots from the street. Everyone turned, tense, searching. Pop, pop, pop, more shots. The listeners and the judge bolted toward the street.

The young man holding the bets started to join the throng, but was gripped tightly by Brad and Rod. "You ain't goin' nowhere, my man," said Brad. "We got business to conduct." He turned to Will, Bonnie and Mack, grinning. "See you later." Brad and Rod, each holding an arm of the bet-holder, hurried to the confines of the livery, followed closely by Jimmy.

Will, Mack and Bonnie were left standing alone, watching cowboys running down the street and disappearing around the corner toward the shooting ruckus.

The trio began walking slowly down the street, now empty but for a couple of staggering drunks that would not notice if they walked in front of a full cavalry charge.

Bonnie stopped, stared at a sign over the door of a building: Asia Doll. "What's that?" she said. "Asia Doll?" Two cowboys lounged beside the entrance, smoking. Another came out through the door, sober-faced, pulling his hat down hard. He looked each way, set off down the sidewalk, suddenly in a hurry to get somewhere, or away from somewhere.

Mack looked at Will, then Bonnie. "That," said Mack, "is where cowboys go to see ladies, the likes of which they haven't seen for many months. Some of these young cowboys *never* seen these types of ladies before." He looked down at Bonnie, a what-do-you-think-of-that look on his face.

"Oh." She looked from Will to Mack. "If I wasn't here, if you didn't know me, would you boys likely go in here to . . . to see the ladies?" She looked from one to the other, unsmiling.

"Wouldn't matter what I wanted to do," said Mack. "They don't let the likes of me in the Asia Doll."

Bonnie frowned. "Hmm. Oh yeah." She turned to Will. "How 'bout you, Will?"

It was Will's turn to frown. "Bonnie, you're always trying to stir up trouble by imagining situations that just don't exist." He took her arm and stepped off, Mack following.

She gently removed his hand from her arm, leaned toward him, whispered. "Bobby."

He squeezed his eyes, spoke softly. "Yeah, sorry, sorry."

They stopped in front of the Long Branch Saloon. "Now here's a place I can go inside," said Mack. "They like my money as much as yours. Course, if I said I'd like to go upstairs to visit the ladies, they'd get a little bent outta shape." He turned to Bonnie, leaned down. "Not that I'd want to go upstairs, you know." He smiled.

"Hmm." She looked at the saloon door. "I bet they'd let *me* go upstairs," Bonnie said. Will and Mack looked at each other.

"Don't you go causing trouble, Bonnie," said Will.

"Bobby," she said, "I'm a guy, remember?" She walked toward the door, stopped and turned back. "You coming?"

"Hang on, Bonnie, uh, Bobby," said Will, grimacing. He turned to Mack. "What kinda gambling do you do? I've not done much gambling."

"Me neither. Most of the games here are faro and monte, but I avoid them. I just like to have a little fun without losing a bunch of money. I play a few games of chuck-a-luck, and when I have lost all I want to lose, I stop."

"What's chuck-a-luck?" Will said. "Never heard of it."

"It's a poor folks' dice game. They put three dice in a wire contraption that looks like a hourglass, rotate it, and the dice fall to the bottom. Before they spin it, players bet five cents on what the dice is gonna show. Takes a long time to lose a lotta money."

Bonnie pushed the door open. The others followed. They stepped into a room filled with patrons busy at cards around a dozen tables. A smoky haze that smelled of tobacco and sweaty bodies hung from the ceiling. A line of cowboys leaned on the bar, boots hooked on the footrail. No one took any notice of the three newcomers beyond a casual glance. Half a dozen black cowboys sat at tables with their white companions.

Bonnie leaned toward Will, keeping her eyes on the room. "This place *stinks,*" she said softly. "I'm gonna have a hard time *breathing.*"

"Hey! Will!" They looked at a table in the far corner. It was Win. He leaned forward and said something to the other players who eyed the three newcomers. Win pushed his chair back and started to leave the table.

"Hey!" said one of the players. Win jerked around. "Cards."

"Yeah, yeah, sorry," Win said. He laid his card

hand on the table, face down. "Just one minute, sorry." He rushed to the door.

"Say, Will, Mack, I'm in a tight spot." He squeezed his eyes, shook his head. "Naw, not a tight spot, just a spot. I got something coming up, I got a feeling—"

"You're losing, aren't you," said Mack, "and you want to borrow some money. Is that what you got coming up?"

"Aw, Mack, Will. Awright, I'm losin', but I feel my luck is about to change. I just need some cash to—"

"Sorry, Win," said Mack. "You've lost your poke, and you want to lose mine. I wouldn't see it again until Montana. Unless you were still in jail in Dodge. Sorry."

Win grimaced. "Will?"

Will shook his head, mouthing a sorry.

Win grimaced. "Bonnie?"

Bonnie shook her head, leaned to whisper in his ear. "Bobby."

Win squeezed his eyes shut, opened them. "Sorry," softly.

Win looked into the eyes of each of his three pards, dropped his head, turned and shuffled back to the table in the corner where the other players had watched, waiting, cards held before them. Win sat down heavily, picked up his cards.

Will shook his head. "Gonna be an early night for Win. Where's the chuck-a-luck table, Mack?"

Mack pointed at a table near the bar and took a step toward it.

"There he is! Sumbitch!"

The room turned to look at the man Will had the set-to with at Wright House. He stood unsteadily, weaving, feet apart and planted. Will and Bonnie and Mack stopped and saw Benjy.

"Give it up, Benjy," said his companion, Walt. "You're drunk as a skunk. C'mon." He took Benjy by the arm. Benjy pulled away roughly.

"He cain't talk to me like that!" Spittle sprayed with the shout.

Will shook his head, took a step toward the chuck-a-luck table.

A collective gasp brought Will around. He saw Benjy pointing a small short-barreled belly gun at him. Chair legs scraped loudly as patrons pushed chairs back, ducked under tables or retreated to walls. Those near the front rushed to the outside door, plugging the exit with their bodies.

Will reached for his six-shooter and found only air.

"Benjy, don't!" Walt grabbed Benjy's arm and jerked just as he fired. Bonnie fell backward, clutching her chest.

Will and Mack caught Bonnie and lowered her gently to the floor. Will looked toward the shooter. He and his companion had disappeared. Will looked sharply at Mack.

"Back door," Mack said.

Will started to rise, looked abruptly for the back door, stopped and bent over Bonnie. She was limp, and her eyes were closed. He looked anxiously at Mack.

"There's a doctor," Mack said. "Just down the street. I saw his sign. Let's get her there."

Will gently lifted her and walked behind Mack to the door. Shocked patrons backed away, opening a path.

Will and Cowboy Mack sat on the top step of the outside stair to the second-floor doctor's office. The landing was dimly illuminated by light from the window. Luckily, it was also the doctor's residence, and he had answered their banging on the door. That was an hour ago, and Will had not taken his eyes off the closed door, waiting for the doctor's report.

The door opened, and the doctor stepped out, holding a lantern. Will and Mack stood. The aged doctor, wearing an ankle-length night shirt, held a lamp, studied the two cowboys a moment.

"She was fortunate, barely missed her heart," the doctor said. "She's got some serious damage to her shoulder, but she'll mend." The doctor frowned. "I was surprised to see her breasts wrapped. Is there—"

"She's been posing as a boy since trail bosses won't hire a girl for a drive," Will said. "It's complicated. I hope you'll go along with that if it comes up in the town."

"Of course, of course. None of my business. Now,

she shouldn't be moved for a couple of days while I watch that shoulder. Is that going to be a problem?"

"We'll do whatever is best for Bonnie. Lemme talk with my pard here, and I'll come in."

The doctor nodded, went inside and shut the door.

Will started to speak, but Mack held up a hand. "If I know you as well as I think I know you, you got some business to tend to. You go in and see Bonnie, and you tell her that the doc and I are taking care of her until she's ready to leave. I'll sit right here on this stair, or maybe the doc can find a spot for me inside. Anyway, I'm staying right here until Bonnie walks out with me."

Will looked his pard in the eyes. "Mack, you're the salt of the earth. How could anybody have a better friend?"

Mack simply nodded. "Git on with it."

"You're right, I do have something I need to do, and you know what it is." He extended a hand, and Mack took it.

Will knocked gently on the door, and it opened promptly. By lantern light, Will and Mack went to the treatment table where Bonnie lay. The top buttons of her shirt were unbuttoned, revealing the bandaged shoulder. Will looked at the doctor who stood at Bonnie's head.

Bonnie's eyes opened, and she saw Will and Mack. She smiled thinly, spoke weakly. "Hello, boys. Ain't this somethin'? Never been shot before. Never been in a doc's office before either." She looked at the doctor, a hint of a smile that became a grimace.

"I've never treated a female cowboy before," the doctor said.

Bonnie's eye opened wide, and she looked abruptly at Will.

Will smiled. "He knows the story. It's all right." He put his hand on her cheek. "You're going to stay here a day or two until you're up to leaving. Mind the doc till then. One of us will be right here till that time. We'll have a soft bed in the hoodlum wagon ready when you're up to traveling." He leaned over and kissed her lips gently, caressed her cheek with a hand.

Will shook the doctor's hand, and he and Mack went out, closing the door. On the landing, he turned to Mack. "That's my life in there, pard. I wouldn't leave her with anybody else. I'll see you . . . when I see you."

First light. Will, Rod and Brad stood in the deep shadow of a cottonwood grove. They watched the stirrings in the drover's camp across the flat as cowboys rose stiffly from bedrolls, stretched and walked to the outskirts of camp to relieve themselves.

The three stepped from the copse, Will leading. The cowboys at the fire saw them, watched them coming.

"Mornin,'" said one of the cowboys. Will didn't recognize him.

"I'm looking for Benjy," said Will. The cowboy

who had spoken looked over his shoulder where a couple of hands were in the process of building a fire. Benjy stood up slowly, without taking his eyes off Will. The other cowboys looked from Will to Benjy. A couple backed away.

"You shot my pard, asshole, "said Will, "and we don't know if he's gonna make it." Rod and Brad stood on each side of Will.

Benjy's jaw dropped and trembled. He jerked his head around at the other cowboys, silently asking for help. They avoided his look, focusing on Will. Two more hands backed away from Benjy.

A frowning cowboy stepped in front of Benjy. "Who th' hell you think you are, coming into our camp and making threats?"

Rod pulled his six-shooter and leveled on the cowboy. "You're gonna find out real soon who we are if you don't back off and stay out of this. This has nothin' to do with you." The cowboy did not move. Rod pulled back the hammer. "I ain't telling you again." The cowboy glared at Rod, then moved a few steps away from Benjy. Rod relaxed, released the pistol hammer, but held the gun at his chest.

Benjy, jaw hanging, looked back and forth at the hands who avoided his eyes. He turned back to Will. "I didn't mean to shoot nobody," his voice quavering. "I was drunk. I'm almost blind when I'm drunk." He searched the faces of his pards. They avoided his look or turned quickly away if they made eye contact.

Will reached for his six-shooter, slowly pulled it from the holster. The cowboys again backed away from Benjy.

"Man, I didn't mean to do it," said Benjy, tears rolling down his cheeks, "it was all a mistake, it was the whiskey did it, not me." He sobbed, his body shaking convulsively.

Will brought the pistol up, leveled on Benjy. The campground was quiet as death, except for Benjy's choking sobs.

Will slowly lowered the pistol, his eyes fixed on Benjy. He shook his head, turned aside, then back to look at Benjy. "You pitiful . . . insect. How could I shoot a sniveling insect?" He turned around slowly, pushing the six-shooter into its holster, looked toward the cottonwoods where the horses were tied.

"Look out!"

Will spun around, drawing his pistol, and saw Benjy pulling a six-shooter from his belt. Before he could level on Will, he was blown backward by Will's shot to the head.

Will walked to the fire circle and looked down at the body, a thin line of blood running from the forehead, another from the side of his mouth and twin streams from nostrils. Will looked back to see Rod and Brad behind him, holding six-shooters at the ready.

Will looked back at the body. "Benjy, Benjy, Benjy, why couldn't you let it go?" Will looked around. "My thanks to somebody for the warning." He pushed his pistol into the holster. Rod and Brad holstered their six-shooters.

"He was a bad un, Benjy," said a cowboy, staring at the corpse. He looked up at Will. "I always figured he would come to a sorry end. He was troubled, never did know what it was. You might've done him a favor."

"Not the sort of favors I like to give," Will said. He looked toward the cottonwoods, paused, pondering. He turned back. "You boys sell your cows at Dodge?"

"Yeah. We're done. Headin' home to Texas."

"If you would like work instead, my boss is hiring. He's three hands short." He looked at the body. "Four, actually. He probably won't want me around now."

He turned back to the hands that had gathered during the conversation. "If you want to work your way to Montana instead of riding unemployed back to Texas, see my boss, Charlie McBride. He's a good boss, a good man. If you hurry, you can catch him in Dodge today before he leaves."

He waved to the cowboys standing at the fire and walked with Rod and Brad toward the cottonwoods and their horses.

Brad and Win had just deposited their empty breakfast dishes at the chuck wagon when they saw Sheriff Bassett riding toward camp. They quickly walked a distance from the campfire and stopped, far enough to be apart, but close enough to hear snippets of conversation from those at the fire. Win and Brad pulled out tobacco pouches and proceeded to roll cigarettes, glancing furtively toward the campfire.

Brad, Rod and Win last night had exchanged stories about their good fortune in Dodge. Brad gave the guitar contest bet-holder ten dollars instead of the promised five and suggested that he might want to make himself scarce. Brad gave Jimmy twenty-five dollars, then split the remainder with Rod. The two entrepreneurs carried away thirty-six dollars each.

Win agreed they had done well, but not as well as he had done at the saloon gambling table. He showed Brad and Rod a bulging pouch. His winnings, he said. Ninety-five dollars.

Now, Brad and Win looked anxiously at the sheriff who had dismounted and stood at the campfire with McBride. Bassett stared at the flames, warming his hands. Cowboys moved about the camp, some walking toward the grazing herd, others just rolling out of bed, nursing headaches brought from Dodge in the early hours.

"I'm satisfied it was self-defense," said Bassett, "and I'm okay with that, but there's a lot of people living in Dodge who are gettin' pretty tired of shootings and killings, so I'm gonna have to investigate. You understand."

Win wanted nothing to do with Sheriff Bassett. He also had wanted nothing to do with the sheriff last night at the Long Branch. At the first shout from Benjy, followed quickly by his pistol shot, while others at Win's game ducked under the table, he reached for the pot in the center of the table and collected as much as he could hold in two hands. He stuffed the stash into pockets and edged slowly along the wall toward the door, looking anxiously back toward the card table where the players still cowered underneath. He finally reached the outside door where he collided with the sheriff who pushed him aside and rushed through, shotgun at the ready. Outside, Win yelled out loud and ran toward the livery, jumping and kicking like a colt.

"Where can I find your man?" Bassett said to McBride.

"You're too late. As you said, it was self-defense, but I don't like trouble-makers in my outfit, so I sent him packin'. He's half way to Texas by now." McBride smiled. "Coffee before you leave?"

Bassett smiled thinly. "Thank you kindly, but I best be on my way." He turned to go, then turned back. "If you should see your man again, you know, if he loses his way and wanders into your camp somewhere on the trail to Montana, advise him not to come back through Dodge on the ride home." He wrinkled his forehead, nodded to McBride.

"I'll sure do that. Thank-ee, sheriff."

Bassett touched his hat and walked to his horse, mounted and set out at a lope.

Win and Brad walked back to the campfire. "Do

you think he'll meet us somewhere on the trail, looking for Will?" Win said.

"Nah, he's glad it turned out like it did. Bassett's a good man, but he has to satisfy the farmers and shop-keepers in Dodge who are just about ready to do what the people in Abilene did, be done with Texas cattle and Texas cowboys.

"Bassett said he arrived at the Long Branch just after Will and Mack left with Bonnie. He asked enough eye witnesses to the shooting to learn something of what hap-pened and the identity of the shooter and his outfit.

"Then this morning, just as Bassett's walking to the café for breakfast, a rider pulls up in the middle of the street and tells him about the shooting at his camp. Bassett wasn't bothered as much by the shooting as he was by missing his breakfast."

The cowboys in the outfit, to a man, had a fine time in Dodge, and they continued to talk about their experi-ence there long after leaving. Most had bought clothes in Dodge and still sported new shirts and trousers that were quickly taking on the look of their old trail clothes.

As much as they had enjoyed Dodge, they were still happy to see the town behind them. Dodge was seen as a halfway point of sorts to the end of the trail in Montana. It was the middle of June, and McBride assured everybody that they would reach their destina-tion in good time: September 1.

The date was mentioned often in talk around evening campfires. Still weeks from that magical date, anticipation had already begun to grow. Not a little talk was about what comes after delivery. Some said they would do what they knew how to do. They would go back to Texas to work on a ranch near the home place.

Some spoke of plans for a return home to folks and a familiar routine. Rod talked about a sweet girl that lived only five miles from his folks' place that he decided he needed to see again. This caused not a few wide-eyed, pulled faces since Rod had never talked about any female but his mare.

The three new hands made friends quickly and took naturally to the joshing and reminiscing about home. The three had been hired by McBride in Dodge. Two were from the outfit where Will had settled affairs with Benjy. The third was a drifter who said little about his past except to affirm that he wanted the job.

The two men from the outfit Will had the set-to with were polar opposites. Renfro was a solemn forty-year-old who did his job efficiently, but took little part in the palaver around the evening campfire. The hands couldn't figure whether he was slow or stuck-up. By bits and pieces, they learned that he actually was intelligent, at one time a successful rancher on a large spread west of Weatherford, Texas. Then his his wife and three daughters were killed in a Comanche raid.

He lost heart and rode away from the ranch, simply abandoned it. He became a drifter, careless of everything but whatever job he happened to be doing at the time. He wore the same clothes every day and avoided any social contact except when others told him to wash himself and his clothes, or they would do both for him.

Marley, thirty-five, knew cows and nothing else. He left home at sixteen and had worked on ranches and farms since then, always tending cows. He still had kin near San Antonio, but rarely saw them. They didn't miss him, he said, and he didn't care.

Sid, the drifter, was a bit of a puzzle. He had little to say on any subject, less about himself. He revealed only that he grew up on a Texas cotton farm and hated the work. When a neighbor offered to pay him to help tend his small herd, he found his calling. He loved it and soon found steady work on a large ranch. This was his first long drive.

Like his cowboys, McBride also had enjoyed Dodge. But he had another reason to feel good about the visit. He had met Ben Collins, a rancher who was returning to his new spread in Montana. The man already had the cattle to populate the ranch, but he needed horses. McBride sold him the remuda, transfer to be made at the end of the drive after delivering the herd to the government. This transaction caused no little concern among the outfit until McBride told them he planned to give each cowboy the horse of his choice at the end of the drive.

The land changed north of Dodge. It appeared to

be drier, though it could have been the arrival of summer rather than the terrain. Trees and down wood for fires were scarce. Cookie stretched a cow skin under the chuck wagon and asked cowboys to pick up scattered bits of wood to carry along for the next cooking fire. It wasn't long before cow chips and buffalo chips were tossed on the skin along with the wood.

Three days out of Dodge, cowboys sat and stood around the evening campfire, supper plates in hand, watching the layers of wispy clouds at the horizon changing colors from bright pink and yellow to darker reds and purple, the land darkening as the sun touched the horizon and slowly slipped away. No hard-bitten, hard-headed, rough-and-tumble cowboy could ignore prairie sunsets.

Rod squinted, stared at the horizon. After a long minute: "There he is." Everyone within hearing turned. A lone horseman rode at a walk, seeming to emerge from the celestial display, toward the campground. Rod turned toward Bonnie who stood at the campfire, her filled plate forgotten, his look a question.

CHAPTER TEN

"Yeah, that's him," she said softly. Bonnie held the plate with the hand at the end of the cloth sling that supported her injured shoulder. The fork in her other hand hovered above the plate.

The cowboys turned back to their plates and coffee cups, silently watching the horseman dismount.

"C'mon in here!" said Rod. "Thought you might uh been bushwhacked out there. Or maybe decided to put all your troubles behind you and head out for Texas." He cut a glance at Bonnie, then jumped aside as she bumped her good shoulder against him, spilling her plate of beef and beans.

She dropped the fork and plate to the ground and walked slowly to Will, stopped when they were almost touching and looked up into his eyes. Every man around the fire and wagons stopped what they were doing to watch.

She ignored the gawking cowboys, as if she and Will were alone in the universe. "It's about time, cowboy," she said. "I was beginning to think maybe you had decided to head out for Texas, leaving all your troubles behind." Rod snorted. She ignored him.

He took her face in his hands. "You are a bit of trouble, but when I decide to head out anywhere, I'll put that bit of trouble in my pack." He put his arms around her shoulders and hugged.

The cowboys responded with a chorus of oohs and ahs. "Git on with it!" shouted Jimmy. The hands grinned and laughed and turned back to their supper.

Will smiled, waved to the boys, put an arm around Bonnie's shoulders and she an arm at his waist. They walked to the hoodlum where he tied his reins to a wheel. She walked him to the back of the wagon.

She wrapped arms around his neck, pulled his head down and kissed him. Reaching inside the wagon, she touched her blankets. "I've got the best bed in camp. If you're nice to me, there's room for you. You got here just in time. Grandpa told me it's time to get back to work, so I figured that means the end of my hoodlum bed after tonight. I've been living pretty soft since Dodge."

"Tell me about Dodge."

"I was at the doctor's place another two days after you left. Doc Anderson's a good man. Cowboy Mack's another good man. Will, he didn't leave that stair for two days. The doc fed him and gave him a pallet at night on the floor right inside the door. The only time he wasn't on the stairs or inside the office was when he went to the outhouse, and he didn't go out there until he got the doc to promise to lock the door while he was away.

"When the doc said I could leave, Mack was like a mama hen, getting' me on my horse and making sure I could ride. We owe a lot to that cowboy."

"Yes, we do. I'll thank him proper when I see him. He wasn't in camp when I got here."

"He's out scouting for water with Charlie. They should have been back by now." She kissed him again. "Now you take care of your horse and eat some supper and come to bed." She patted his cheek.

"You sure that arm feels okay for driving those ornery mules?" Will said. He stood beside the hoodlum wagon, holding the reins of his horse, looking up at Bonnie on the wagon seat. Cookie had finished cleaning up after breakfast and just pulled out, motioning ahead with an arm without looking back.

"Yeah, yeah, Grandpa Cookie, hold your horses, I still know how to do this," she mumbled, knowing he could not hear. She looked down at Will, smiled. "This arm?" She held the arm up. "It's fine. I'm just keeping the sling on for the sympathy. The boys have been real helpful. 'Can I do that for you, Bonnie?' 'Here, Bonnie, let me carry that for you.' Guess I can't milk that cow much longer."

"You sure the boys are trying to be kind, and not trying to get close to you? They ever ask any favors in return for the help?" He frowned, then smiled.

"Git away, cowboy, you know I can take care of myself. They know I'm not available." She cocked her head. "Well, some of 'em do get a little playful."

"Tell me names. I'll kill 'em," stern-faced, playful.

She turned to the front, shook the lines. "Giddap, mules." The wagon pulled away. She looked back at Will. "You take care of yourself, sweetheart. That's a full-time job. I'll take care of myself. See you at dinner."

He watched her pull away. Mounting, he turned aside and rode back where the other hands were just throwing the herd onto the trail. Win, riding point on the near side, motioned ahead. They saw McBride and Mack coming at a lope.

The two riders reined up. McBride pulled a bandana from a pocket and wiped his forehead. "Closest we saw to water was the damn mirages. We were both sure we had found a good pond and rode toward it till it disappeared. We'll just have to drive 'em slow till we find water. Good thing we watered 'em good yesterday."

Win nodded and rode back to his point position. Will rode across the front of the herd to take up point on the left side.

Spring had given way to summer, and the land had turned from green to tan to brown. From the sweet soft breezes at dawn to the early promise of a hot, still day.

The only constant in the flat dry landscape was the mirages. They were not the imagination of a single person at any one point. If two or three were riding together, the mirages were seen by all, distorting the land

and the objects in it. A vision of a lake bordered by lush forests seen at a distance became more distinct as they approached, promising water and shade, only to blur, shimmer and disappear as vapor.

As well as landscape, animals were distorted. A deer seen a half mile away appeared as an imaginary or prehistoric tall, long-necked beast. Cowboys riding drag saw point riders at the head of the column as tall, broad, lumbering giants. Only evening brought relief when images and landscape regained their true features.

For two days, they saw no water. The cattle were becoming more difficult to manage. On the trail, individuals walked away from the herd, head down, and had to be turned back to the column.

At night, some restless cows would not bed down. They bellowed, wandered. They seemed not to hear the night herders' songs.

"Pretty," said Bonnie. She and Will sat their horses on a stark, treeless, sunburnt plain. They stared at a pond of blue water in the distance, dense willow thickets at water's edge. A grove of oaks lined the far bank, their dark foliage almost gray in the heat waves that blurred the image. The dark banks appeared to be covered by lush grass.

This was the fourth promise of water they had discovered since setting out from camp at dawn. On this third waterless day, McBride dispatched Will and

Bonnie and two others, Rod and Jimmy, riding solo due to the shortage of hands to watch the unruly herd. Rod rode straight ahead on the trail. Jimmy angled off to the right.

Bonnie and Will took the leftward search. They were hardly a mile from camp when they saw what appeared to be a substantial creek bordered by tall green grass on the banks and groves of Osage Orange and cottonwoods. They kicked their tired mounts into a gallop toward the creek, Will waving his hat and Bonnie shouting, sure that they would carry this good news to the outfit.

They slowed their mounts as the oasis shimmered, blurred, withdrew, faded and vanished.

The next sighting was a small pond and a narrow watercourse that fed it. They approached this water more slowly, stopped and watched it disintegrate and disappear. They saw the third apparition at high noon a couple of miles ahead and approached only because it was on their route. It dissolved at their approach.

The fourth sighting was little different from the others. Inviting, deceptive, seductive.

"Yeah, it's pretty," said Will, "like a pretty horse, or a pretty woman that bolts as soon as you show interest." She turned to him, unsmiling, then looked back at the pond.

"I feel like we've been chasing a dream all morning," she said. "You know, something that we want real bad, something we can be a part of, something to grab hold of."

Harlan Hague

Will pulled a bandana from a pocket, removed his hat and wiped his face and top of his head. "I think you've been in the sun too long." He turned to her. "Are you feeling dizzy?"

She frowned, staring at her horse's ears. "No, and I haven't been in the sun too long." She looked over at Will. "Isn't that what dreams are? Something we conjure up and want to be real?" She looked back at the pond and bordering trees. "That's the sort of place I want. Clear blue water, deep shade, green grass."

He shook his head, replaced his hat and pushed the bandana into a pocket. "C'mon, let's ride up a bit and have a look. Then we'll give it up for the day and head back to the herd. You need to sit in shade." He turned to her. "Wouldn't it be nice if we could mount a big umbrella on the hoodlum driver's seat?" She looked at him, frowning. He squeezed his legs, pushing his horse to a walk. She followed.

As they approached the pond, the heat waves from the scorched plain intensified, blurring the pond and woods. Then something miraculous happened. Instead of the pond and woods shimmering and vanishing, the heat waves thinned, swirled and disappeared.

"Will! It's real! The water and the trees and the grass are real." They kicked their horses ahead and galloped to the pond. Pulling up at the bank, they slid from saddles as the horses dipped muzzles into the clear water. They knelt beside their mounts and drank from cupped hands.

Will stood, wiped his mouth with a sleeve, enjoying the shade and the view of the calm pool fed by a narrow creek. He closed his eyes, inhaled. At a sound, he opened his eyes abruptly and saw his horse stepping from the bank into the shallows. He backed up and pulled on the reins.

"C'mon, pard, don't want you to founder on too much water. Still work to do. Pull her back, Bonnie. We need to get back to the herd with the good news."

Will mounted, looked down at Bonnie who still stood by her horse, staring at the pond and the trees. "Bonnie?"

She looked up at him. It was a face he had not seen before, a look of inexpressible sadness. She pulled her horse away from the water and mounted.

"Are you okay, sweetheart?" he said.

"Yeah. No. Let's get on with it."

They kicked their horses into a lope down the back trail.

Little more than an hour after leaving the pond, Will and Bonnie saw the chuck wagon and hoodlum approaching. Cookie waved and pulled up. Brad, driving the hoodlum wagon, was especially glad to see Bonnie. He had long since told anyone who would listen that he hated mules, declaring that God made mules of the scraps after he had finished creating horses. Now he told Bonnie how happy he was to turn the beasts over to her.

As if on signal, Rod and Jimmy rode in. Cookie told all to rest a bit, and he would have a late cold dinner for them in two shakes of a lamb's tail.

The two single water searchers had found nothing but tantalizing mirages. They breathed a collective sigh of relief at their pards' good news.

The tired cowboys and Bonnie sat in the shade of the chuck wagon. The men shared tales of mirages and heat and disappointments. Unlike the others who ate leisurely, Rod ate quickly, scraping his plate with the fork. He stood and walked to the chuck wagon where he deposited his empty plate, fork and cup in the dish bucket. He walked back to Will and Bonnie, brushing something imaginary off his hands.

"Okay if I ride back to tell the good news? I've not been in Charlie's good graces lately, and he's going to be mighty pleased to hear your news."

"Sure, if you don't mind me and Bonnie staying with the wagons and meeting the outfit when you catch up for supper." He glanced at Bonnie who concentrated on her plate, pushing the beans around. He looked back at Rod. "I don't suppose that's going to please Charlie none, me staying here instead of gettin' back to the herd, but when he hears about the pond, maybe he'll forget about me."

Rod grinned. "Let's go, Jimmy. Since the herd is coming this way and we have tired horses, we'll take it slow."

"I'm ridin' with you, now that Bonnie's back,"

said Brad. Bonnie looked up, and he smiled at her. She nodded and looked back at her plate.

"Take our horses," said Will, "and leave us yours. Ours've been watered, and we're not goin' anywhere fast."

"Good idea," said Rod. "Thank-ee. We'll take good care of 'em." While Cookie packed up the chuck wagon for traveling, Bonnie and Will went with the others to the hoodlum where the horses were tied to wagon wheels. Saddles were transferred, and the two searchers set out on the back trail at a walk. Brad hurriedly untied his horse from the back of the hoodlum, mounted and followed, whistling.

Will took Bonnie by the arm, and they walked around the hoodlum to a solitary cottonwood. She sat in the shade, and he leaned against the trunk. He glanced back to see Cookie leaning over the tailgate, fussing with something inside the wagon. Will looked down at Bonnie.

She pulled her hat off, raised her chin, closed her eyes and shook out her hair. With fingers extended, she pushed both hands through the hair. Wiping her face with a sleeve, she replaced the hat and pulled it down in front.

He waited.

She drew her legs up, wrapped her arms around them and rested her chin on her knees. She stared across the flat plain toward the horizon, looked up at him.

"What's it all about, Will? I'm not unhappy, I like what I do, what we do, but is this all there is? Forever?" She looked across the dry flat toward the horizon. "Isn't there something else, something we look forward to, something like that pond today, something that we can cling to, something that satisfies us?" She looked down at her feet, spoke softly. "I'm not making much sense, am I?"

"You're making a lot of sense. Some of these waddies we work with would say that they don't need anything different. They're happy and doing exactly what they want to do the rest of their lives. Other folks are not satisfied with what they have and want something that will fill the empty places."

She looked up at him. "What do you want, Will?"

He squatted and sat beside her. "What I want is what I think, what I hope, you want. You just keep on wondering, sweetheart, and we're gonna talk about lots of things when we get paid off in Montana. Until Montana, we keep doing what we're doing, taking some satisfaction in doing it, and thinking about what might come after."

She wrinkled her forehead, leaned toward him. "Are you saying—"

He put a finger to her lips. "I'm just saying that we have a job to do, and we keep doing it as best we can. When this drive is done, we can talk about anything we want to talk about, and we can do whatever we want to do. For now, just love me half as much as I love you.

And keep thinking about that clear blue pond and shade trees."

McBride shouldn't have worried about crossing the Republican River since reports this year said that it was a shallow stream without much current. But he worried about crossing any water. In any event, he was pleased to find a good ford and low water. The herd was driven over in less than two hours. Camp was set up on the north bank in a patch of the only good grass in sight.

Next morning, they watered the herd again at first light and were on the trail shortly after sunrise. McBride was all too familiar with the forty-mile waterless drive from the Republican River to the South Platte. A friend had told him that last year when he was driving a herd to Montana, he had pushed the herd onto the trail immediately after crossing the Republican. The herd had not been rested on either side of the river, and cattle were lost on the drive. McBride vowed that would not happen to him this year.

It was a slow, hot drive, but they arrived as expected at the South Platte at noon on the third day. The thirsty cows smelled the water and ran the last stretch to the bank and walked into the shallows to drink. The river bed was a mile wide at this point, and the shallow stream meandered among sandbars and islands. The refreshed herd was moved across with no difficulty.

On the north bank, the outfit approached railroad tracks that seemed to come from nowhere and go to nowhere. The cattle balked at the rails, and tired cowboys cussed and shouted and quirted the critters until the leaders moved across. The rest of the herd followed in regular order.

McBride called a halt for dinner, and the herd was thrown on a patch of dry grass. McBride, Will and a few others walked back to the tracks.

Standing between the rails, they looked in each direction and saw no evidence of life or habitation. It was eerily quiet. No sounds, no movement in sight but the slightest waving in the sage from a whisper of a breeze.

"Where the hell does it go, boss?" said Marley.

"Well, if you go in that direction," McBride pointed eastward, "you'll come to Ogalalla. Not much of a town there at the moment, just a few tents and shacks. But wherever there's a settlement of any kind on a railroad, there's bound to be a town coming. Next year, it'll be a different story, I'll wager." He pointed westward. "If you go in that direction, you'll come to Cheyenne."

Marley shook his head. "What's the world comin' to, railroads all over the place gettin' in the way." He and the other hands walked toward the wagons. Only McBride and Will remained.

"Do you think you'll be shipping your cattle north by rail anytime soon?" Will said.

McBride looked westward at the rails that ran through the flat prairie to a turn and disappeared behind a rise. "I heard rumors last winter that the railroad is coming to Fort Worth. They've already started building a big stockyard north of town to handle the herds that they expect the railroad will attract. Am I going to ship animals on the railroad? Who knows?" He looked at the distant mountains in the west. "Probably be expensive to ship cattle north for stocking. Anyway, I don't think I'd like the view from inside a railroad car.

"What are your plans, Will? You'll be paid off before long. What then?"

"Ah." Will looked toward the camp. He figured that he should be busy at something in camp, but Charlie seemed to want to talk, so he was content. "Not sure. I've thought about it and talked about it with, uh, . . ."

"With Bonnie," said McBride. "I'm not blind or dumb."

Will smiled. "What do you think, Charlie? I hear some ranches are setting up in Wyoming and Montana, around where we're traveling."

"That's true. Thought about it myself, in fact. That's why Mack and I rode over to have a look at Cheyenne. Not far west of here. I figured I could meet some people who run cattle around here. This railroad track reached Cheyenne a few years ago. Should be real handy for shipping cows back East. Or West. Hell, this track goes all the way to the Pacific Ocean now! Maybe I could sell cows to China!"

"Learn anything useful in Cheyenne?" said Will.

"Yeah, I got an earful. Locals say their ranches are doing pretty good, but that things are gettin' a little edgy lately. Looks like there's liable to be some Indian troubles up in the Black Hills north of here.

"Seems that gold was discovered there a few years back, and miners began moving in. That was in violation of a treaty that recognized the Black Hills as Sioux country. Course, you know that treaties with Indians have never been worth the paper they're written on if white people want the land. Just last year, the government sent in an army unit to investigate, the Custer Expedition they called it, and Custer reported back that sure enough there's lots of gold there. So more miners flooded the hills.

"The government tried to keep the miners from going into Sioux lands, but that didn't work, so they tried to buy the Black Hills from the Indians. The Sioux weren't having it. Some Sioux leaders even went to Washington last spring—yeah!—to try to persuade the government to abide by the treaties and make the miners leave their country. Word is, they actually met with the President and some of his top people. The President's men told the chiefs they would pay them $25,000 for the Black Hills, and the Sioux would be relocated to Indian Territory down south, a really fine country. That's what they said.

"Spotted Tail, one of the Sioux leaders, said something like, that's not my country, and I want nothing to do with it. He said if it is such a good country, send the white miners there, and leave us alone. You can imagine how the meeting ended. The Indians went home with nothing settled and hoppin' mad.

"There's a rumor in Cheyenne now that the government is sending people this fall to meet with the Sioux to try to pressure them to sell the land. The Sioux have heard the same rumors, and now they're madder'n hell. Least, that's what the boys in the saloon said, and they were cold sober when they said it. Everybody I talked with in Cheyenne was pretty uneasy about the future.

"So you can see why I'm not fixing to put down roots in Wyoming or Montana just now. No sir, after we deliver the herd and I settle up with all you yahoos, it's back to Texas for me. Anyway, I don't think I'd be satisfied any place else. Home to Texas for me. Might even take the train. I'll bet a few of the boys would join me. We'd catch it in Cheyenne."

Will frowned, looked at the prairie beyond the herd that was now grazing peacefully. "Well, that clears my mind of any thought of settling up here. I sure don't need problems with Indians. Had enough of that with the Comanche. There was lots of troubles the last few years in north Texas, but it was pretty quiet when I left home for this drive. I 'spect by now it's all settled with the Indians around there."

McBride looked down, pondering. "We got plenty of time to think about the future." He looked toward camp. "Right now, we need to finish this drive. We got four hundred miles to the Crow agency and plenty of time to get there . . . if the troubles in the Black Hills stay in the Black Hills. We'll be driving this bunch on a trail that's too close to the Black Hills for my liking." He beckoned. "C'mon, Cookie's dishing out dinner. We don't want him to run out before we git there."

After dinner, Bonnie put the mules in harness on the two wagons and helped Cookie pack up the chuck wagon. That done, they moved out while the hands watered the herd once more. Then the cows, full of water and grass, were thrown back on the trail, heading north.

"Montana just over that hill!" shouted Sid, grinning, then looked around nervously at his outburst. The response from hands riding near him suggested that his attempt at humor was not appreciated. He sobered, dropped his head and studied his horse's ears.

Holding his reins, McBride stood on the trampled dry grass where the cattle had grazed. He watched the herd moving out on the trail, the wagons already a half mile ahead.

He looked up when a single grasshopper flew lazily past him, rising, drifting in the light breeze, disappearing from view over the river. He mounted and kicked his horse to a lope toward the herd.

Will stood near the chuck wagon, watching the day come. The top of the orange sun disc brightened the eastern horizon and colored the wispy cloud layers above in pastel shades.

He looked up when a grasshopper glided by, borne by the light, cool breeze. He jerked his head aside when two others drifted toward his face before veering off. He saw McBride nearby, standing at the grassy edge of the trail, studying something at his feet. Will walked over to him.

McBride pointed at the ground. A dozen grasshoppers crawled about in the dry grass. The men looked up to see a dozen more gliding high above them.

"Call the boys to come over here," McBride said.

"They're at breakfast," Will said.

McBride leaned into his face. "Did I ask what they're doing! I don't give a rusty rat's ass what they're doing! Tell 'em to leave their plates and git over here! Now!" He glared at Will.

Will recoiled at this uncharacteristic bluster and hurried to the fire circle, frowning. He spoke to the hands, sitting and standing, chatting and laughing. They sobered and listened, and all jollity ended. Setting their plates on the ground, they strode to McBride.

"Okay, look up and listen up," McBride said. The hands looked up to see a flurry of grasshoppers flying and drifting toward the camp. "I told you about the grasshopper trouble last year. Looks like we're in for it."

The cowhands had paid unusually close attention on a couple of occasions recently at the evening campfire when McBride told about the locust plague last year. What's a locust, one hand had asked. When it's only one or two, they're grasshoppers, McBride had answered. When it's thousands or millions, they're called locusts.

McBride heard about the locust troubles from a couple of friends who had been in the thick of it on drives to Montana, and he heard more stories in Texas last fall and winter. Most of the hands heard something of it back home in Texas, but not from people who had actually experienced it.

Last summer when McBride's friends were driving herds through Nebraska, hordes of grasshoppers darkened the sky, millions of them, then descended on the land and the herds. They ate everything in sight and stampeded the terrified animals. When the cloud of insects passed, they left a bare landscape, devoid of grass and leaves. It took the hands days to recover the cattle, and many were never found.

"Didn't expect this would happen again, least not so soon. But there they are." They looked up and watched the northern sky gradually filling with a gray-green mass that thickened and obscured the sun.

"Button up," said McBride. "Tie your pant legs at the bottom. Tie your bandana around your face below your eyes. We can't do nothing about the grasshoppers. They're coming, no doubt about that. Just try to keep the herd milling. Keep on your toes! The cattle are likely to go plumb loco." He looked up. "Okay, git to it! They're comin' fast!"

Cowboys buttoned shirts and tied cuffs and scattered. Some ran to saddled mounts; others collected saddles and ran to the remuda. Cookie and Bonnie hustled to the chuck wagon, pulled down flaps and tried to cover openings. Once mounted, riders went to the herd, hallooed and waved and put the cattle milling slowly.

Now the churning cloud of millions of locusts were overhead and suddenly descended on the encampment. Wings whirring, they beat against canvas wagon covers, assaulted cowboys who dodged and swatted and horses and cows that whirled and bucked, shaking heads and switching tails to ward off the buzzing insects.

Terrified cows bolted from the herd and ran in all directions, ignoring cowboys who tried to hold them. Will and Bonnie rode together, back and forth, trying to head off running cattle. The cows stopped, shook their heads, backed up, bucked and whirled.

Reining sharply to turn a steer, Bonnie's horse brushed it, and the enraged animal charged her, colliding hard with her mount, and the horse went down. Bonnie fell on her side and rolled away from the plunging horse that struggled to stand. The steer turned on Bonnie and charged with lowered head, butting against her. The wide horns did not touch her, only the hard head of the animal as she tried to roll away.

Riding behind Bonnie, Will saw her go down and kicked his horse toward the steer, drawing his pistol. He emptied the six-shooter at the animal's neck and head, pulling back when the steer was too close to Bonnie. Finally, the steer's knees buckled, and it collapsed on its side. Bonnie, wide-eyed and panting, scooted backwards and scrambled up. She looked up at Will.

"Wow, that was fun," she said, still shaking.

"You okay?" Will said.

"No." She wiped her face with both hands, pulled the bandanna up to cover her nose and mouth. "I'll be okay as soon as I get my breath. And my mare." She looked around, pointed. "There she is." The horse stood twenty paces away, shaking its head and tail twitching under a swarm of locusts. "Good girl," she said and walked to the horse. She stroked the mare's neck, calming it. She mounted and rode to Will.

"We'll be cow hunting for a couple of days," he said, swatting grasshoppers away from his face. "You okay to ride? We need to hold as many of these critters here as we can." They began to ride the perimeter of the few cows still milling.

Flying locusts swarmed about the campsite, others covered the ground, making crunching sounds when stepped on. Cowboys rode in all directions, swatting the insects that swirled about their heads, trying without much success to hold the cattle together.

Renfro's horse had enough of the locusts. It whirled and crow-hopped across the flat, throwing its rider. The cowboy rolled away from the horse that continued to buck as it moved away. Renfro stood slowly and looked around, confused, ignoring the locusts that buzzed around his head. He walked toward the meadow, away from the encampment, his head twitching.

Then it was over. The buzzing, whirring pandemonium had continued all morning till mid-afternoon when the swarm, as if on some intelligent signal, vanished. The cloud of insects simply lifted and moved southward.

Cowboys, mounted and afoot, looked around. It was still, quiet, but for the crunching underfoot when the hands walked about the site. Some cows, no more than a third of the herd, milled and wandered without any order or restraint.

Renfro walked slowly toward camp, a faint smile creasing his sunburnt face, as he looked about, fanning his face with his hat. Nobody looked his way. He replaced his hat, looked around for his horse.

McBride dismounted and tied his horse to a chuck wagon wheel. He stared at the wagon interior. Cookie walked around to stand beside him.

"Be damned," said Cookie. "They ate the canvas." The wooden wagon bows were bare of any covering, but for a few tattered shreds. "Might be able to rig a replacement from the tents in the hoodlum. If they didn't eat them as well."

McBride nodded, still staring. "Do what you can," he said softly. He turned and surveyed the camp. Cowboys were already moving scattered cows into the semblance of a herd.

*****

McBride and Win sat their horses at noon, watching cowboys bringing in cows, a dozen from the west, fifty or so from the northeast, more bunches from every direction. Hands had been hunting cows since mid-afternoon yesterday, when the locust swarm moved off.

"How many do you think we lost?" McBride said.

"Hard to say till everybody comes in," said Win, "but I wouldn't be surprised if we lost two or three hundred head. They were pretty spooked. Some of 'em might be swimming the Rio Grande about now." He pointed at a bunch approaching from the north. "Here comes a good lot, hundred head, I'll bet. Wouldn't you know it's Will and Bonnie."

Bonnie and Will waved as they moved the cows toward the herd. "All right if I help Bonnie and Cookie with the wagon tops?" Will called. Will took McBride's wave as an okay.

They moved their bunch to the herd where some exhausted animals had already bedded down, then rode to the chuck wagon. They were delighted to find Cookie working on a late dinner featuring slabs of roasted beef butchered from Will's kill.

"Charlie wasn't happy to see that carcass out there," Cookie said, "but he grumbled a glad-she's-okay after I told him the story. In fact, he said he could use a good steak after all the excitement. I'm sure all the boys are gonna agree. I wouldn't be surprised if some one or two of the boys might even decide that

Will had such a good idea that they might look for the occasion down the road to do something of the same." He smiled.

"I do think old McBride would see right through that little scheme," said Bonnie. She took a grip on Will's shirtsleeve. The sleeve ripped at the shoulder and slid to his wrist. Bonnie frowned. "Will, the grasshoppers almost ate the shirt off your back. They ate a good part of my britches too. Didn't know it till I heard Rod and Sid looking at my backside and giggling."

Will turned her around and, sure enough, her buns were exposed. "Yeah." He patted her bottom.

She pushed his hand away. "C'mon, let's see if we can do something about the chuck wagon cover. Hope the damn grasshoppers didn't eat the tents. They were rolled up pretty tight in the hoodlum."

Supper was a drawn-out affair as bone-tired cowboys shuffled in ones and twos to the chuck wagon after putting their collected bunches of cattle with the herd. McBride and Win calculated that they had lost over two hundred head, and the boss was still on edge. Nobody cared to sit near him at the supper campfire.

Sid walked slowly to the fire, carrying his plate of beef, beans and biscuits. He stopped and looked around. A couple of cowboys looked up at him and returned to their plates.

Bonnie looked up. "Sit down, Sid." She gestured with a nod of her head at the ground beside her.

"Oh, uh, thanks, Bonnie." He sat down a couple of feet from her. He looked at her and started to say more, but she had returned to her plate. He took a couple of bites, glanced at her nervously. "That was pretty exciting today. Pretty scary, too."

She looked up at him, returned to her plate. "Sure was. Hope we don't have to do that very often."

"Where's, uh, where's Will?"

She forked the last chunk of beef to her mouth. "Ridin' herd. I usually ride with him, but I'm still hurting from my dumb tussle with a longhorn, and Charlie gave me the night off."

"I heard about that. That was really somethin'. Glad you weren't hurt worse."

"Thanks. Me too." She turned to him. "What do you think about the outfit so far? Everything okay?"

"Yeah, it's fine; they're a good bunch." He pushed the beans around on his plate with a fork, looked at her as she soaked up meat juice with her biscuit. "Uh, Bonnie, do you know what bonnie means?"

She looked up, her face a question.

"I had a friend back in Texas who told me that bonnie means, uh, pretty."

She leaned back, frowned. "Hmm. Well, I don't think that's what my parents had in mind when they named me. My real name is Barbara. I was first called Bonnie by a little neighbor kid who couldn't say Barbara." She looked around. "Don't you tell anybody," she said softly. "I haven't told anybody my real name, even Will."

He leaned toward her. "I won't, Bonnie! I won't. I like Bonnie better, too. It's, uh, it's a better name for you. Cause you are, uh, you *are* pretty." He glanced around nervously to see whether anyone had heard. No one looked his way.

"That's nice of you to say so, Sid." She touched his hand, stood, looked down at him. "I'm headin' for the barn. This has been a tough day. I'm really tired. Night, Sid."

He looked up. "Goodnight, Bonnie . . . bonnie." He smiled broadly. She smiled a hint of a smile and walked toward the chuck wagon.

Bonnie deposited her dishes in the chuck wagon bucket and went to the hoodlum where she pulled out her bedding, at least what the locusts had left. Happily, most of the bedrolls were under planks in the wagon bed, so they were intact for the most part, but for small holes made by the persistent hoppers.

She had hardly finished laying out the bedroll when Will shuffled in, dropped his saddle. He inhaled deeply. "Whoo. Glad I wasn't ridin' herd in the middle of the night. I'm plumb wore out. That was some day."

She pulled the covers back, removed her boots and britches and crawled in. Will sat down, pulled off his boots and wriggled out of his britches. Lying beside her, he pulled up the cover, unbuttoned her shirt and caressed her breasts, then moved his hand down her body.

"Hey, I thought you were worn out."

"I am. All up to you."

She rolled over on top of him, and they were caught in a slow-motion frenzy of gasps and moans, each shushing the other, both panting at the end.

She fell off him and lay still, breathing heavily. Wiping perspiration from her forehead with the blanket, she rolled over to face him, her lips at his ear.

"You might have some competition, honey," she said softly.

He moved over to face her and kissed her cheek, then nibbled her ear. "Who is it? I'll kill 'im."

"Oh, yeah, big man. Everybody run." She kissed him. "It's Sid."

"Sid. Don't mess with Sid, sweetheart. Can't figure him out. He's had serious problems somewhere in his past. He's a fragile kid."

"Kid? He's nineteen, same as me. You think I'm a kid?"

"You're a grown woman. At least, in comparison to Sid." He put his hands on both her cheeks. "But you're still my little sweetie pie girl."

She pushed the cover down and sat up. "So now I'm a little sweetie pie girl. Maybe I *will* encourage Sid. Might be interesting to compare a rough old cowboy to a soft, sweet kid."

He rolled over to face away from her. "Go to sleep. You know I'm joking."

She lay down, scooted to the edge of the blankets, pulled the cover to her chin. *I'm not.*

CHAPTER ELEVEN

Breakfast finished, cowboys ambled toward the remuda, carrying saddles, chatting, some smoking a last cigarette before setting out on the day's work. Bonnie, standing beside the chuck wagon, watched the cowboys passing.

"Sid!" she called. He stopped, turned to her, surprised.

"Mornin', Bonnie." He smiled broadly.

"Sid, I got a favor to ask. Grandpa's feeling a little out of sorts this morning. Can you give us a hand? I think you said you can drive a wagon?"

"Sure, Bonnie, I been driving wagons since I was a sprout." He pursed his lips, confused.

"I already asked Charlie. He and Win rode out early to hunt for water. He said it was okay."

"Well, that's good. Uh, where's Will?"

Bonnie frowned, impatient. "He's riding in Win's trail boss position since him and Charlie are gone. Can you do this for me?"

"Sure, I can Bonnie. I'll do anything for you. All you gotta do is ask. I'll get my horse and tie him on the back of the wagon. Just in case something comes up."

"Good idea. Hurry. We need to get the mules in harness and move out ahead of the herd."

Sid didn't move. He studied the chuck wagon cover, frowning.

Bonnie looked at the wagon. "What?"

"You did a good job on that cover."

"Yeah, Grandpa and I used up a lot of tents, but we got 'em covered. Means a lot of you boys will have to sleep under the wagons when it rains." She frowned. "Now, can we get moving?"

"Right on it, Bonnie." He hefted his saddle to a shoulder "I'll be right back." He hustled toward the remuda with long strides, his head thrown back. He skipped once.

The herd was lined out on the low banks of a narrow, flowing creek. After McBride and Win found the creek, Win had ridden back down the trail and passed the word to Bonnie to noon at the creek. He continued to the oncoming herd where he relieved Will and sent him ahead to tell Bonnie when to expect the herd.

Will set out at a slow lope, alone with his thoughts. He smiled, contented, a bit proud of himself. It was the first time he had ridden in the trail boss's position, and he flattered himself that he had done a good job and felt like a trail boss. Why not? Though this was his first long drive, he had proven himself a first-rate, reliable hand.

He reined up as he approached the wagons. Cookie was nowhere in sight. Bonnie and Sid stood side by side at the back of the chuck wagon, working at something. They were enjoying whatever they were doing, chatting and laughing. They looked up at Will's approach. Will dismounted, frowning, and tied his reins to a wheel.

"Where's Cookie?" Will said.

She looked at Sid, turned back to Will. "Hello, Will, I'm fine, and everything's fine here. Are you fine?" She smiled.

Will looked from Sid to Bonnie. "Where's your grandpa?"

Bonnie sobered, turned back to the biscuit dough. "He had an uneasy stomach this morning, took to his bed in the hoodlum wagon. Sid's been helping out. Sid knows mules, wagons and potatoes." Sid laughed, showed Will a potato he was peeling.

Will nodded, turned and walked to his horse. "Herd will be here in half an hour," he said, untying his reins.

"Afraid the boys are going to have to wait a bit for dinner. Me and Sid aren't too skilled at this, but it won't be long." She looked at Sid, smiled, turned toward Will. "Want to help?"

He looked back at her, saw her smile, mounted and rode toward the herd that was being held at the creek.

Bonnie bent over the dough, pounding, kneading, squeezing and rolling. "This is no fun," she said. "Glad grandpa has me tending mules and wagons most of the time 'stead of helping with the cooking."

Sid frowned. "Uh, Bonnie . . ."

Bonnie stopped, her hands on the roll of dough, looked at him. "What?"

Sid frowned, wrinkling his forehead. "Uh, Bonnie, I . . . I don't think you're supposed to pound biscuit dough like you do bread dough. I used to help my ma in the kitchen."

Bonnie straightened, looked over at him, frowning. She softened. "Hmm. Is that so? I may just give this chore to you if I'm ever set to work fixing meals again."

Sid brightened, grinning ear to ear. "Bonnie, if you ever get stuck with cooking again, just tell me, and I'll do anything you say. I like to work with you, beside you. Bonnie, you're the only person in the outfit that pays me any mind. The others kinda, sorta, look at me like I'm not there. They don't much want to talk with me. I don't think they like me."

Bonnie frowned at him, smiled. She touched his hand, and he looked down at the hand. "I think it's your imagination, Sid. Do you talk with them? Don't wait for them to say something to you. You say something to them first, and I bet they'll answer."

He smiled broadly. "I'll try that." He moved a step closer. "It makes me feel so good to talk to you, Bonnie. I like to be with you."

She smiled thinly, sighed, turned grim, rolling the dough. "Thanks, Sid, that's sweet of you to say so." She looked toward the stream. "You better get back to the herd, and check in with Win. I'll finish up here. Put some more wood and chips, whatever you find in the cooney, on the fire, would you?"

"Okay, sure." He took his hat from the hook on the wagon side, started to walk away, then turned back, frowning. "Cooney?"

"The cowhide stretched under the chuck wagon." She pointed. "You never heard of a cooney?"

"All I've heard is 'hide' from the others."

"Grandpa calls it a 'cooney', so I call it a 'cooney'."

"Okay, I'll do it. Bonnie, I really enjoyed helping. If Cookie isn't up to driving this afternoon, tell me, and I'll come back. Bonnie, I really . . . really . . . like to help you. I like to be with you."

She straightened, flexed her back. "Thanks, Sid. You've been a big help. Now you better hustle. Win's gonna start wondering what's keeping you."

He put on the hat, pulled the brim down. He took a step toward Bonnie, stopped and simply looked at her, sober. He touched her hand that was covered with flour. She looked up at him, smiled.

"Right. I'm off," he said, softly.

She watched him go for a moment, then wiped her hands on a cloth and went to the cook fire. She shook her head. Sid had forgotten to feed the fire, now only glowing embers. Collecting an armful of cow chips from the cooney, she dropped them on the fire. She straightened, flexed her back, watching Sid walking toward the remuda. His head was thrown back. He was whistling.

No one sitting around the campfire later complained about the dinner of beans, potatoes and the biscuits that had a soft, doughy center. Some of the hands even complimented Bonnie for stepping in and preparing the meal. She thanked them for the kind words, frowning, unsure of what they really thought of her efforts.

She pointed out, for any that did not know, that Sid had been a great help in the fixings. Sid beamed. Will, sitting beside Bonnie, looked from Sid to Bonnie and back to Sid. Pushing the beans around on his plate, Will forked a hunk of potato to his mouth, glanced at Bonnie.

"Before we finish here," said Rod. He waited until he had everyone's attention. "Before we finish here, may I ask that we all say a little prayer for Cookie's quick recovery." This was followed by a roar of laughter and Bonnie throwing what was left of her soggy biscuit at Rod.

As hands deposited their dishes in the pail, Cookie climbed down from the back of the hoodlum wagon, walked to the campfire and announced to all that he was well and hungry. He shushed Bonnie's protests and said he would rustle something up to eat, and furthermore, he would drive his wagon this afternoon.

Sid, standing nearby, caught Bonnie's eye and smiled. She smiled thinly, then turned to Will when he said something to her. Sid's smile vanished, and he headed toward the remuda, his head hanging. He looked back over his shoulder to see Will and Bonnie walking toward the chuck wagon, chatting and laughing.

The drive in the afternoon was long and dry. The herd arrived at the destination, a narrow creek of good water, at sundown. After watering the cattle and putting them on the bed ground, all but the first shift on night herd put their horses with the remuda and shuffled to the waiting campfire, bone tired.

While Cookie worked at the cook fire, Bonnie plates and forks from the wagon bed. She looked up to see Sid coming. He whipped off his hat, smiling.

"Anything I can do?" he said.

Bonnie smiled. "I think everything's under control. I really appreciate all your help, Sid. That was kind of you." She leaned inside the wagon, reached in with a grunt.

"Can I get it, whatever you're reaching for?" Sid stepped up quickly beside her, looking into the wagon, brushing against her arm.

"Sid, don't bother Bonnie. She's busy." Cookie held a steaming pot of beans that he had just removed from the cook fire. "I'll call supper in a couple of minutes. Scoot!" His wave was a get-away gesture.

Sid backed away, still holding his hat at his chest, his face sober. "Well, if I can . . . holler if there's somethin' I can do."

Bonnie withdrew from the wagon, with a hint of a smile that disappeared quickly as she hefted a stack of plates. Sid started to step toward her but backed off when she shook her head without a word. He turned and shuffled slowly toward the campfire.

During supper, the tired cowboys said little but an occasional comment about an ornery beast or the heat or the sweet relief when the sun set and a soft cool breeze picked up.

Jimmy, sitting a few feet from Bonnie, waved a biscuit at the chuck wagon. "Cookie," he called, "we sure are happy to see you healthy and plying' your trade. We missed you." He pulled a face, glanced at Bonnie and dodged her backhand swipe.

One by one, the hands finished their supper, stood and stretched, walked to the chuck wagon to return plates, forks and cups. Some walked outside the waning light of the campfire to darkness, others ambled to the hoodlum wagon to retrieve bedrolls. A couple of cowboys, chatting and smoking, walked to the remuda to get their horses for night herd.

Bonnie and Will walked around the chuck wagon toward the hoodlum. She held his arm, pulled his head down and kissed him as he squeezed a breast. She wriggled, laughed and pushed his hand away.

Sid stood at the edge of darkness, watching Will and Bonnie who were dimly illuminated by the low flames of the campfire and cook fire.

*****

Next morning, breakfast finished, the cowboys walked to the remuda, hefting saddles and bridles, quiet for the most part, save an occasional soft laugh and muted morning conversation.

McBride was first in the saddle. He watched the parade of cowboys moving toward the horse herd. "Anybody seen Sid? Hadn't seen him this morning." The cowboys didn't pause, just looked up at McBride and shook heads. McBride rode to the hoodlum where Bonnie had just finished putting the mules in harness.

"I notice that Sid has been paying you some attention lately," said McBride. "Have you seen him this morning?"

Bonnie looked up. "Sid? Nope, haven't seen him since supper."

McBride frowned. "Well, he seemed a drifter when I hired him. I suppose he got tired of settled life." He rode toward the herd that cowboys were pushing onto the trail.

Cookie had watched this exchange from his seat on the chuck wagon. "Good riddance, I'd say. The kid was getting too . . . helpful." He shook the lines. "Giddap, mules!"

Bonnie shook the lines and pulled in behind the chuck wagon. She waved to Will and Mack who returned the wave as they rode past at a lope. Will told her earlier that he and Mack would ride ahead this morning in the daily ritual of searching for water.

*****

"Looks real," said Mack. They sat their horses, looking across a dry flat toward a line of trees with a heavy growth of some sort of bushes at their feet. Though they could see no water, they agreed that it likely was there. They feared that the grove would disappear as two mirages earlier this morning had vanished, but this one grew more distinct as they drew nearer.

"How 'bout you checking the pine grove there on the right," Will said, "and I'll have a look at the cottonwoods on the left. I think we'll find a good creek." Mack nodded, and they moved off.

Will rode to the left and pulled up at a pool about ten feet wide and twenty yards long. The water was still but for a few ripples at the far end where a narrow, slow-moving stream flowed between lush banks. He dismounted and led the bay to the pond edge.

"Will!" His head came up at Mack's shout. He mounted hurriedly and galloped on the bank. He pulled up when he saw Mack standing in a knee-high growth of ferns and rushes. Mack looked at Will, then at the ground.

Will dismounted and saw the body at Mack's feet. The body lay on its side, dried blood on a cheek and temple where a slow trickle of blood still oozed from the hole. The grip of the six-shooter lay in Sid's open hand.

They stared at the body, neither knowing where to begin.

"I knew the boy was troubled," said Will, "and

wondered about him." He shook his head. "We should have talked with him more. We might have been able to help."

"It ain't in the nature of an outfit like ours to get inside a cowboy's head, if the cowboy don't welcome it," Mack said. "Lots of boys join a cattle outfit to get away from something, and they don't cotton to somebody trying to git too close. Sid didn't talk to nobody very much . . . 'cept Bonnie." He looked up at Will. "Only time I ever saw him smile was when he was talkin' to her."

Will looked up at Mack. He bent, took the six-shooter from Sid's open hand and examined it. The grip was chipped, the barrel tarnished and showing some rust. "I didn't know he owned a gun. Never saw him wearing it."

"Some cowboys own guns like some people own jewelry. I bet he never shot it before." Mack reached for the six-shooter, and Will gave it to him. Mack opened the cylinder and showed Will the five cartridges, a residue of lightly caked dust encircling each rim.

Will looked around. "Wonder where his horse is."

"Over yonder," Mack pointed, "in that pine thicket. "When I saw the horse, I knew somebody was about. I'll get it."

Will still stared at the body when Mack walked up, leading the horse. "He didn't bother to tie him. I s'pose he knew from the start that he wasn't going back for it."

"Well, let's get him on his horse," said Will. "Never tied a body on a horse before."

"Sad to say, I have. Help me pick him up, and I'll tie him on." They lifted the body and draped it over the saddle. Mack took some leather strips from his saddle bags and secured the body to the saddle.

They found their horses and mounted, Mack holding the reins of Sid's horse.

The meadow was wide here, with only a slight breeze from straight ahead. Bonnie pulled the hoodlum up beside the chuck wagon. Cookie looked aside, nodded to her and looked back to the front, gently shook the lines.

"How're you feeling?" she said.

"Right as rain," he said, without looking at her.

They rode silently. She studied the trail ahead, the parched prairie grasses, the sparse trees and bushes. She frowned when she saw horsemen in the trail ahead. "Grandpa, is that Will and Mack coming?"

He leaned forward, straining. "Appears to be."

She frowned. "There's three horses. They didn't have a packhorse when they passed this morning. Wonder what's goin' on."

He stared at his mules. "We'll find out soon enough. Let 'em come."

They watched as the riders drew closer. She sat up. "Grandpa, that's a body tied on that horse!"

"Yeah, 'pears to be."

Cookie and Bonnie pulled up, set brakes, and

waited for the riders. Will and Mack reined up beside the chuck wagon. Bonnie stared at the body. The head was on the offside of the horse, out of Bonnie's view.

"What happened?" she said. "Either of you know him?" She jumped down from the hoodlum, dusted her pants and walked around the chuck wagon toward the body.

"Bonnie," said Will.

She looked up at him as she walked around the horse bearing the corpse. She stopped suddenly, and her hands went to her face. She looked up at Will, wide-eyed.

"It's Sid!" She stepped backward, staring at what had been Sid. "What . . . how did it happen?"

Will looked at Mack. "He shot hisself, missy," said Mack.

Bonnie collapsed to her knees, her hands still on her face. "Oh, no. Oh, no." She looked up. "I did this, Will. I asked him to help, and he wanted so much to help. He smiled at me, and he touched me, just my hand and my arm. It was nothing, but it must have been something to him. I just wanted to be kind to him, to be a friend." Her hands covered her eyes, and the tears came.

"And I wanted to make you jealous." She sobbed. "I killed him, Will, just like I pulled the trigger." She looked up at Mack, tears streaming down her cheeks. "I killed him, Mack," almost a whisper.

Will dismounted and went to Bonnie. He took her

shoulders and helped her stand. He pulled her to him and held her, her arms stiff at her side.

"It wasn't your fault," he said. "You were kind to a fella who was used to people ignoring him. He read too much into that. Sid was troubled. You weren't responsible for whatever demons were chasing him."

He raised her chin. "Mack and I are going to ride slow toward the herd. Charlie needs to know about this. He'll decide what to do." He turned to Cookie. "There's a good nooning spot just an hour or so ahead. Look for the line of pines and cottonwoods a mile or so off the trail to the left. There's a good pond and grass." Cookie nodded.

Will put his hands to Bonnie's cheeks and kissed her. "See you in a while. Until then, you just think about blue water, pretty sunsets, bluebonnets and cold beer."

She pulled back, frowning. She wiped tears from a cheek. "Cold beer? I don't like beer."

He smiled. "Okay, I'll think about cold beer, and you think about me. Is that okay?"

She put her arms around him and hugged. "Okay, cowboy," softly. "Do what you gotta do." She pulled his head down and kissed him.

"Are you two finally done?" said Cookie, looking down from his wagon seat, frowning. "We got some dinner to fix."

Will mounted and kicked his horse to a lope to catch up with Mack who had already set out with their mournful burden.

*****

Cowboys sat on the ground near the chuck wagon, bent over dinner plates. The campground was strangely quiet. A sharp breeze rustling the streamside pines was the only sound. Some looked up at the whistling trill of a meadowlark, searched for it without success, then turned back to their plates.

"Where did you put him . . . Sid?" Bonnie said to McBride.

"Buried him near the pond where passersby will see the grave. Didn't have much to put on the marker. I have addresses of family of everybody in the outfit but Sid. All he told me was that he was from northeast Texas. When I asked for names and addresses, he just repeated 'northeast Texas'. I got the impression he didn't have family or didn't have any contact with them. So all we put on the marker was R.I.P. and his name and 'Northeast Texas'. Maybe somebody passing this way will recognize the name and notify kin."

When dinner was finished, all but those left to tend the herd went to Sid's grave. After Mack recited the Lord's prayer, McBride asked if anyone would like to say something. The men looked at the others, nervously, and said nothing. Some glanced, almost furtively, at Bonnie. She clung with both hands to Will's arm, her head pressed against his shoulder, and said nothing.

When they returned to camp, Will and Bonnie went to the hoodlum, passing Cookie who sat on the chuck wagon seat. He had already put the mules in harness on both wagons. Cookie nodded to them, and Bonnie's attempt at a smile was not successful, ending in a choking sensation.

They stopped at the hoodlum wagon, and she leaned against the side. Will put a hand to her cheek, wiping a tear. She turned to him, touched his hand, her face blank, and climbed up to the wagon seat. She looked down at him, then faced front and shook the lines.

Will and Cookie watched the hoodlum pull away. "She'll be okay," said Cookie. "She's a tough lady. You know that." Will looked down, nodded. Cookie shook the lines, and the wagon pulled away. Will watched the wagon a moment, then walked to his picketed horse.

The afternoon drive was mostly silent. The cattle had watered and grazed some on the banks of the pond and were herded easily. The cowboys were unusually quiet. There had been little comment on the return from the gravesite. Death was not uncommon on the trail. Hundreds of graves had been seen on the drive, beginning just a few miles north of the Rio Grande. Most were old and covered with grass, but there were recent ones as well. A few of the mounds were bare of any grass, and some of the markers confirmed that the deaths were this year. The cowboys had taken little notice of them.

But this was the fourth death in the outfit on this drive. The others had been caused by risks normally associated with trail driving, stampede and altercations with other outfits. While sad in the extreme, the cowboys could understand these deaths. Sid's death was different. They had a hard time understanding suicide.

McBride rode into camp at dusk. He had gone ahead to visit a herd that was spotted a few miles ahead on the trail. At least, the boys spotted a huge cloud of gray dust hugging the trail, and it was assumed that a herd was below the cloud. He had hoped to find somebody who knew more about the trail ahead than he knew. He was not disappointed.

McBride tended to his horse, then went to the chuck wagon where Cookie handed him a full plate. He walked to the campfire and sat with the hands who had set aside empty plates, now smoking or sipping from coffee cups.

"What's it look like, Charlie," said Win, "green grass and clear water up ahead all the way to Montana?"

McBride frowned, forked a mouthful of beans. "Not hardly. Here's what's comin'. We move the herd slower than usual tomorrow morning, let 'em graze a bit more till we reach a little crick. We'll water 'em good. Here's the hard part. That's the last water for a dry stretch of over fifty miles. Least, that's what it was last year. Boss of the herd ahead sent a rider up the trail who confirmed that's the way it looks this year.

"So it's gonna be a tough haul. We'll do some

driving at night and stop in the heat of the day. That means we're changin' our sleep habits too."

The cowboys looked at each other. "Don't sound like much fun," said Renfro, wearing a hint of smile. He looked around for support or comment. The others, silent and grim-faced, stood and carried plates and cups to the chuck wagon.

At the creek next morning, cattle and horses stood in the shallow water to drink. Afterward, the herd grazed on green grass on the banks and dry grass beyond.

After an hour, McBride gave the signal. "All right, boys, throw 'em on the trail. Don't push 'em hard. They'll not get water again till we reach the next stream. Fifty miles."

The drive this day was slower than the everyday pace. Cowboys were quieter than usual for they knew what was coming. They stopped for supper before sundown. Cows were put on dry grass and grazed till dusk. They were slow to settle, and some refused to bed down, lowing softly. Cowboys on night herd were kept busier than usual turning back the occasional bovine that wanted to stray from the bed ground.

The next day was a trial, the hardest some of the cowboys had experienced on the trail. They pushed the herd at a steady pace in the morning, slowing when the cattle found dew on grass and grazed, only slightly slaking their thirst.

A stop was called before noon when cows grazed

or lay down, exhausted from lack of water. Except for those watching the herd, cowboys tried to snatch a few minutes of sleep in the shade of the wagons. After a light supper, the cattle were again thrown on the trail and driven until the eastern horizon brightened with the promise of another hot day.

The morning of the third day brought no relief but the expectation that they should reach water by sundown. The cattle were becoming less a herd than individuals that tried to move away from the column, lowing, heads hanging, shuffling. Only with shouts and curses and quirts were the cowboys able to keep the cattle together and moving. The effort was complicated since the cowboys rode horses that were in no better condition than the cows.

The noon stop under a scorching sun was punctuated by the lowing and bellowing of cows on the patch of dry grass where they milled slowly, grazing little, as riders tried to intercept their wandering.

Cowboys not on herd duty stood around the chuck wagon in any shade they could find, bent over dinner plates. Everyone looked up when a light shower began to fall. Most returned to their plates, ignoring the scattered raindrops.

"Hey, everbody, it's raining!" said Marley, wide-eyed, holding his hands out to catch the raindrops.

"Never mind, devil's beating his wife," said Jimmy, concentrating on his plate. He forked a chunk of beef to his mouth.

"What's that?" Marley said.

Jimmy turned to him. "Devil's beatin' his wife."

"That's the dumbest thang I ever heard. What's it mean?"

"You a Texan, and you never heard about the devil beatin' his wife?" Marley shook his head. "It means when it rains when the sun is shinin', the devil's beatin' his wife."

"But what's it *mean*?"

Jimmy lowered his fork and stared at him.

Marley frowned, looked around and found no one was interested in this conversation. The shower had ended, and he returned to his plate.

In late afternoon, when the heat had only slightly begun to dissipate, the herd was again thrown on the trail. After hours of hard slogging, men and beasts had just about reached the limits of their endurance. Cows hung their heads, walked slowly, some stumbling.

Then it happened, something the cowboys always looked for on a dry drive. The cattle became alert, restless, heads up, looking ahead. They quickened their pace.

Almost simultaneously Win, who was riding at the head of the column, stood up in his stirrups, staring ahead. He turned in his saddle and shouted. "There it is! See that dark line? Trees! The river!" A cheer rose from the cowboys. They shouted and laughed, causing the cattle to shy and become even more unruly. The riders, who had been having so much trouble pushing the cattle ahead, pulled away as the beasts, smelling the water, quickened their pace and began to run.

They approached the banks of the stream as the orange sun disk touched the horizon. The cows, previously exhausted, ran, stumbling and weaving, until they walked into the shallows, standing motionless, drinking deeply. The loose horses galloped to the bank and into the water. Riders dismounted on the bank and knelt to drink from cupped hands.

"Another river that's a mile wide and an inch deep," McBride said to the cowboys nearby. "That's what they say. It's a bit more than an inch deep right now. Must have had some rain upcountry." He looked off to the west. "Doesn't look like any weather up there now. We'll camp on this side and cross the herd tomorrow. Everybody could use some rest. Grass looks better on this side as well."

While Cookie and Bonnie worked on supper, cowboys tended to their horses and drifted back to the campfire that Cowboy Mack and Will were stoking with buffalo chips and cow chips. Jimmy sat cross-legged beside the fire circle, lightly strumming his guitar and humming, oblivious of what was going on around him, in his own place.

Cowboys hovered around the chuck wagon and eagerly took the filled plates that Bonnie handed them. Shuffling back to the fire, they squatted slowly, grunting and blowing, near exhaustion. They paid attention to their plates and ate silently.

Jimmy set his empty plate aside and picked up his guitar. He strummed a chord. "Would you boys like a little inspiration to help you get across that river tomorrow? I'm working on a song about crossing a river that may help you some. I heard a dark cowboy in a San Antonio saloon singing a piece about crossing a river, and I'm changing it a bit." He smiled.

"Sure," said Brad. "Maybe we can use it next time we want to brag about our git-fiddler." He grinned.

Jimmy bent over the guitar, played a few chords and began to sing softly, looking at the strings as he played.

Another river to cross, a wide river
Don't know how to reach the other side,
Wide river
Jesus gonna help you reach the other side,
Wide river
Old Satan gonna fight you,
Wide river
Reach out to Jesus, his nail-scarred hand
Reach the other side

Jimmy paused, looked up. "Well, that's all so far. Still working on it."

"Good song," said Cowboy Mack. Everyone turned to look at Mack. He rarely had anything to say at the supper campfire. "I like it." He bent over his plate, forked beans over a biscuit and took a bite.

Mack leaned back, looked into the flames. "I

know the song that black cowboy got his piece from. We used to sing it in the quarters. I learned it as a child." He closed his eyes and lowered his head.

"Do you still know it?" said Bonnie.

He looked at her a long moment, looked down, nodded.

"Would you sing it for us?" she said.

Renfro and Marley looked at each other, grinning. Bonnie glared at them until they sobered, Renfro pulling a face.

Cowboy Mack closed his eyes, raised his chin.

Oh, wasn't that a wide river?
That river of Jordan, Lord,
Wide river!
There's one more river to cross!

At the first note, all conversation ended suddenly as the cowboys were stunned, jaws hanging. Mack sang softly, but in a strong, rich bass voice, full of tension and feeling.

Oh, the river of Jordan is so wide,
One more river to cross!
I don't know how to get on the other side,
One more river to cross!

The listeners leaned forward, trying to see the singer more clearly in the glow from the dying fire.

Oh, wasn't that a wide river?
That river of Jordan, Lord,
Wide river!
There's one more river to cross!

Mack's face reflected the anguish, the emotion, in his song. He squinted, nodded, a single tear rolling down his cheek. He sang with restrained passion, struggling, eyes clenched.

Old Satan ain't nothin' but a snake in the grass,
One more river to cross!
If you ain't mighty careful, he will hold you fast!
One more river to cross!

The cowhands were captivated, silent, staring at Mack.

Oh, wasn't that a wide river?
That river of Jordan, Lord,
Wide river!
There's one more river to cross!

He drooped, eyes tightly closed. Listeners looked at each other, speechless. Not a few of the hard-bitten cowboys wiped tears from cheeks.

Mack set his plate on the ground beside him, stood and walked slowly from the fire circle to the edge of darkness. He stopped there, chin raised, staring up into the void.

"Should I go to him?" Bonnie whispered to Will. She had left the chuck wagon to sit by Will when Mack began singing.

Will still looked at Mack. "Leave him be, sweetheart. He's not in this camp right now. He's somewhere else, by hisself. I hope he'll talk with us later. Thought I knew Cowboy Mack. Don't seem I do."

The cowboys finished their supper, now cold on their plates. There was only muted conversation, mostly soft comment about Mack's song. They stood, stretched, and walked to the chuck wagon to deposit dishes. Marley walked beside Renfro, asking questions about the song that Renfro said he could not answer.

The hands strolled into the darkness to relieve themselves or to the hoodlum wagon to retrieve bedrolls. They stood about, smoking, still subdued. Renfro and Marley walked to their picketed horses to take their turn at night herding. The others found places around the dying fire and the wagons and dropped bedrolls.

Bonnie and Will had gone to the bushes where they parted a minute, then came back together. They walked along the edge of firelight, Bonnie holding him around his waist, and he with an arm around her shoulders. They stopped when they saw Mack still facing the darkness.

Mack turned and saw them. He walked slowly to them. His face was soft and wore a hint of a smile. He looked down at Bonnie.

"Mack, that was just wonderful," she said. "You really rattled the hands. They might have a hard time thinkin' about you as just one of the boys now."

"I'll disabuse them of any of that thinkin' real fast," said Mack, smiling.

"I'm guessing you haven't sung that song in years," said Will.

Mack looked aside into the darkness. "Oh, I've sung it many, many times in my head. It still speaks to me. It said a lot to us when we sung it evenings after dark in the quarters. We thought about what it said. One more river to cross. The Ohio was that river for us. It was our Jordan. One more river to cross, one more river to cross to freedom. Oh, we thought about it, and we sung about it.

"And some of us sung it in our hearts as we snuck away in the dark and ran toward the Ohio, to the Promised Land.

"Most of the runners didn't make it. We thought we was gonna make it. My mama and daddy and I saw the trees on the bank. We was in spittin' distance. But the slave catchers came outta those trees, and they caught us, right on the bank. We was almost there. One more river to cross. They killed my mama and daddy right there. I fought, but they had me and dragged me back to the plantation. That's where they beat me so long and so hard, I almost died. I wished then they had killed me. I wanted to die." He looked away.

Bonnie took Mack's hand. "Cowboy Mack, we're

glad you didn't die. You're the best cowboy I know and one of the best men I know." She put her arms around his waist and hugged, her head against his chest. Mack's eyes opened wide, his arms dangled, and he looked anxiously at Will. Will smiled, and Mack put his arms lightly around Bonnie's shoulders, still looking at Will.

CHAPTER TWELVE

The trail ran through a valley of gently rolling plains, dry shortgrass prairie with scattered sagebrush. The general absence of trees made their infrequent sightings notable since the sparse cottonwoods usually lined the banks of waterways.

A range of forested high mountains lay well west of the trail. Riders dispatched early each day to look for water told of seeing what they thought were bighorn sheep on the distant crags, and they saw dozens of pronghorn antelope in the valley. The howl of wolves at dusk both startled and thrilled.

At the evening campfire, cowboys leaned against the chuck wagon and sat around the fire circle, supper plates in hand, too occupied for conversation.

"We got a visitor," said Win.

All looked up at the solitary rider that approached at a walk. McBride handed his plate to Cookie and walked toward the horseman. He waved to the rider who pulled up at the edge of firelight. The man dismounted, and they talked. McBride clapped him on the back, and they walked to the fire.

"Boys, missy," McBride said, nodding to Bonnie,

"this is Ohanzee. He is going to ride with us for a while. He knows this country like the back of his hand, and he speaks better English than most of you yahoos. I met Ohanzee in Cheyenne. He works on a ranch north of town. His boss said that it would be my good fortune if Ohanzee would ride with us for a few weeks, and he said it was okay with him.

"You see, Ohanzee is Sioux. We're going to be driving the herd close to his country, the Black Hills, where the army and the Sioux are not in real good relations at the moment. If we meet any of his countrymen, he can explain that we're just passing through, and we have nothing to do with what's happening in their country.

"Course, if they ask where we are taking this bunch of fat cattle, and we tell them we're taking the herd to the Crow reservation, this might cause some agitation. The Sioux and the Crow have been enemies forever, and they might decide that they would just as soon have this herd as see it go to their enemies.

"That's where Ohanzee comes in. He will explain that the Crow are poor now and will never be able to make war on the Sioux again, and they will never be able to encroach on their hunting grounds." He turned to Ohanzee, smiling. "Does that sound about right?"

Ohanzee had stood behind McBride, frowning, during his discourse. McBride stepped aside.

"Yes, it sounds okay," Ohanzee said. "Yes, I will try to convince them that you are good white people, and they are in no danger from you. And I will try to convince them that they are in no danger from the Crow people. But I do not know what they will be thinking. If they are angry at the army and all white men, they may take the herd. All of it." Cowboys looked at each other, nervously.

"If they are not angry, they may be satisfied with taking only a few cows. But they will require some cows, even if they are not angry. They have been pushed too hard by white people, miners and soldiers. If they are very angry, they may kill me for riding with you."

The cowboys stared at Ohanzee, grim. "Then why are you doing this?" said Will.

Ohanzee looked down, then looked past the fire circle into the darkness. He looked back to the fire and spoke slowly. "I have been among whites for two years. I have seen good white men, and I have seen bad white men. Just like in my tribe. I know times are changing. We cannot go back to a time when there were only Indian people in the country, before white men came. Now the whites flow into our country like a swift river. They settle and become like the blades of grass on the prairie. They will keep coming.

"I do not wish to see the Sioux way of life end, but it is ending. I do not know what is coming, but the old ways are gone. I wish to survive, so I look for a place in this new world."

Cowboy Mack, sitting at the fire circle, stared into the flames, nodding slowly, his supper forgotten.

The hands listened quietly. In the past, sitting at campfires, they talked often of changes in lifeways that they had seen and were a part of. Progress, some had called it. They had thought little, if at all, about what those changes meant for the Indians, the native people who were being displaced and their cultures altered forever. They figured that Indians were just part of the wild landscape that had to be tamed and civilized or neutralized in some fashion.

McBride gestured toward the chuck wagon and walked there with Ohanzee. Cowboys returned to their supper and conversation that was uncharacteristically muted. Bonnie and Will deposited their dishes in the bucket at the chuck wagon and walked toward the herd. The cattle were watered late in the afternoon and had grazed just before stopping. Full of water and grass, they bedded down easily and now were quiet. The soft whistling of an unseen night guard came from the darkness.

"That's sad," said Bonnie. "I don't think I ever gave any thought about what's happening to the Indians till we saw that bunch from the Texas panhandle crossing our trail, heading for a reservation or a jail. I mean, I hadn't given any thought about them from their point of view. Every time I thought about Indians, I just thought: enemy. I guess I never thought they had any feelings. I was wrong."

"What th' hell, Charlie! What's this?" Bonnie stared, open-mouthed and eyes squinting in the bright sun.

Bonnie, Will, Mack and McBride had left camp at first light to ride ahead. Now they sat their horses near the banks of the Platte River, looking up at a wire strung between widely spaced poles.

"That's the telegraph," said McBride, "come to Fort Laramie years ago, then just kept on going west." He turned to Bonnie. "Ain't you seen the telegraph?

"Sure, I've seen it in Texas. Just didn't expect to see it way up here."

"C'mon, we'll follow the wire and the river to the fort. It's on the Laramie River near where it joins the Platte. I need to decide whether we should stop there or pass on by and cross the river further on. The fort's always been caught up with Sioux affairs, and they should be able to give us some advice."

Bonnie and Will rode close behind McBride and Mack. "Charlie, is it true that somebody in New York City can talk with somebody in San Francisco?" Bonnie said. "Well, I don't mean talk, but send messages?"

"That's right, missy. And somebody at the fort might look out the window right now and see us and tell Washington that Charlie McBride is coming their way, and how should they receive us." He turned and smiled at Bonnie.

She stared at her horse's mane. She pulled back on her reins to fall behind. Will slowed.

She leaned toward him. "Will, I'm not sure I want to be in touch with the whole country. What happens when you want to be by yourself?"

Will frowned. "Bonnie. You're not required to send or receive messages from anybody unless you want to. Nobody's going to watch you or interfere with whatever you want to do. Well, not if what you're doing is not illegal or immoral. What do you mean, be by yourself? You want neighbors, friends, when you settle down, don't you?"

"Hmm. I s'pose so. I just don't want neighbors to live too close. Maybe I can tell them we'll keep in touch by telegraph." She kicked her horse to a trot to catch up.

"Okay, here's what's happenin'." McBride spoke to the hands at the campfire after breakfast. "The people at the fort yesterday told me that the Sioux are mad at the miners and the army, but they shouldn't give us any problems as long as we stay away from 'em. Well, we'll try to do that, but we'll be driving through their hunting grounds.

"We're going to pass west of the fort, but if curiosity is going to get the best of you, you can ride in for a visit. You won't need more'n a couple of hours. Mind your manners. This is an army post. By the way, if you're goin' in to see what an old-timey fort looks like, forget it. It looks more like a town.

"At the fort, you're going to hear about the Fort Laramie Hog Ranch, a few miles west of the fort. Stay away from it. It has nothing to do with Fort Laramie, and it has nothing to do with hogs. It's gambling and liquor and women you don't want to mess with."

*****

Rod and Jimmy stood inside the Fort Laramie Sutler's store, wide-eyed at the display of merchandise. There were shelves of household goods like bowls, plates, cups, cutlery. Clothing and cloth, shoes and boots, bonnets and hats, all manner of food, from nuts and jellies to vegetables, sugar and canned seafood.

"Why, Jimmy," said Rod, "this store has more stuff than our store at home. I thought we were driving through a wilderness. But this whole fort is just like a town and better laid out than anything I've seen around our place at home."

"Yeah, it sure has its attractions," Jimmy said. "I wonder what the attraction is over there." He stared across the counters and shelves of merchandise at a passel of soldiers crowded around a woman. They leaned toward her, grinning, laughing. She smiled, touched a soldier's cheek, the tip of another's nose. She fended off a soldier's hand that reached tentatively toward her waist. Or a breast.

"Wonder who she is?" said Rod.

Jimmy caught a passing soldier by the sleeve. "Say, who is that?" He motioned toward the woman. "Seems to be real popular."

The soldier grinned. "That, my good man, is Martha Jane Cannary."

"Those fellas are falling all over her," said Rod. "Why's that? She ain't no beauty."

The soldier leaned toward Rod, spoke softly.

"Jane has talents that are not readily visible. If you want to know more about Martha Jane, you'd best visit her at the Hog Ranch."

"Ooooh, I see," said Jimmy. Well, I'm gonna leave Martha Jane Cannary to you soldiers." He turned away. "C'mon, Rod, I have seen Fort Laramie." He waved to the soldier, put an arm on Rod's shoulder, and they walked toward the door.

Rod looked again at Martha Jane Cannary and the cluster of admiring soldiers. "My goodness. These soldiers must have been away from home a long time. My mare's better lookin' than that woman."

Stepping outside, they saw Will, Bonnie and Ohanzee who stopped and greeted them. "Anything interesting inside?" said Bonnie.

"Well, if you need to do grocery shopping or clothes shopping or any kind of shopping," said Rod, "you'll find it here. Will might be interested in an article on display, but he'll have to go to the Hog Ranch to buy." He grinned.

Bonnie took Will's arm tightly with both hands and moved off. "No, thanks," she said, "he's not shopping here or there." Will looked over his shoulder as Bonnie dragged him along, following Ohanzee.

They walked past frame buildings that bordered the parade ground, past the post hospital, to a trail that led to the entrance of the cemetery. They walked silently among the graves, looking at headstones and wooden markers.

After a few minutes, Ohanzee stopped and held up a hand. "This is it. This is what I want to show you." They stood before a Sioux burial scaffold that was erected over a grave.

"You've heard much talk about why whites and Indians cannot live in peace," Ohanzee said, "why they cannot find a path to a new way of living together. This is the grave of a young woman who wondered the same thing. She was the daughter of Spotted Tail, a famous Sioux leader. She and her father believed that whites and Indians must find a way to live in peace. She visited Fort Laramie many times with her father and enjoyed watching the soldiers at parade and sitting on a bench in the sutler's store, watching the customers come and go. She refused to marry a young Sioux man who was interested in her. Stories said she wanted to marry a soldier as other young women in her tribe had done.

"She became very ill one winter and told her father that when she died, she wished her burial scaffold to be erected in the fort cemetery. She died that winter, only eighteen years old.

"Her father did as he promised and approached the fort commander. The commander saw an opportunity and made this an occasion that combined military show and Sioux tradition. Sioux and soldiers attended a Christian burial service for the young woman at the cemetery. She was not Christian, but Spotted Tail agreed to the ceremony since he felt it meant something to the whites. Someone said later that the fort commander believed that all this showed that Indians after all were not wild animals, but had human hearts. I wonder whether some of the Sioux said the same thing about whites."

Bonnie wiped her cheek with a sleeve. "What was her name?"

"Her name was Mni-aku, Hinzinwin, Ah-ho-ap-pa."

"She had three names?"

"Yes, Sioux are often named something to identify important things that happened in the lives of their parents, a vision or an event. Her names mean 'Water Bringer' and 'Yellow Buckskin Girl' and 'Wheat Flour.'"

"I hope her death, and life, had a good influence," Bonnie said.

Ohanzee nodded. "Some people, Sioux and soldiers, thought her life and her death could mean that Indians and whites could find peace and lasting friendship. But the bad times did not end. They have not ended today."

Leaving Fort Laramie, the drive turned northwestward. Spirits lifted with the sure knowledge that they were on the last segment of the journey. Montana just ahead! The lightheartedness vanished quickly. Nothing had changed, except the sure knowledge that every day that passed meant that they were nearer the Crow reservation and the end of the drive.

The trail now ran along the Platte, so water was no problem. McBride took care to avoid the few emigrant wagons on the storied Oregon Trail. Since the completion of the transcontinental railroad, there was little attraction for overland travel inside an ox-drawn wagon.

Becoming increasingly anxious to see the end of the drive, McBride decided to bypass remote Fort Fetterman without a visit. The herd was turned northward, generally following the route of the old Bozeman Trail, now abandoned. The trail had been heavily traveled in the 1860s by argonauts hoping to strike it rich in Montana's gold fields. Now the trail was but a memory.

Leaving the Platte, once again every day began with a search for water. A pair or pairs were sent out at first light or after breakfast, depending on how critical was the need for water. Will and Bonnie seemed to be the most successful in the hunt, and they now went out most mornings. On this day, riding in hilly and undulating terrain, they topped a low rise and Bonnie held up an arm.

"Will! Look."

She pointed down the gentle slope at a mother grizzly and two cubs less than fifty yards away. The mother looked intently at the two riders while the cubs continued to paw at leafy debris at their feet.

"I see them," Will said. He reached down slowly and grasped the stock of his rifle, still watching the bears.

"Don't," said Bonnie, almost a whisper. "We're in no danger, and we don't need meat. And this is their home." She did not look at him.

Will frowned. He pulled his hand from the rifle and rested it on his leg. "Gut reaction." He turned to her. "You're a puzzle sometimes, Bonnie. Lately you've been concerned about what's happening to Indians. Now it's bears."

She frowned in turn, stared at her horse's head, then turned to Will. "Why is it white people think they own everything, and whatever happens, it has to benefit white people? Even if everyone and everything else suffers?"

"Whoa." Will grimaced. He paused, forehead wrinkled, pondering. "That's the strangest thing I've heard in a long time. I don't even know how to respond. Sweetheart, you're going to keep on till you make my head hurt." He turned his horse up the slope. "C'mon, let's get back to doing something that doesn't require any serious thought. We need to find some water for that thirsty herd."

After riding an hour on the rolling plain covered with shortgrass gramma, green from recent rains, they saw a line of cottonwoods a mile ahead at the base of a low hill and pulled up. From the wood, three thin spirals of gray smoke rose vertically before thinning and vanishing.

"They camped there for the same reason that we'll need to stop there," Will said. "Water."

"Can't we drive the herd around them, tell Charlie to leave the trail and avoid them?"

"They've seen us. Likely this party is hunting. They'll have men in the hills that've been watching us for some time. Besides, those hills on each side of this meadow are too steep to drive cattle over them. No, we've no choice but to move straight on to the stream and the Indian camp. Now that they know we're coming, they'll not leave."

He wheeled his horse. "C'mon. This is not our problem; it's Charlie's." They set out at a lope down the back trail. She looked over her shoulder toward the camp.

"You won't see anyone back there. You'll see 'em over there. He gestured with a nod toward the grassy slope on their right. Fifty yards away, at the base of the slope, two feathered warriors sat their horses, watching them.

Nooning. The cattle were let to graze over an extended area, loosely herded by a few riders. The other cowboys sat or stood around the chuck wagon in twos and threes, eating, talking, smoking. Ohanzee and Cowboy Mack leaned against the side of the hoodlum, plates in hand.

"We are alike, you and me," said Ohanzee. "The whites take from us what we care most about."

"That's true, but we're different in a way, too. You still have much to lose, and things are going to get worse for you. For me, we got our freedom, and things are going to be better for us. At least, that's my hope."

"That's true," Ohanzee said. "That's why I am trying to find a place in the white man's world, as you have. I am still Sioux, and I will hold to what that means, but I will earn my living in the white man's world. There is no other way. What will you do, after the herd is delivered, and you are paid?"

Mack paused, his fork held over his plate. He pushed the beans around, forked a chunk of beef to his mouth, chewed a moment. "I don't know for sure. Probably follow the boss, like always." He looked up, stared at the grazing cattle. "Sure would like my own place someday. Don't know when that's gonna happen. Or how."

"Why don't you stay here? My boss is looking for good cowboys. He is building up his herd and needs more men. He is a good man to work for. Maybe you could ask him to pay you partly in cows. He told me once that he would do this so I could have my own place someday. He would do this for you, if you ask."

Mack looked down, frowning, his plate forgotten. "Mmm. Sounds interestin'." He looked up at Ohanzee. "He would do that? Maybe I'll think on it."

They lapsed into silence, studying their plates as they forked the last of the beans and beef, finished their biscuits. At the sound of hooves, they looked up and saw Bonnie and Will coming at a lope. They walked to the chuck wagon, deposited their dishes in the bucket and waited.

The riders pulled up, and Mack held Bonnie's reins as she dismounted. "Howdy, boys. Save any dinner for us?" she said. Mack handed Bonnie's reins to Will, and he rode toward the remuda.

"I 'spect Cookie has somethin' in the pot," Mack said. "Did you find water?"

"We did," said Bonnie. "Maybe found some trouble as well. You'll have to help us on that count, Ohanzee. We saw an Indian camp on the banks of the stream where we will need to camp for water. I'm assuming they are Sioux, but you'll know better than me. They saw us."

McBride, Ohanzee, Will and Cowboy Mack sat their horses, staring down the valley toward the cottonwood grove and the Sioux camp. They had set out at first light. Now they saw the four mounted Sioux ahead on the right and four on the left, stationary, waiting.

"Let's git on with it," McBride said. They set out at a lope. Hardly had McBride and the others begun to ride when the warriors on each side of the trail kicked their mounts to ride on a parallel course, gradually moving closer to the cowboys. McBride and the others slowed to a walk.

As they approached the Indian camp, men emerged from the wood and watched the riders come. By the time they arrived at the camp, the Indian riders were alongside the cowboys. All pulled up before a contingent of Sioux, now numbering twenty or so. Others in the camp had stopped what they were doing and watched the meeting.

The cowboys dismounted, holding their reins, while the eight Indians rode into the camp. An elderly Sioux in the group stepped forward.

Ohanzee raised an arm in greeting and spoke in Lakota. The Sioux spokesman replied crisply. A warrior stepped up behind him and said something. After a brief exchange, the spokesman turned back to Ohanzee, and they talked.

McBride grimaced, impatient. "What's he saying, Ohanzee?"

Ohanzee held up his hand to McBride, still talking with the spokesman who was becoming agitated and raising his voice. Some in the group behind the spokesman shouted angrily, shaking fists at Ohanzee and brandishing rifles. Ohanzee ignored them, spoke softly, gesturing often toward McBride.

"Ohanzee." Said McBride. "What th' hell's he saying?"

Ohanzee turned to McBride. "He is Otaktay, a war chief. He says they are hunting. He says they had to leave their country to hunt because the whites in the Black Hills have killed the animals or driven them away. He says they have seen no buffalo for many days.

"He is very angry at me. He says I am dressed like

a white man and sound like a white man. He says I have become a white man. One of the men behind him says he knows me, and I remember him. I told them what I have told you, that I am Lakota and will remain Lakota, but I know that change is coming, and I am trying to make a life in the new world, and that includes accepting that whites and Sioux must learn to live together in this new world.

"He is not happy with this talk. Ohers with him are very angry. They say that nothing will change. They say they will kill all white men in their country and live in peace. As Sioux, not Indian white men.

"He asked me where we are taking this herd. I told him you are taking them to the Crow people. This made him and the others very angry. The Crow are the enemy of the Sioux. They have always been enemies. He says maybe he will take the entire herd for his people. I said that the government surely intends sending a herd to the Sioux soon. I said if he takes your herd, the government will not like this, and the Sioux will never get a herd. And the army will come to the Black Hills to punish the Sioux. That is when some warriors behind him shouted that they should kill us now."

McBride frowned, looking down. Mack and Will watched him. Will thought he could almost hear McBride's brain churning.

McBride looked at Ohanzee, then at the chief. He smiled. "Tell him I'll give him twenty steers. He probably knows already that cattle taste better than buffalo, and it's a hell of a lot easier to kill them. Tell him if he doesn't agree to this, I'll send fast riders to get the army."

Ohanzee blinked, shot a quick glance at the chief, back to McBride. "Are you sure?" said Ohanzee. This will make them very angry."

McBride's jaw was set. "Tell him."

Ohanzee looked down, hesitated. He looked up to the chief and relayed the terms of McBride's offer. As he spoke, the chief's face turned grim, and the mutterings from the warriors behind him grew to rumbling, then angry shouts and fist waving. Warriors brandished rifles and bows.

A young man who had shouted the loudest pushed others aside, quickly brought his rifle up, leveled on Ohanzee and fired, startling those around him. The shooter immediately was blown backward, a bullet hole in his forehead. A dozen warriors jerked their rifles up to level on Mack and fire. Cowboy Mack, riddled with bullets, dropped his six-shooter, stumbled backwards and fell heavily to the ground.

Will and McBride drew their six-shooters and were bringing them up when Ohanzee, gripping his shoulder, blood flowing between his fingers, stepped in front of them.

"No! No!" said Ohanzee, "they will kill us all! It's over. Don't do this."

Will and McBride stopped their pistols chest high, looked past Ohanzee to see the chief, arms raised, facing the warriors, calming them as they lowered their weapons.

Will pushed the six-shooter into its holster and knelt beside Mack. He lay on his back, gasping, blood soaking his shirt in a dozen places. His eyes fluttered, fixed on Will's eyes. He gripped Will's hand tightly, coughed, and blood streamed from his mouth down his chin.

Mack gasped, trying to speak, looking over Will's shoulder to the sky. His eyes were blank, unblinking. "One more river . . . one more river . . . Lord . . . mama . . .daddy . . . one more river . . . I'm coming . . . one more . . ." His eyes fluttered, closed, his mouth almost closed, and he was still.

Will released Mack's hand and stood. He looked at the Indians who were walking away, carrying the body of the slain young warrior. Some looked back at Will and McBride, their faces hard. Others looked back, their expressions soft, asking questions.

McBride looked at Mack, serene in death. McBride inhaled deeply, exhaled. "What a waste, what a goddamned waste. One of the best cowboys I ever knew. One of the best men I ever knew." He spoke to Will, still looking at the body. "Get him tied on his horse, Will." He turned to Ohanzee, who gripped his bloody shoulder. "Can you ride?"

"I can ride," Ohanzee said.

"Let's get back." He walked toward the horses. "Bad business," he muttered under his breath, his head lowered.

*****

"No, no, no." Bonnie said, softly. She stood beside the horse that carried Mack's body. Her hands were on her cheeks, tears flowing between her fingers. "No!" She collapsed to her knees, her hands still on her cheeks. McBride took Mack's reins from Will and rode away, leading the horse bearing what remained of its rider.

Will took Bonnie's shoulders and helped her stand. He gently pulled her hands from her face and held her. She wiped her eyes on a sleeve and leaned on his chest, her arms around his waist.

"He was too good . . . for his own good, Will. Why do good men have to die? I wish he had kin I could talk to. I would tell them what he meant to me, what he meant to everybody who knew him." She buried her face in the folds of his shirt, gripping fistfuls of the shirt, sobbing.

"He's at peace now, Bonnie. He's with his mama and daddy. He crossed that river, and his journey is done."

They watered the herd that evening upstream from the Sioux encampment, then crossed the stream and bedded the cattle down in a grassy meadow.

Some of the Sioux warriors had grumbled at the transfer of but twenty cows, but most appeared satisfied, no doubt anticipating the taste of fresh beef, judging from their smiles as they moved the bunch toward their camp. Much to the relief of McBride and the outfit, the Indians broke camp before sundown and moved out. Their eastward track suggested that their hunting foray was at an end, and they were headed for their own country.

Ohanzee had come off better than at first feared. The bullet had passed through the flesh of his upper arm, and no bones were broken. Cookie washed the wound with water and whiskey, bandaged it and put the arm in a sling. He predicted a speedy recovery.

Bonnie was surprised to learn that her grandpa had done doctoring. He had never talked about it. She was impressed with the result and told him so, surprised that Grandpa actually blushed.

Some of the cowboys had mixed emotions about the doctoring. They expressed themselves happy that Ohanzee was healing, but lamented the loss of the good whiskey that was expended in the process.

They buried Cowboy Mack just back of the bank on the north side of the stream. Rod fashioned a wooden cross from sideboards of an abandoned wagon and carved on the horizontal crosspiece: "R.I.P. Cowboy Mack. A Good Man." He pushed the cross into the loose soil at the grave's head.

When all had gathered at the grave, McBride asked if anyone could sing or recite something appropriate. Heads down, cowboys looked around at each other, and no one responded.

"Uh, Charlie." Everyone turned to look at Renfro. It was the first time most had heard him speak in days.

"I got a Bible." He pulled a small, worn Bible from a vest pocket. "I can read something that I read often. Means a lot me, and I think Mack would like it."

McBride nodded.

Renfro thumbed the pages, settled on a page and read.

> The Lord is my shepherd; I shall not want.
>
> He maketh me to lie down in green pastures; he leadeth me beside the still waters.
>
> He restoreth my soul; he leadeth me in the paths of righteousness for his name's sake.
>
> Yea, though I walk through the valley of the shadow of death, I will fear no evil; for thou art with me; thy rod and thy staff they comfort me.
>
> Thou preparest a table before me in the presence of mine enemies; thou anointest my head with oil; my cup runneth over.
>
> Surely goodness and mercy shall follow me all the days of my life; and I will dwell in the house of the Lord forever.

"Amen," said Bonnie and Rod together.

Renfro closed the book, looked at McBride. Most of the cowboys had closed their eyes during the reading. They opened their eyes now, and not an eye was dry.

McBride cleared his throat. "Thank you for that, Renfro. Mighty good verse." He looked at the others who had not moved, all waiting for an ending. "Look around and get every rock you can find, and spread 'em on the grave. Don't want any critter to disturb it. C'mon up to the fire when you get that done. Gittin' late. Cookie's already waving at us."

Cowboys replaced hats and wandered about, collecting stones of all sizes, placing them on the grave until it was covered with two layers of rock.

Bonnie and Will, dusting off hands and trousers, stood at the grave after the others left. She sighed, wiped her eyes with both hands. "I think he would tell us not to be sad. He's in a better place." She took Will's arm, and they walked toward the campfire.

Day followed day on this last leg of the drive. The hands pushed the herd, usually strung out a mile at least, through a rolling prairie. The pace was steady, but permitted some grazing on the dry gramma grass, lush and nutritious.

Ohanzee urged the outfit to be vigilant because they were still in traditional Sioux hunting grounds. Since the party they encountered at the stream would have returned to their villages in the Black Hills by now, the tribe would know that this herd was moving northward to the Crow, their bitter enemies. McBride veered westward at every opportunity, trying to put miles between the herd and the Sioux.

On more than one occasion at supper campfires, Ohanzee talked about the attraction of ranching in Wyoming and his boss's hope to hire some Texas cowboys.

Ohanzee said that his boss had given up on hiring drifters.

Ohanzee described the ranch in some detail. He noted that it was one of the largest, best equipped spreads, located in wild country but near enough to Cheyenne and the railroad to enjoy all the advantages. He was obviously coached by his boss. Some in the outfit began to wonder whether this appeal for hands was the real reason Ohanzee had ridden with them on this last stretch to Montana.

Ohanzee particularly tried to persuade Will to consider his boss's offer. On one evening after an early supper, while the other hands were yarning and playing cards at the campfire, Will and Bonnie strolled outside camp with Ohanzee.

"I want you to work with us," said Ohanzee. "You would be good friends. And you would have your own ranch in a few years." He smiled. "Maybe I will have a ranch of my own someday. It is my dream." He looked down, then at Will. "Mack told me he was thinking of visiting the ranch. He wanted to talk with my boss. I think he might have stayed. I am sad. I liked Cowboy Mack and wish I could have him as a friend."

They stood a moment, silent. Ohanzee nodded and turned to walk toward camp. Bonnie and Will watched him go. Then Bonnie took Will's arm, and they strolled away from camp, talking softly. They stopped to watch the sun sinking on the horizon, the filmy cloud layers turning from pink to blue to gray, finally to heavy black churning masses. A low rumble, like the sound of a kettle of boiling water, issued from the mass. The cool breeze quickened, and the dark cloud moved overhead. Bonnie shivered and stepped behind Will, her arms about his waist, pulling him close.

A light shower of cold raindrops began to fall, and they walked, then ran toward camp. Hardly had they reached the campfire when the rain was replaced by snowflakes, soft, light, swirling in the breeze. Everyone in camp, around the campfire and standing about in idle conversation, stopped and looked up, smiling, hands outstretched to catch the flakes. The snowfall ended as quickly as it began, replaced by a soft, cool breeze.

The sun rose the next morning in a cloudless sky, pleasantly warm after a cold night. Bonnie and Will rolled up their beds, deposited them in the hoodlum and walked their separate ways into a nearby cluster of sage.

Will had hardly lost sight of Bonnie when he was startled by her cry.

"Oh! Oh!"

Fumbling with his trousers, Will ran into the clump of sage where she had disappeared. And there she was, arms held high, beaming, looking up at dozens of green butterflies swirling about her head. She spun, laughing, hands reaching, trying to touch the drifting butterflies.

She saw him. "Will! They are beautiful!" She lowered her arms, turning slowly, looking up as the swirl of butterflies lifted and drifted away. She turned to Will, smiling. She wiped a single tear from a cheek.

"I love this country," she said.

On this last stretch of the drive, talk at campfires turned to what comes after. Going home. How to get home? What awaits at home? And then? Rod said he would do what he always did between drives. He would go back to the family ranch near Sweetwater where his father and brother raised horses. He mentioned again the young woman he decided he needed to look up, which raised a few eyebrows. Win worked with Charlie and would go wherever Charlie went. Renfro and Marley simply shrugged when questioned about plans.

One evening, Jimmy proclaimed, grinning, that he had had enough of cows and itinerant cowboys and would find some way to make a living with his guitar. Maybe he would get some kindred spirits to join him in a group to play in saloons, perhaps in dance halls as well. Maybe he would call the band something that would grab people's attention, *The Cowboy's Day,* or some such.

"You be sure to tell us where you're playin', " said Rod, "so we'll know . . . uh, so we'll know where to drink whiskey." He turned to the others, pulled a face. Jimmy ignored him, bent over his guitar.

Will and Bonnie stood, and Will stretched. "You tell me where you're planning to play. If I'm within a hundred miles, I'll ride over."

Jimmy looked up with almost a hint of a smile. He bent over the guitar and strummed a chord. "Sure you will," he said, softly. Will touched Jimmy's shoulder.

Bonnie and Will strolled to the hoodlum wagon, fetched their bedrolls and laid them out. Unlike most evenings, they prepared for bed without comment. Once in bed, Bonnie pulled up the cover, and they faced each other, silent, pensive.

"What do you plan to do after the herd is gone, and you have money in your pocket, Will Bishop?" Rolling over to lie on his back, he looked up into the clear sky, filled with sparkling stars. She raised on her elbows, leaned over, kissed him on a cheek and lay on his chest.

"You're going to have money in your pocket, too, sweetheart. Exactly what I have." He rolled back to face her. "On that point, don't let old Charlie pay you less than what he pays the others. He hired you as a cowboy, not a lady cowhand. If he tries to pay you less, you let me know, and I'll remind him that he called you the best cowboy in the outfit." He rolled over on his back, put his hands behind his head. "Charlie's okay. I don't think he'll shortchange you."

"You didn't answer my question," she said.

He stared at the heavens. She punched him lightly in his side. He jumped, startled. He pulled her head down, kissed her on the lips and bit her ear lightly.

"Ow, are you going to answer me, or should I punch you hard?"

He put an arm around her shoulders and held her.

She rested her head on his chest. "The question, sweetheart, is not what *I'm* gonna do, but what *we're* gonna do. Let's get this herd delivered and get some money in our pockets. Then we'll be happily unemployed and obliged to no one but each other. Then we'll do some serious talking."

Delivering the herd was easier than most had expected. The government agent rode into the camp during breakfast, accompanied by half a dozen young Crows riding spirited horses, charging about the campground, showing off, the agent said, until he calmed them.

After breakfast, the outfit pushed the herd ahead to the reservation where it was officially delivered. The agent, accompanied by a few government men and half a dozen Crows, drove the cattle to a grassy meadow. The herd would be kept there only a short time. The plan was to distribute cows to Indian families for their own use. The agent had impressed on the Crows, he hoped, that the animals should become the nucleus of personal herds, with the exception of the steers that would be kept for slaughtering.

McBride and a few others who had nothing else to do, now that they had turned the herd over, stood by idly, watching and chatting.

As they saw their charges and employment moving away, the cowboys naturally mused on what comes next. Home and how to get there were prominent subjects of conversation. McBride had announced days ago that he intended to ride back to Cheyenne by a route farther west, determined to avoid another encounter with the Sioux when he would have no beeves to surrender. He was still inclined toward taking the train from Cheyenne and had invited any and all to join him.

The cowboys wandered away, heading toward the wagons. They would have supper there and breakfast the next morning and then watch the wagons driven away. They had already been sold. McBride had passed the word earlier that he would pay off the hands after breakfast. Then it would be finished. He had already given each person their favorite mount.

"It's just you and me now, pard," Bonnie said. She and Will stood watching the cowboys walking away.

"Yep." He put an arm around her shoulders. He nodded toward the west where the rim of the orange sun rested on the horizon, bright orange turning gold as they watched, coloring the lower fringes of wispy cloud layers.

She took his hand in both of hers, leaned on his arm.

They watched the sunset in silence. Then he turned to her. "On the trail, seemed like we were in our own little world," he said, "like it was the whole world. But it's changing. Railroads and telegraph poles everywhere, towns popping up and growing. Ranches and farms where only buffalo and Indians used to be.

"Driving cattle seemed to be the most natural

thing when we were doing it. But it can't last. It's important, though. Served a purpose. And it was grand. Someday they're going to write stories about these cattle drives. And we were part of it. Sort of makes it important, what we did." He hugged her shoulders.

She put an arm around his waist, held him. "You're going to have me blubbering, if you don't stop."

He inhaled deeply, chin raised, eyes closed, his mind racing. He turned suddenly and grabbed her with both hands, squeezing hard. She squealed, laughed, struggling. He released his hold, took her by an arm and headed for camp, pulling her along.

"C'mon, we need to talk."

AFTERWORD AND ACKNOWLEDGEMENTS

If I were to list all of the people who assisted in the writing of this narrative, the dozens who offered snippets of information, suggestions, musings, advice, criticism and glasses of wine, the list would be very long. So I simply thank them and hope they find that I have distilled their data satisfactorily.

Particular thanks to the dozens of colleagues and perfect strangers who graciously responded to my appeals for assistance and information. I am grateful to the scores of unnamed historians and diarists whose works I consulted in order to place my characters in the appropriate places and predicaments.

For editorial comment, I am indebted to the Pacific Critique Group for their reading of the narrative and for their suggestions, corrections, inspiration and useful tirades. Particuar thanks to Rod Miller for his detailed nitpicking, particularly on horses, cowboys and cattle. I could ask for no better support than all these kindred spirits.

Special thanks to Pam Van Allen for formatting and to Donna Yee who designed the cover.

ABOUT THE AUTHOR

Harlan Hague, Ph.D., is a native Texan who has lived in Japan and England. His travels have taken him to about eighty countries and dependencies and a circumnavigation of the globe.

Hague is a prize-winning historian and award-winning novelist. History specialties are exploration and trails, California's Mexican era, American Indians and the environment. His novels are mostly westerns with romance themes. Two are set largely in Japan. Some titles have been translated into Spanish, Italian, Portuguese and German. In addition to history, biography and fiction, he once wrote travel articles that published in newspapers around the country, and he has written a bit of fantasy. His screenplays are making the rounds.

For more information about what he has done and what he is doing, visit his website at harlanhague.us. Hague lives in California's Great Central Valley.